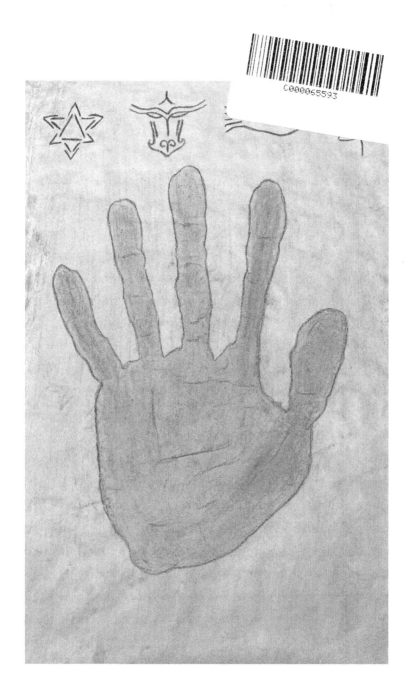

1

About the Author

Emma Flowers is a mother, an artist, a writer of fantasy fiction and poetry, she has also written an inspirational chapter, for a bestselling book series, A Journey of Riches – Discover Your Purpose, and is the author of her own novel series, The Crystal Masters, S(available on Amazon.com).

Emma was born and raised in England, and from a young age showed a passion and talent for writing and storytelling. As a young adult, while trying to figure out what she wanted to be, Emma worked in various jobs, like hospitality, sales, and other corporate duties. She also speaks two languages, English and Italian. It wasn't until Emma started a family of her own, that she realised her true purpose was to write stories. On moving to Australia with her husband and two little boys, she learned the craft of 'Law of Attraction'. This opened unlimited creative possibilities, among them the penning of her first novel.

Emma is currently working on a sequel to The Crystal Masters, with plans for a full series; other fantasy novels are in the pipeline. She hopes her stories and illustrations,

will bring a level of escapism and pleasure to peoples'
lives, just as it does for her.

Contact details:

Facebook – Emma Flowers

Instagram – emma.fantasyauthor

The Crystal Masters
Part One

by Emma Flowers

Dedication

I would like to dedicate this book to my family and friends who have supported me on my creative journey, including my husband, David, my boys for their imaginative input, Jo Smith, my enthusiastic editor, Angela Flanagan, for her creative magic with the book cover design, and not forgetting of course, you dear reader.

List of Main Characters

Lady Rose
Gallium McLarty
Malachi
Borago—The Shadow Master
Morgana—The Fairy Queen
King Yarrow
Queen Aveena
Prince Burdock
Sir Dill

Table of Contents

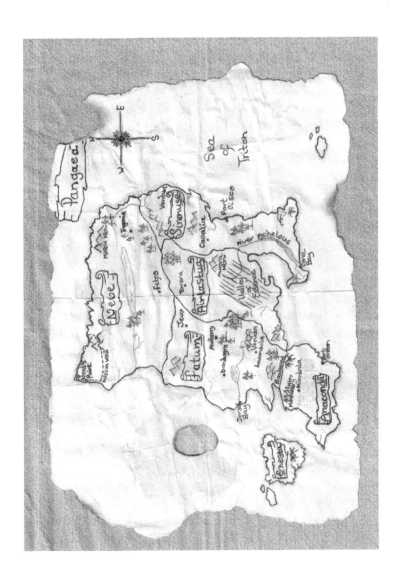

Introduction

At the time of creation, the God Omnio, with the help of the Crystal Masters, created an idyllic land known as Pangaea. Born from the earth's most precious crystals, the Crystal Masters' duty was to spread peace and harmony throughout Pangaea. Now, the crystals lay dormant in a secret location known only to the Gnomes of Jurien, who are the Keepers of Crystals and Guardians of the Book of Legends.

Pangaea has five vast and individual realms. In the north is the bitterly cold Neve realm. Towering above it are the snow-capped Mystic Mountains; while distant chimes from icicles add to the sense of intrigue. At the centre of Pangaea is the bountiful Airlastua realm, with its panoramic Aurora Mountains and mesmerising waterfall. In the east is the Sirenuse realm, where the river Achelous meets the ocean—an infinite waterway surrounded by a rich fertile ground of flowers whose exploding pods release their seeds for continuity. In the west is the vibrant green Fatum realm, with verdant forests and undulating hills.

Later, there came the south realm of Anaconda; a treacherous place, created by the titan God Helidor, brother to the God Omnio. Helidor, consumed with jealousy at his brother's creation, manifested a different world of his own—a wicked world. Thus betrayed by his brother, Omnio banished the titan with all his might, into the sun's core, thereby rendering Helidor powerless. And that was the day the sun shone so brightly that man's gaze cannot withstand it still.

Now, a gigantic gorge separates Anaconda from Fatum and all the other realms. At the centre of this dry and barren land is the Moora Desert; to the north-west are the Mercury Mountains, shadowing the infamous City of Mumbala.

Chapter One—Another

High up in the Mercury Mountains, contoured by the desert plains of the Anaconda realm, is the obsidian castle of the Shadow Master Borago, ruler of fear and conjurer of curses—a tall figure of a man with a smooth, bald head decorated with a leafy tattoo running right from the top and down the side of his face. The Orbicular Rock is the source of his powers, being the most powerful crystal known to the ancient world of Pangaea; he carries it everywhere, mounted in a gold clasp on top of a wooden staff. The Orbicular Rock is like a huge, mottled-brown glass egg; and something smoke-like can be seen moving within.

Borago stole the Orbicular Rock a time ago from the Gnome King Draile, while he and another gnome were secretly returning it to their Kingdom of Jurien. Borago killed the good king with his dagger, loosening him from the ownership of the rock; but before his last breath, King Draile uttered the name of one greater than he—The Illuminata. Then, with the same offensive blade that killed the king, Borago made an incision on the palm of his hand, and, under a full moon smeared the Orbicular Rock with his own blood, thus completing the ritual. The blood seeped through the porous rock, tainting its core for a brief moment. Hence, the Shadow Master was born.

Subsequently, mountains cracked and seas roared, as this dark force was slowly ignited.

At this time, on a humid evening within his igneous castle, the Shadow Master was making his way down a series of steps, lit only by wall-mounted torches. The steps led to a cool chamber in the basement of his castle; a smell of decay wafted from below, leaving a faint metallic taste in the mouth. This was the Mercury Well chamber. Beside the round stone well—which was offset from the centre of the dim, damp room— stood a giant troll, mute and hideously deformed by warts the size of walnuts, his ankle shackled to the well. Lonely in his miserable existence, Otto was always pleased to see his master.

'Otto, my troll, here, I have a treat for you', Borago greeted Otto slyly, throwing a leg of roast turkey up to him, before striding over to the mercury-filled well. Otto devoured the leg in seconds.

'I summon the Witches of the Mercury Well for their full moon prediction and the coming of the Illuminata.' Borago paused. There was an eerie silence, then the mercury in the well started to glow; so too did the Orbicular Rock.

The thick silvery mercury began to swirl slowly. A cackling of laughter grew louder, followed by some coughing and spluttering. Marelda and Hemmatia were once dark witches of the north, before being imprisoned in the well by the Shadow Master.

'Oh, I can't keep this up, my throat is too dry', a rather plump, translucent figure said, hovering above the well. It was Marelda. Next, with a yawn and a stretch, appeared her more slender, gaunt-face sister Hemmatia.

'What is thy bidding, master?' Hemmatia asked keenly, a slight strain in her voice.

'I wish to know when the Illuminata is coming to darken my reign.' The Shadow Master's voice held a mulish undertone.

'On the eve of her birth, there will be a blazing star, as a sign', Hemmatia murmured in a trance.

'And directly below it, will be the birthplace of the Illuminata.'

'Yes, but when?' Borago pressed, while snatching a passing cockroach from the edge of the well, and crushing it with his bare hand, before tossing it up to Otto who caught it neatly in his mouth.

'Master, these mercury conditions have rendered our powers weak, and as a result, time does not exist in our world', Hemmatia explained, lowering her eyes.

'By the pits of lava, why do I bother with you crones?!' boomed the Shadow Master, gripping his staff ever tighter and rolling his eyes.

'Oh, he's even more handsome when angry', swooned Marelda. 'Err, I can sing for you sir—la, la, la, la!' she crooned in not-so-dulcet tones. Hemmatia, embarrassed by her sister's blatant display of affection, gave Marelda a quick jab with her bony elbow to shut her up.

'You simply need to keep watch every night, but I can tell you it will be soon, as our predictions are based on forthcoming events', Hemmatia ended. 'Will that be all, my lord?'

'Very well, I accept your prediction—for now.' The Shadow Master turned away quickly and with a bang on the floor of his staff, the witches disappeared back down the well, before frantically vacating the chamber.

Meanwhile, out at sea, the pirate ship Exodus was on another voyage.

'Flinders, where are you?!' bellowed a deep gruff voice from the captain's cabin.

It was Captain 'Nine-tails' Johnson, the most feared pirate king of all the seas, so called because he used a braided, nine-tail whip to punish his victims. As for the captain, he had long, wavy black hair, with streaks of grey through it, and a short, braided black beard. He wasn't very tall, but had shoulders broad as a butcher's board, a belly you could bounce a baby on, and boots the size of a cabin boy's bucket.

'Where's that idiot?' he muttered.

Flinders, a wafer of a man, came rushing in, followed by a scruffy looking, young cabin boy, his clothes in tatters, carrying a bottle of rum in his arms.

'Here...it...is, captain', he spluttered, trying to catch his breath and not drop the silver tray of gastronomic delights. 'I am frightfully sorry, I had a bit of a disaster in the galley so I...'

'Quit babblin' man and give's it here', the captain shouted, banging his fists on the table. He began tearing shreds off a leg of ham and munching, jaws drooling like it was his last supper. 'What you lookin' at boy?'

The cabin boy stood solemnly by the door, and with bloodshot eyes stared unfazed at the big lug. The young boy's name was Gallium, and up until a year ago the ship had belonged to his father, Captain Aiden McLarty. McLarty was a dedicated buccaneer who had served a good king, transporting special cargo and keeping watch out at sea for any threatening foe. Flinders used to be his first mate until Captain Nine-tails had seized the vessel, with the help of his own pirates, and traded McLarty in to Borago. In return, the Shadow Master gave ownership of the Exodus to Nine-tails. Borago used McLarty for information; no one had seen him since he was apprehended. Gallium vowed from that day forward that he would find his father and reclaim the ship Exodus.

17

As the sun set, filling the whole sky with vibrant crimson and glowing amber, soldiers in every land prepared for their night watch duties on top of castle battlements. This included Borago's army of centaurs. These were a feral race—horse from the waist down, but with the torso and head of a man. The centaurs had a bad reputation for taking what didn't belong to them; they found pleasure in fighting, drinking and looting. Borago, through his powers of persuasion, recruited them and now they served only him. His most loyal was Taurus, a strong young centaur who, at the command of the Shadow Master, would lead his race.

That night, high above the land, a flicker of light travelled over a cloud-blushed moon and across the purple-black sky. It was the predicted star and it hung high above the Fatum realm like a blazing ball, creating a shine that could be seen from miles away. A centaur on night watch duty told Taurus, who immediately went to Borago's bedchamber and knocked loudly on his door.

'Master, come quickly, the star has appeared', Taurus announced excitedly.

Borago, not quite asleep yet, grabbed his staff and without hesitation, opened the door. 'Do you know its location?'

'It is in the direction of the Fatum realm, master.'

'Very well, I will summon the Salamanders at the Magma Pit. Meet me inside the Magma Cave, with a few of your centaurs', Borago ordered, as he prepared himself.

The Magma Cave, at the foot of the Mercury Mountains, appears dark on entering, but soon the heat and glow from the liquid lava gives some light to the obsidian walls.

Moments later, the Shadow Master arrived at the Magma Cave to find Taurus already inside, waiting. He walked over to the pool of burning hot lava. Once again Borago held his staff aloft and the Orbicular Rock shone with power.

'Salamanders, I command you to awaken!' barked the Shadow Master.

The lava began to swell into a huge vortex. Before long, balls of fire the size of coconuts were shooting from the whirling mass and onto the floor of the cave. Two, four, five, ten...Borago was surrounded by a circle of miniature, fire-engulfed beings. The Salamanders were stick-thin, fiery sprites, great seekers and highly destructive.

'Salamanders, I have summoned you to seek out and destroy the Illuminata', the Shadow Master commanded. 'Go forth and head for the Fatum realm.'

The Salamanders left the cave like flaming cart wheels, leaving a faintly scorched trail behind them. Taurus followed to ensure they reached Bloodwood Gorge, the deep ravine that separated the Anaconda realm from all the others. When they arrived, the Salamanders propelled themselves through the air and over the Gorge, landing on the other side.

After the countless surprise attacks the Salamanders had executed, the next village to be targeted was Lavandula, situated at the foot of Vervain hills, next to the fields of lavender. A watchman from the nearby battlements of Vervain castle witnessed the inferno on Lavandula and told the first knight, Sir Dill, who rushed to report to his great leader—King Yarrow of Vervain. He was a noble and honest king, just like his forefathers, born into a dutiful life of maintaining peace and harmony throughout Fatum. He and his kind and loyal wife,

Queen Aveena, had a young son named Prince Burdock, who was not yet old enough to ride a horse.

'Gather your best men-at-arms and let us depart immediately', King Yarrow instructed Sir Dill, as he prepared for whatever malevolent force was out there.

'Be careful, my love', Queen Aveena implored, clasping his hands in hers. King Yarrow smiled lovingly, and placed a gentle kiss on her forehead before departing.

The king's horses galloped as fast as they could, their thundering hooves marking out divots in the soft damp ground, as they rode away from Vervain towards the scene at Lavandula. Upon arrival, it became apparent from the charcoal remains that the situation was worse than first feared.

'Sir Dill, order your men to spread out', the king ordered. 'Check for survivors and be on your guard.'

'Right away, Your Grace.'

King Yarrow slowly dismounted from his horse and, armed with a sword, walked carefully through the burnt village. The torched houses lit the night sky; the grounds still warm with embers. He was too late. The once pretty village of Lavandula had been destroyed; a foul smell of smoke and cremated victims filled the air. It was a scene of total devastation.

All at once, King Yarrow saw something not far off. He approached with caution, each step he took crushing the charred soil. The thing was a pulsating sphere of light, which became smaller as he got closer, until it faded into the darkness. King Yarrow came to a halt and, looking down, saw a baby lying in a woven willow basket, nestled in a lavender bush. As he lifted the basket, his eyes didn't blink; then a strong gust of wind suddenly swept through the village putting out every last flame. Instantly, the ball of light appeared again from the nearby lavender field; with it came an enchanting voice whispering King Yarrow's name. It grew louder with the movement of the sphere. Again, the ball of light faded to black; then, into the moonlight stepped a captivating young woman, with long, black hair, a hint of lilac running through the locks. Her emerald eyes seemed to sparkle and she wore a flowing gown made of ivy, her head fittingly decorated with a silver coronet.

'King Yarrow, I mean you no harm', she spoke softly.

At this point the guards arrived, ready to defend their king.

'At ease men', the king commanded undeterred, and turned back to face the mysterious lady. 'Who are you?'

'I am Morgana', she answered, 'Queen of the Fairies and Magical Creatures of Fatum.'

'Morgana...yes', King Yarrow said, staring curiously at her.

The story of Morgana was legendary; how she had helped nurture the forests of the Fatum realm in its infancy and protected them thereafter.

'Please King Yarrow, order your men to leave, for what I am about to reveal to you is not for their knowledge', she said, leaning close.

The king, with a sense of trust, did as Morgana asked. His men rode back to the castle while King Yarrow held the basket cradling the baby.

'The child you are holding is no ordinary child; she is the prophet Illuminata', Morgana declared.

The king fixed his gaze upon the sweet infant.

'Her name is Rose, and you are to take good care of her, as her guardian', Morgana affirmed.

21

'You are the last good king, entrusted by God to take care of the prophet. She must be protected at all costs.' Morgana opened her hand to reveal a silver chain; attached was a tear-shaped pink crystal. It was a rose quartz.

'This powerful crystal symbolises all that Rose will radiate in time—unconditional love and infinite peace. It will also protect her.' Morgana placed the precious gemstone in the basket.

'On the day of her eighteenth birthday, you must present it to her, but do not reveal any of this information to Rose or anyone else.' The king listened attentively and nodded respectfully.

'When the time is right, I will send for the Illuminata to fulfil the prophecy. Remember, trust no one.' Whereupon, like a wisp of smoke from a burning candle, Morgana disappeared into the nearby woods.

The king took a moment; he needed to digest the information and to think of an explanation to give the court. Using the long reins, King Yarrow strapped the basket onto the horse's mane, before climbing up himself. Holding tight to the precious bundle, he rode non-stop towards his castle.

Chapter Two—The Search

Continues

After days of wreaking havoc and destruction in the surrounding area of Vervain, the Salamanders went back to their place of origin, as witnessed by Taurus's men from the battlements of Borago's castle.

'Master, the Salamanders have successfully returned', Taurus rapidly advised. He stood tall and strong before his master.

'I see. I will consult the hags just to be sure their mission was complete. Take leave for the night, I will summon you again if need be.' Borago went into the Mercury Well chamber and called for the sinful sisters.

'What is your bidding, master?' they spoke in unison.

Borago peered closely at them, with a frown and pupils like tiny dots.

'I need to know if the prophet Illuminata has been destroyed.'

There was a slight gap before one of them replied.

'Go on, you tell him', Marelda whispered and nodded to her sister.

'Oh, all right, you coward', Hemmatia sneered and poked Marelda with her long finger.

'Tell me what?' Borago asked, alarmed.

'The prophet still lives, master', Hemmatia answered, with one eye tightly shut as she braced for an eruption. Marelda was hopelessly trying to hide behind her beanpole sister.

'No! I must know its exact location.' Borago did indeed erupt, pointing his staff with the glowing rock at the trembling crones.

'Please, master, it's not that simple', the witches wailed. 'The prophet, we are told is a baby girl, held somewhere in the Fatum realm, but she is being shielded by a crystal. Therefore we cannot locate her exact spot. We speak the truth!' Hemmatia bowed her head.

'So, she has a crystal...' thought Borago aloud, lowering his staff and rubbing his prickly chin. '...then we will seek out the girl with the crystal.' Borago knew that only a Crystal Master had the privilege of owning a crystal; it was said to be their symbol of greatness and power. 'I will not rest until she is found and brought to me.'

The following day Borago woke up with a plan. From the grounds of his castle he called out to his most trusted chariot, a golden gryphon named Castro. This majestic bird, which resided at the top of the mountains, flew down and landed heavy-footed beside him. As Castro crouched down, Borago mounted the ornately-plumed creature and set course for the Moora Desert. The air was warm and dry as they flew, arriving a short time later at the centre of the Moora—what could only be described as a harsh environment of the most dehydrated kind. The sun's unceasing rays beat down on the dusty, dry red plains. Even the trees grew flat along the ground, their bare branches scratching the surface, as though in search of water. In one area, the carnivorous crows were feasting on an oversized rodent—the latest victim of the Moora—mercilessly pecking it bare, with their sharp beaks. Casting the occasional shadow were hundreds of colossal termite mounds. Borago walked casually over and stood among them and, in a strident voice, spoke.

'Rock Men, hear me. I, the Shadow Master, release you from your slumber!'

Suddenly, the termite mounds began to shudder and out of the cracks came millions of tiny white ants, hurriedly escaping the shape-shifting lumps. One by one they evolved and grew into Rock Men. These boulder-sized beasts had beady red eyes of lava, arms like giant clubs and feet wide enough to squash a large dog.

'Rock Men, your task is to build me a bridge over Bloodwood Gorge, so that all of Anaconda can unite as my army, and travel across to the other realms to enable my rule.' Borago rotated slowly on the spot, demonstrating his powerful stance. 'Use the rocks from the Mercury Mountains and throw them into the gorge until a path has been made. Go now and do not fail me.'

The Rock Men gave out a unified roar, scaring the crows away, and then began their journey towards the mountains. Meanwhile Borago, with the help of Castro, returned to his castle, feeling certain of his plan.

Chapter Three—Coming of Age

As a child, Rose was a contented princess. Her given title was Lady Rose of Vervain and the king and queen adored her as they would their own daughter. Prince Burdock, their son, not much older than Rose, played happily with her. Queen Aveena understood full well the implications of her husband's duty to Morgana, for the king had revealed the secret only to his loyal wife the same night that Rose was found, and he explained why she was never allowed to go outside the castle walls unaccompanied.

But one day in particular, one which the queen would never forget, Rose went missing, briefly. She was only five years old and had managed to slip away unnoticed. All the courtiers and guards were ordered to search the grounds immediately. Eventually one of them found the little girl in the stables and informed their Royal Highnesses, who rushed over to where Rose had been found. To their amazement, she appeared to be conversing with Belle, the queen's horse. The mare seemed to understand, responding by nodding or tapping its hoof on the ground. The royal couple continued to watch in awe, until Rose sensed their presence and turned to address them.

'Look, Belle has a baby in her tummy', Rose said, pointing to Belle's underside. 'It's a boy horse.' She smiled sweetly, blissfully unaware of the panic she had caused.

'That is wonderful news, my dear. Now, let us get you ready for supper', Queen Aveena said, not really sure how she should react, but taking Rose lovingly by the hand and leading her back inside the castle.

'Bye, Belle', Rose said, waving sweetly.

Later that evening the king and queen discussed the day's event.

'And do you really think Belle is expecting?' the queen asked, getting into bed.

'Impossible, she has never been with a stallion.' The king looked curiously into the night sky from his window. 'From now on, we must be extra vigilant with Rose's identity. She is starting to show her uniqueness.'

'I agree, the gentry will think her odd, different.' The queen slipped under the blanket of the bed and gave out a long sigh.

'Don't worry', King Yarrow said, huddling up to his pensive wife. 'Morgana will come for her when the time is right, of that I am certain.' He kissed his dear lady before turning over to blow out the candle. 'Goodnight, Aveena.'

'Goodnight, dear.'

Several months passed, and Belle did indeed mysteriously give birth to a fine colt, pure white except for a dark blaze like a crescent moon on its forehead. From the moment it was born, the foal showed strength and character. King Yarrow believed it to be a gift from the God Omnio, but chose to say nothing. So as not to raise any suspicions, he confessed to having himself taken the mare to a breeder. Rose was allowed to visit Belle, who lay on the floor still exhausted from her labour.

'Can I keep him, please?' Rose asked the king, while hugging the king's leg.

The king patted her gently on the head. 'Certainly; what shall we name him?'

'Um, I think Noble is a nice name', Rose said, greeting her new friend, 'Hello Noble, my name is

Rose and I will love you forever.' She hugged him gently and the newly born foal graciously responded with a tiny neigh.

As time went by, Rose developed many artistic talents, one of which was the ability to play the harp from a very young age. Rose had a special visitor, who frequented her window ledge; it was a blue wagtail, a small bird, with a slightly fanned tail which it would wag from side to side as it sang. Rose loved to listen to its melodic chirp and named it Mr Wags.

As Rose grew older she would write poetry, which clearly showed her longing for adventure and to see the world beyond the castle walls.

As I sit and observe from my window,
The birds are calling me,
I wait as serene as a flower in bloom,
Knowing one day I will be free,
Roaming every hillside and mountain,
Sailing across the sea,
There is a place of longing,
And that is where I will be.

In the meantime, back on board the ship Exodus, someone else had a similar plan of their own. Gallium had become a strong young man with rugged, dark good looks. He wanted so much to get away from the clutches of Captain Nine-tails and seek his own fortune, while avenging his father.

'Ha, is that the best you can do lad?' declared one of the shipmates, Knuckles, a walrus of a man who was rightly named for his unbeatable bare-fist fights.

'I'm just warming up', Gallium said, charging towards Knuckles, fists at the ready. He swung with his right, but missed as Knuckles swerved and grabbed Gallium's arm and bent it behind his back, before pinning the young buccaneer face down on the wooden floor.

'D' you gives up?' Knuckles asked, applying so much pressure that Gallium's cheek rubbed against the splintered deck. The crew watched in amusement, jeering and betting among themselves (with not much to trade) on who would win.

'All right, you win.' Gallium realised he was no match for this fighter.

'Get back to work you no-good, flea-infested cretins!' Captain Nine-tails boomed, cracking his whip on the deck and nearly taking a privateer's eye out.

Knuckles released Gallium, amused by his efforts. Gallium got back to his feet, wiping the blood from his slightly grazed cheek with the back of his hand, and giving the captain who prowled back down to his cabin, a daggered stare.

'If you thinks I'm going easy on you 'cause we're mates, you can thinks again. Welcome to the real world', Knuckles jested, giving Gallium a friendly slap on the back, which nearly sent him overboard. The slurry of a crew chorused with laughter before returning to their duties.

Gallium also practised another form of defence— the art of sword fighting. He would train with Mr Flinders most evenings, as the rest of the crew and the captain fell asleep drunk. Before Captain Aidan McLarty's capture, the valiant mariner had given Gallium his sword as a gift. His beloved son kept the sword hidden under a loose board where he slept below deck, along with a few gold coins that had been shared out over the years among the privateers. Once old enough, Gallium practised every day, with one mission in life—to avenge his father's death. Tomorrow the ship Exodus would dock at Dorsal Bay in the Fatum realm; there he would make his great escape and begin his search for the Shadow Master.

From his monstrous castle in the Mercury Mountains, Borago was awaiting another evening's entertainment. He sat tapping his seafaring fingers against the armrest of his elaborate obsidian throne. Taurus finally announced that the entertainers of Mumbala had arrived outside the castle's huge wooden double doors. Bored, Borago raised his hand, signalling to the two well-built doormen. They proceeded to heave open the heavy doors.

Spilling into the Great Hall came a procession of artists, dancing and leaping their way in. First to enter were the musicians, playing an upbeat tempo on traditional oud guitars, and the rhythmic tablah drums used in and around the City of Mumbala. They were closely followed by a harem of belly dancers, whose hypnotic hips and brightly coloured organza costumes flowed with their movements; one of them even had a snake around her neck, draped over the arms like a fashion accessory! The women jiggled and glided their way across the floor, to finish, bowed down at the feet of their master, whose mind was clearly elsewhere as he sat poker-faced and not moved in the slightest. Next were the three jugglers extraordinaire. Walking on stilts, their faces heavily defined with theatrical make-up, they tossed beribboned clubs high into the air, while working to keep their balance. After these came the big finale; six acrobatic male dancers, performing their forward rolls, heart-stopping somersaults and amazing back flips. To finish off was a fire-eater with flaming batons that he tossed high in the air, before extinguishing each one in his mouth.

One of the belly dancers, a young woman of Mumbala, suddenly caught the Shadow Master's eye.

He studied her every move intensely. Azria was her name; a young beauty with raven dark hair, cinnamon skin and almond shaped eyes, who danced devotedly in front of her master, moving ever closer to enrapture him. But Borago had been betrayed a long time ago by another, and had vowed never to let a woman enter his blackened heart again.

On the day of Rose's eighteenth birthday, King Yarrow was true to his word and presented her with the crystal pendant.

'Rose, now that you have become a young lady, I feel it is time to give you this special gift', he said, handing Her Ladyship a small wooden box with a floral carved design.

With Rose's eyes wide as to what it could be, the wait was soon over.

'It's a precious gem stone, one we discovered with you the day you came to be in this family', the queen said, assisting with the fastening of the chain around Rose's neck. The light pink crystal glowed ever so slightly, just for a few seconds, as it touched her milky skin.

'Thank you', said Rose graciously, as she smoothed her thumb over the shiny piece. 'It's beautiful.' She gave each guardian a kiss on the cheek. 'I will treasure it forever.'

Later that evening, there was a celebratory feast held in honour of Lady Rose. Rose loved every moment of merriment, especially as it didn't happen often. The culinary smells spread into the Great Hall; upon the tables were a full hog roast; numerous cooked chickens; fresh crusty bread, crisp and golden; and other fancies, complete with a steady flow of mead, which the court happily indulged in. There were musicians softly blowing on wooden flutes, a lady plucking the strings of a harp to create a winsome sound, and dancers in long flowing dresses with flower garlands in their hair, waving colourful ribbons in the air. Not forgetting Sid the court jester, clowning around as usual with witty songs, wearing his rainbow-coloured motley costume and his big floppy hat with tiny bells sewn on the tips. Rose never failed to laugh at Sid, especially when he tried to impress Flora, her maid, by producing a rather crushed bouquet of flowers from up his sleeve. While the evening ended well, with the royal guests positively rolling out of the Great Hall, with their contented bellies and wine-blushed cheeks, Rose secretly wished for a life far beyond the reaches of the castle walls. A life filled with more adventure and purpose. 'Maybe one day', she thought.

A short time passed after her birthday, and Rose was now a beautiful young woman with long, chestnut-brown hair and large doe eyes, which at times clearly demonstrated her emotions. There was still one thing Rose specifically wanted—to unmask her true identity; who she really was and where exactly she came from. It was time for answers.

After a morning ride with the king and Prince Burdock, Rose mustered the courage to ask.

'Your Grace, may I have a quiet word with you about something of a personal nature?'

'Sounds serious, Rose; very well, walk with me', King Yarrow said, as he led his horse back to the stable. Once inside he turned attentively to Rose. 'What is it my child?' King Yarrow asked.

'Well, the thing is, I would really like to know who I am. I feel sheltered from the truth. Please do not think me ungrateful', Rose blurted, hands nervously fidgeting with the edge of her cloak. 'I love living here with you all, but there is a part of me that is missing.'

'I see.' The king pondered for a moment, while gently brushing down his horse's mane. He understood her frustration, but unfortunately it was not his place to reveal the truth.

'Please, can you help me?' Rose asked, with a tremble in her voice.

The king ceased grooming his horse and faced his troubled ward. 'I understand your curiosity, but as I have explained before, you were found abandoned after the fires of Lavandula.'

'No note, no clue?' Rose interrupted, now flattening the straw where she stood.

'I fear not. I wish I could help you more, but that is all I know.' The king hoped that Morgana would be in touch soon. He hated lying to Rose, even though it was for her own good.

'Very well Your Grace, I appreciate what you and the queen have done for me, and I will press no further.' Rose slowly walked back up to her chambers, heart sinking and eyes welling with emotion, wondering if the king was really telling her the truth. That night Rose lay in bed mulling it over; eventually she cried herself to sleep.

A glorious morning dawned, as Rose was experiencing a vivid dream. In this dream she wandered aimlessly in a nearby wood, feeling lost and alone. But then, up ahead past some trees, she noticed something resembling a large white animal. Rose stepped bravely through the undergrowth. The animal ambled in her direction, it was a white hart, an adult male deer, 'Follow me to your destiny', the white hart said in a low calm voice, while leading her down a sandy path. Rose saw a bright light up ahead, and then she woke with a start.

'Flora, Flora!' she called to her maid, a kind old soul who had been with Rose for much of her upbringing.

Flora raced through the door. 'Whatever is the matter, milady?' she asked, a hand on her large bosom, trying to catch her breath.

'Oh Flora, I had the most amazing dream, no wait, it was a sign', Rose divulged, jumping on her bed. 'I know', thinking aloud, 'I will ride into the nearby wood. I feel sure that is the place to start.' She leapt off the bed giddy with excitement.

'You want to go into the wood, you say? Well, in that case I will go and ask Prince Burdock to accompany you.' But as Flora turned to go, Rose grabbed her by the apron.

'No, please, I need to do this alone; Burdock will only take me as far as Dorsal River', Rose pleaded. 'I have never asked you for anything as important.' Her eyes had a look of desperation as she held Flora's hands firmly.

'Yes, but what will I tell the king? You know how protective he is of you', Flora said, cradling Rose's hands in hers.

Rose gave a huge sigh, and slumped back onto her bed. She knew Flora was right. King Yarrow would send out a search party as soon as she stepped foot outside the castle. Flora felt Rose's anguish and sat beside her. At that moment, a chirping sound came from the window. It was the beloved Mr Wags. He appeared to be carrying something around his neck. Rose went over to the window to greet him.

'What is this you have?' Rose unfastened the string; tied to it was an object wrapped in parchment. She unravelled it to reveal a note addressed to her, with a miniature bottle.

'Oh dear, maybe we ought to tell the king', Flora said, poring over the note.

'No, wait let me read it first', Rose said studying it curiously.

'As you wish, milady', Flora said, paying very close attention.

Rose read the note aloud, it read:

Dear Rose,
Whoever drinks me,
Will set you free,
But beware,
They must drink just a drop,
And leave enough to spare,
For each swap.

Rose held the curious little bottle of pink potion up to the light; she studied its colour, then sniffed at it; it was odourless. Her curiosity grew from within as Rose wondered who would have sent such a thing, and how they came to know about her.

'Oh, I do not like this, I do not like this one bit!' Flora paced the floor hoping Rose would agree. 'We should tell the king immediately.'

'Wait, I have a good feeling about this', Rose professed, using her whole body to block the door.

'But it could be poison, milady. I would never forgive myself', Flora stressed with her hands now clasped in prayer position.

'If it were poison then they would want me to drink it, not someone else, someone say, like, you.'

'Me!' By now Flora was starting to panic.

'Do not fret, I will try it on Mr Wags first. Mr Wags, would you be so kind?' Rose said turning to the little bird now perched on her bed.

Mr Wags was more than obliging, poised with beak open, as she delicately poured a drop in.

Flora and Rose waited with conflicting sentiments, to see what would happen. For a moment: nothing, as the tiny bird swooped onto the chamber floor. Gradually it started to grow, as feathers shrunk deep into its body, revealing pink skin. Then, arms and legs grew, and hair on its head. The creature didn't appear to be in distress, even though the scene was rather disturbing, but the results were outstanding.

It had morphed. The bird was now Rose or at least someone who looked like her. Flora's jaw dropped and Rose stood back in amazement.

'Good heavens! He looks just like you milady', Flora exclaimed, staggering over to lean on a chair.

'This is wonderful!' Rose clapped.

Mr Wags, who was now Rose, seemed to be confused, staring around the room and then down at its new naked body. Rose quickly grabbed a blanket to cover its now female form.

'Hello Mr Wags. How do you feel?' Rose asked.

At first Mr Wags said nothing, and then out came a squawking sound. The female may have resembled Rose in every way, but its soul was still that of a bird.

'Oh dear, that won't do at all. If someone is to imitate me, they must at least sound human', Rose said.

She poured another drop of potion into a cup before handing it to Mr Wags. Flora was now turning pale at the very idea of what just happened. Evidently, some convincing would be needed before Flora would accept the role, and not to mention the need for a plan to get the real Rose out of the castle unnoticed.

Chapter Four—The Plan

Evening fell. The Shadow Master, Borago, was pacing the floor in the Great Hall of his mammoth castle. He stopped abruptly and turned to address his subjects, who had just arrived by his command. They were Taurus, Captain Nine-tails (with some of his misfit crew) and the Bandits of Mumbala, a devilish-looking lot who owed their wealth and power to Borago. Sporting black silk headscarves over their long dark 'manes' and dripping with gold as a mark of their worth, they wore sleeveless shirts revealing identical tattoos of a three headed cobra to symbolise their brotherhood.

'Gentlemen, welcome. With the bridge at Bloodwood Gorge almost complete, the time has come for us to unite.' The Shadow Master strode calmly over to his enormous fireplace and picked up a hand-sized ornate silver box from the mantel. From this he took a small red-back spider, the bite of which was fatal. He placed the spider carefully onto the palm of his hand and, holding it up to his face, whispered a curse. At first the spider did not appear to move.

Borago released the lethal spider onto the floor of the Great Hall. The men observed closely, poised to reach for their weapons if needed.

'Is it not the most beautiful creature you have ever seen?' the Shadow Master asked, with cold superiority.

Then, the spider started to grow rapidly. The onlookers stood transfixed, eyebrows raised and mouths open. Cautiously they took a few steps back as the creature grew to the size of a horse. Some of the pirates felt threatened and fled from the hall through the huge doors—which were then shut tight by the heavy-duty guards, preventing further escape. The leaders armed themselves for an attack, as the spider crept slowly towards them, its bulbous black body suspended above eight lanky legs. Then it leapt quickly to the back of the hall, blocking the only way out.

Borago sat on his throne and observed with a sinister grin. Captain Nine-tails drew his cutlass ready to defend himself, while Taurus and the remaining men followed suit. With beads of sweat on their brows, the arachnid had its prey on their toes. Fronting the giant spider, the men tried desperately to dodge the great long legs and lethal bite.

'What you playin' at Borago!?' Captain Nine-tails spat, hot-footing it away from the creature. 'We had a deal!'

Borago casually got up from his throne and pointed the Orbicular Rock at the spider.

'Cease, arachnid!' he commanded. With a glow from the rock, the spider was instantly reduced to its former size and crawled back into the silver box. 'Gentlemen, forgive me', he said shrewdly, 'but I had to test your courage and loyalty before offering you my next plan to defeat the Illuminata.' He then placed the box back on the mantel.

'Why you...I've a good mind to slit your throat!' the captain cursed, brandishing his cutlass.

'I would not if I were you, captain!' the Shadow Master replied, throwing him a severe stare and firmly gripping his staff.

'What about the treasure?' Captain Nine-tails badgered, putting away his weapon.

'You shall get your reward, captain, and more. Now, let us discuss this in detail.' The Shadow

Master led the group of men to the main dining table for further instructions.

Curvaceous maid servants were on hand in scanty attire, ready to pour wine into jewel encrusted goblets, and to hand feed the pack with fresh grapes, while all sat around the grand table, which gleamed with pewter candelabras down its long centre.

'Gentlemen, it has been brought to my attention that the Illuminata is a young maiden', the Shadow Master announced, sipping wine majestically. 'We know her to be located in the Fatum realm. She can be identified by a crystal worn around her neck.'

Borago went on to explain that the plan of action would be for each brigand to take on and complete a task, in order to capture the Illuminata. Captain Nine-tails and his crew were to cover the oceans and ports; the Bandits of Mumbala were to search every village and town, while Taurus and his army were to scan the lands and mountains. No stone was to be left unturned, no mountain untouched, no person unnoticed.

'Let me make this perfectly clear.' The Shadow Master leaned forward with inverted eyebrows. 'As long as the Illuminata lives, we are all threatened. You will deliver her alive to me and I will destroy this prophet.' He paused, casually producing a dagger from his belt and flinging it across the table, slicing the tops off the candles and narrowly missing a serving girl before the blade thudded into a wooden chair. 'Do not fail me.'

For a moment there was an uncomfortable silence.

'My lord, my men and I are ready to serve you', Taurus vowed, head down and fist on heart.

'Fine, it's a deal, but we'll need supplies', the captain said reluctantly.

The bandits grunted in accord and with that in place, the plan was set.

Chapter Five—The Escape

A few days later in the Fatum realm, in her bedchamber at the top of Vervain Castle, Rose was gracefully plucking the strings of her harp when the door quietly opened. In crept her maid, Flora, carrying a bundle of clothes. She placed them on the bed and looked suspiciously up and down the corridor, before closing the door behind her.

'Lady Rose', Flora said, 'I have a plan of how to get you out of the castle unnoticed.'

'What is it, Flora?' Rose asked eagerly, and stopped playing.

Flora picked up an item of clothing from the bed. 'These are stableboy clothes, just about your size. If you were to wear these, while I transformed into you, I could escort you to the castle gate with Noble.' Flora proceeded to unfold the garments. 'Then, I will explain to the guards that you are to take Noble to the local blacksmith for new shoes, and they will let you out. What do you think?' Flora didn't have to wait long for an answer.

'Oh Flora, you are a genius!' Rose hugged her tight and without a second thought, began to undress. 'May I ask what changed your mind?'

'Well the truth is, I also had a dream', Flora replied with a knowing smile.

The brown tunic had a hood that disguised Rose by covering most of her face; Flora assisted by carefully tying Rose's hair back. Having lived such a sheltered life, Rose felt nervous and excited all at the same time, but truly believed this had to be the life-changing adventure that she had been waiting for.

With both of them knowing what was at risk, they continued without a pause, speaking not a word the whole time. Rose mindfully removed the cork from the miniature bottle and poured a drop into a cup, before handing it with a grateful smile to Flora, who then hastily and with a shaky hand, drank the potion before she could change her mind.

'Thank you, my dear Flora', Rose whispered, as they waited for it to take effect.

A few seconds in and Flora's appearance began to transform. First her papery skin grew plump and soft, then her hair colour changed from grey to chestnut (like Rose's), and finally her body became slender and strong. Even the colour of her eyes dissolved into another colour. In no time at all she had indeed become Lady Rose.

'Huh', Rose looked up and down at Flora in astonishment. 'How do you feel?'

'I feel lighter than air! do I look like you, milady?' Flora asked, her hands trembling slightly, as she examined them.

'See for yourself in the mirror.'

Except, when Flora stood before the mirror, they were both alarmed to see not Rose's reflection, but Flora's.

'Oh dear, milady, what shall we do now?' Flora didn't want to disappoint her.

'No matter, it just means you will have to stay away from mirrors', Rose instructed, fetching Flora one of her dresses to wear.

'You won't be gone long, will you milady?' Flora asked, changing into the dress.

'I shall be back before the sun has set', Rose answered, as she wrote a detailed note. She was writing to the king, in order to protect a most loyal guardian, Flora.

'If I fail to return by sunset, you must resume your true form, and give this to the king.' She handed the wax-sealed parchment to Flora. 'It will explain everything.' And then Rose helped fasten the back of Flora's dress. 'Right, I will follow you Flora. Remember, you are now me.'

Flora nodded and opened the chamber door slowly.

Drawing in a deep breath, they hurried quietly along the corridor and down the winding staircase. Rose kept her hood up and head down at all times. She had never felt such exhilaration; her stomach was in knots. Just at that moment, voices could be heard coming from the bottom of the circular stairs. Peering around the bend, Rose could see that it was Sir Dill. He was conversing with the king and they were on their way out into the courtyard; the two women were about to run into them!

'Quickly milady, come this way.' Flora ushered Rose behind a huge, wood-carved statue at the foot of the stairs until His Grace was out of sight.

The quick-thinking maid then took Rose by the hand and rushed her out into the courtyard; but the king caught sight of them out of the corner of his eye.

'Ah, there you are Rose. I was just talking with Sir Dill about a forthcoming visit from our distant cousins, the Van Sprouts', the king explained, at the same time suspiciously eyeballing the young lad standing sheepishly to one side, not having any clue who it was.

'Where are you going with this boy, my dear?' the king enquired, referring of course to Rose.

'Oh, yes well, I was just taking err, Tim, to fetch Noble from the stables. He needs new horseshoes, Your Grace.'

'Well no matter, we can discuss the plans later.' The king made a swift half-turn and then added 'You sound unwell, Rose.'

'Perfectly fine...thank you...Your Grace', Flora said, diverting her gaze towards the stables, aware that her voice didn't sound exactly like Rose's.

'I see. You might want our local physician to take a look at you', King Yarrow concluded, walking back into the castle, leaving Sir Dill to mount his horse and exit the grounds.

Flora gingerly escorted Rose to the stables. Once there, Rose whispered in Noble's ear 'It is I, Rose; I need you to accompany me out of the castle grounds.'

Noble tapped his hoof on the ground and then miraculously spoke to her telepathically, for the first time.

'I understand, my lady', Noble said in a warm-hearted voice. 'Your time has come and it is my duty to assist you in your quest.'

'You just spoke to me', Rose gasped.

'Yes, you have the power to speak using thought, as do all magical creatures.'

Rose smiled at Noble's information and took him by the reins.

'We are ready to leave now', she whispered eagerly to her faithful maid.

Rose and Noble followed Flora to the castle entrance. As they approached the guards, every step was unpredictable; 'fake Rose' instructed them to open the portcullis. By now, Rose's heart was beating as fast as a bird's wing, her mouth was dry and her hands gripped Noble's reins tightly. 'This is it', she thought. 'No turning back now.' She had been waiting for this moment for so long. The portcullis began to open, the sound of its rusty chains unnerving them all.

'Courage, my lady', Noble voiced, offering Rose his support.

The rising sun shone on this most momentous of days. Rose took a deep breath, and, with a farewell look at Flora, began to walk steadily out of the castle and away from the stony grey walls. Leading her horse by the reins at a careful pace, they followed a dirt track in the direction of the market town of Vervain. Rose could feel every little stone underfoot, but couldn't risk being seen riding a royal's horse. A while later they neared the High Street; Rose kept her hood on and peered out at the sides. The noise of vendors and locals from the market grew louder. Through the town they ventured, avoiding any stares or contact, so as not to draw attention. Rose wasn't familiar with these surroundings and peered with great interest at the way of life in these parts of the kingdom: how locals greeted one another with friendly banter, or a cheeky slap on the back; how the dusty street was lined with market stalls and merchants plying their goods. The stalls had long wooden tables loaded with produce, shaded by large cloths suspended over wooden posts. The smells from the fresh produce filled her nostrils—some sweet, some savoury and some unidentifiable. Soon they came across a blacksmith who was busy hammering an iron horseshoe into shape. The heat from the forge made the blacksmith sweat profusely; drops fell from the end of his nose, evaporating on impact with the hot iron. Close by, a lady sold freshly picked apples; next to her was a man selling all kinds of cheeses and yet another dispensing from barrels of apple cider—just a few of the many traders, all shouting their wares to earn a living. A tired old farmer limped by, leading his equally aged horse and cart out of the town. At the centre of town was an old well where local women congregated to gossip as they filled their pails with water; and to one side of a lane was a man with one leg, begging for alms. Rose felt deeply for him, but all she could do was secretly wish him well. On the village green, a young man was locked in the stocks, probably for stealing, as passing locals pelted him with rotten vegetables. A group of little boys were kicking a pigskin football on the green too, and the young man in the stocks became an easy target for the energetic youngsters; occasionally he'd receive a direct hit to the head from the ball! Suddenly, Rose noticed some familiar faces outside 'The Old Boot' pub; they were the musicians who had come to the castle for her birthday celebrations. 'What if they should recognise me?', she thought.

'I think it best we leave now and make our way to the Whispering Wood', Noble suggested and Rose agreed hurriedly.

Once out of sight, she mounted Noble and off he galloped to the Whispering Wood, as though he knew exactly where to take her.

Back at the castle, Flora was finding it a little awkward to fill in for the Lady Rose, as the role of a princess involved things she wasn't accustomed to, like playing the harp (in Flora's case badly), and drawing some odd-shaped things, all the time trying to avoid reflections of herself. Flora prayed Rose would not be gone too long, otherwise she might have to explain things to the king. Even though the important note was in Flora's possession, she still felt responsible for the king's precious ward who, by now, was goodness-only-knew-where.

Noble galloped as fast as the winds across the ocean; he knew Rose had very little time before she must return to the castle. Soon, they neared Dorsal River. Noble crossed the bridge and was continuing through pastures green, when in the distance, Rose spotted a group on horseback. They appeared to be heading towards her. Quickly it dawned on her that Prince Burdock was out on his morning hunt. Rose had to think fast. To her right was the Flower Forest. It would be a great diversion and hiding place, a temporary measure until the prince had passed by. Once again her loyal steed obeyed and changed course of direction.

Chapter Six—What a Find!

Prince Burdock and his party were oblivious to Rose's escapade, and after a successful morning hunt, were headed back to Vervain. Noble trotted deeper into the Flower Forest; it grew dense and prolific with wildlife. The earthy ground was scattered with colourful blooms that delicately skirted the humongous trunks of the towering trees. Rose gazed up at the entwining branches laden with leaves shading the mossy ground, and breathed in the fragrant scent. The sun's rays were streams of light breaking through the foliage that gently kissed the earth. Swooping from tree to tree, were blue fairy wrens, twittering merrily. Rose lost herself completely in the captivating setting.

Dismounting from her horse, Rose closely observed some honey bees busy collecting pollen. Noble decided to rest awhile and lay down at the foot of a tree, as butterflies the size of his hooves fluttered by.

Rose, busy absorbing nature's gifts, stumbled on an oversize tree root growing above ground, and lost her footing. Picking herself up without concern, she noticed something strange about the tree in front of her. On closer inspection, she saw that the entrance to the tree's trunk was covered with some kind of animal skin, nailed along the top. Rose explored a bit further. Just outside the entrance were the remains of a campfire.

'Is anybody there?' she called, but there was no answer.

Curiosity took hold as Rose pulled the make-shift door to one side. It appeared to be inhabited—like a tree house, except within the tree trunk. 'What kind of person would live here?' thought Rose. On the ground inside the huge hollow tree was a bed made from woven willow with an old grey woollen blanket placed on top. A few items stood around: a burnt-out candle welded onto a large stone and, on the bed, a spyglass, compass, leather satchel and a pocket-sized book. Curious, Rose picked up the leather-bound book titled, 'A Traveller's Tale'. She ran her fingers over the smooth cover and held it up to her nose; its old scent made it all the more mysterious. It appeared to be someone's journal. Just as Rose delicately began to open it, there came a rustling sound from nearby branches. Straightaway, Rose prepared to leave, for fear the owner had returned and wouldn't take too kindly to her trespassing. Breathing shallowly, she replaced the item and stepped back outside. Suddenly, Rose was stopped in her tracks. She gasped. An arrow had landed on the ground just missing her foot. Turning to run to Noble, Rose tripped once again over the same exposed tree root, this time falling hard, causing her hood to drop, revealing her long hair. Looking up she saw a young man on a black stallion who seemed as stunned as she was.

It was Gallium on his black horse, Ironbark.

'Who are you?' he enquired sternly. 'And what were you doing in my tree house?'

'I...I was just curious, I meant no harm', Rose answered, hands shaking as she tried to shield her face.

By now Gallium could see that she was no threat. He noticed the crystal around her neck and remembered Captain Nine-tails speaking of a hidden place with such gems.

'You ought not to be poking around these parts alone.' He put away his bow while keeping a close eye on her.

Rose didn't respond; instead she tried to get up, but her ankle was sprained from the fall.

'I cannot move it', she said, her face creased with pain.

Noble woke with a jolt and trotted over to where she sat; he noticed the threatening company and in her defence, reared up on his back legs.

'Whoa boy, I mean her no harm.' Gallium dismounted from his horse, slowly lowering his weapons to the ground.

'Lady Rose, use your crystal; it has healing powers', Noble communicated, as he backed away from Ironbark and went to stand beside her.

Unaware of the special communication gift the two possessed, Gallium was about to help, when something magical happened.

Rose instinctively unfastened the crystal, placed it in her hand, and held it against the injured ankle. The light pink stone began to shine brightly. In her mind she repeated, 'I am healed, I am healed, I am healed'. Moments later, she felt a surge of energy through her leg, and she began to get up slowly. Gallium witnessed all this in amazement.

'Impressive', he commented. 'You do not look like a witch, and yet...'

Rose threw him a hard look.

'Of course not, I am a mere traveller.' Rose couldn't think of what else to say, and tried to avoid his alert gaze.

Gallium suspected there was much more to this beautiful traveller from the moment she healed herself, not to mention the fine horse and precious stone were evidence enough to suggest she was no ordinary lady. Still he thought it best not to question her further.

'Forgive me, but I have learnt over time, never to trust anyone.' Gallium held up his hands and took a step closer.

Rose looked at him with a subtle smile. Feeling fully recovered, she replaced the pendant round her neck. By now she had been away from the castle for far too long, at least for Flora's sake. It was time to journey back to Vervain.

'You are forgiven and now I must leave at once', Rose said, as she straddled her horse. 'I bid you good day, sir.' And off she rode before Gallium could interrogate her further.

'Wait!' Gallium stood watching as the beautiful stranger rode out of the forest, leaving him in wonder.

Once back at the castle, Rose led Noble into the stables and thanked him for his service. She hurried inside the castle, trying not to be seen, and scurried back up the stairs like a frightened field mouse and into her room, hoping to find Flora.

'Merciful God, you have returned! I have been so worried', Flora babbled, accidentally pricking her finger with a cross-stitch needle.

'Flora, there is no time.' Rose picked up the bottle of potion from her dressing table. 'Quickly, take some of the potion.'

Flora resumed her normal self almost immediately, with huge sighs of relief from both ladies. They quickly dressed in their original attire and normality was resumed.

'Oh how was it, milady?' Flora asked, as she fastened herself into her clothes.

'It was not how I planned', Rose confided dolefully. 'I had to hide from Burdock in the Flower Forest, but I *will* try again.'

Rose thought it best not to mention the stranger she had encountered in the forest, so as not to worry the old dear. Instead, she lay on her bed, held the crystal pendant round her neck and rubbed it soothingly between her fingers, staring dreamily up at the ceiling. Flora placed the stableboy disguise beneath Rose's bed, before returning to her duties.

'Who was that man? And why was he hiding in a forest?' Rose wondered.

Chapter Seven—Morgana

On another glorious day, and dressed as a stableboy, Rose attempted once more to venture away from the castle of Vervain on her loyal horse, Noble. So as not to risk being seen a second time, she left after Burdock's return from his morning hunt. Noble carried Rose instinctively in the direction of the Whispering Wood. As he galloped over brooks and meadows, clouds were forming overhead and winds were gathering momentum, forcing Rose to hold on tight to both her hood and the reins. Her blood was pumping from excitement; this time everything felt right.

The Flower Forest came into view. Tempting as it was for Rose, they did not go through it, as the Whispering Wood was past that point. Soon, up ahead, there appeared a clearing that led into the Whispering Wood. Once inside the thick woodland, the pair could hear faint whispers seeming to come from the trees. Rose couldn't decipher the softly spoken incantations. Looking over her shoulder, she checked to see if anyone was following, but there was only wood, after wood, after wood. Nestled at the foot of every peppermint tree was a group of vivid red toadstools freckled with white spots. Noble slowed down to a more pleasant pace and continued to guide Rose through this enchanted place that seemed somehow familiar, even though she had never been there before. All at once it dawned on Rose that this place was just like the one in her dream! They followed a similar path of dry twigs, fallen leaves and mossy ground, which wound its way beneath the peppermint trees, aptly named for their pungent minty scent that filled the air. The stretching branches had formed into a curve at the top, creating a sort of woodland archway.

'Noble, can you hear something? Sounds like...music. It's getting louder', Rose remarked, quivering with delight and looking to see what or who could be making this merry tune.

Jumping down from her horse she led Noble by the reins, treading watchfully through the undergrowth towards the sound of the music. When Rose was able to see ahead, there, dancing along the path, were strange four-legged creatures. She was curious, but unafraid. She and Noble kept walking closer until all was revealed. The creatures were in fact magical fauns, with the body of a goat but the head and torso of a man. One faun led the merry dance while blowing on his pan pipes, followed by another strumming a lyre and yet another beating a small drum. Glittering flower fairies the size of small birds, skipped and pirouetted to the music behind the fauns. By now Rose was in a trance, lured by these tiny beings further and further into the wood. Many more fairies fluttered over to join in the soirée, coming out from behind toadstools or emerging from crevices in tree trunks, leaving a sparkling trail of fairy dust upon the ground. Deeper and deeper into the wood they all went, and as they went, Rose felt happier and lighter. Eventually, the group came to a glade—an area of daisy-filled grass in the middle of which stood an ancient tree. This was the Sacred Tree, the heart of all things growing and living in this magical realm. As wide as a horse cart, its twisted light grey trunk had knobbly bark while its branches interwove in every direction, their wide, clustered leaves forming a generous canopy. Swiftly the music stopped and everyone came to a halt. A faint rumbling noise could be heard from beneath the earth.

'What is happening?' asked Rose alarmed, as she struggled to move her feet. It was as though they had been nailed to the ground.

The terrain started to vibrate ever so slightly, but Rose managed to keep her balance. One by one, the creatures all disappeared behind the Sacred Tree. Rose then watched as large grey stones appeared from the earth, forming a huge circle round the tree, with her in the centre. Next, from the base of the magnificent tree, there floated up and around its trunk hundreds of tiny points of light. These bright specks cocooned the twisted trunk, then dimmed to nothing, revealing the more familiar form of a female, carved from wood and standing against the trunk. Emerging from the carved image like an awakened beauty, came Morgana. She stood before Rose with great majesty, in a flowing gown made entirely of ivy.

'Welcome, Rose of Vervain, to the Whispering Wood', Morgana announced. 'You are now standing inside a fairy circle.' Morgana started walking around Rose who stood firm, her eyes fixed on the maiden's presence. 'Relax; no harm can come to you while you are inside. Anyone looking in from the outside cannot see us, nor may they enter.'

'Who are you and how do you know who I am?' Rose asked, slightly nervous as she began to regain movement in her feet.

'I am Morgana, Queen of the Fairies and Magical Creatures within this realm', Morgana proclaimed in a soothing voice.

Then, to Rose's amazement, Morgana quickly transformed herself into a little blue wagtail.

'Mr Wags?' Rose said, astonished. 'Or should I say Mrs Wags?'

The vibrant blue bird flew towards the Sacred Tree and disappeared into the trunk leaving a rippling effect like water.

'The answers you seek lie with me', Morgana's voice echoed from within the tree, as she commenced narration by vision on the trunk, like a reflection in water.

'The God Omnio released you from the heavens, and by magic you were born from a crystal. King Yarrow is your guardian; he vowed to protect your identity until the time came for me to call upon you.' Morgana fell silent and next reappeared from the tree, as herself, to explain further. 'The crystal you keep is part of who you are; it is the source of your power.' The Fairy Queen lightly touched the stone pendant with her finger, as if anointing it. 'Should it end up in the wrong hands, you and the ancient world of Pangaea will be destroyed.'

'So, am I to understand that I am a *stone*?!' Rose asked mystified, studying herself.

Morgana blew some fairy dust on to an exposed root of the Sacred Tree, and it magically transfigured into two wooden chairs. Morgana sat on one and gestured for Rose to sit on the other. Rose walked over to the other chair and sat seated face to face with the magical queen; the conversation continued.

'Rose, you are the prophet Illuminata, born to save our world.'

The young princess jerked back in her chair, her hands gripping her knees, eyes wide and ears catching every word. This is what Rose had always dreamed of; finding out who she really was, but— saving the world?

Morgana then signalled to the Sacred Tree's trunk, creating another vision, and continued with the story.

'The God Omnio created our land with the help of the Crystal Masters, who, like you, were born of the four powerful crystals of Pangaea. They helped create all the realms of Pangaea except one; Anaconda, which was created by the God Omnio's jealous brother, Helidor, now banished to the sun. Once the masters' work was complete, the crystals were returned to their birthplace, each in a different, secret location. The Crystal Masters were then laid to rest at another secret location. The truths and secrets are known only to the Gnomes of Jurien, as written in the Book of Legends.'

Rose promptly stood up. 'I feel...I feel strange.' She started to glow from head to toe like a moonbeam. 'What is happening to me?' she asked, rubbing her sweaty palms on her thighs.

'Please Rose, take a breath and sit down. I am here to help you.' Morgana held her hands gently as the startled Rose sat down again.

'The Sacred Tree is forming a bond with you; the crystal and your powers are growing stronger. In time, you will learn to control it through your emotions.'

Rose composed herself and listened attentively to her informer.

'All right, it would appear this is my duty, so I accept. What must I do?'

The vision faded and Morgana turned to face her pupil.

'Your quest is to go to Jurien. Announce who you are to the Gnome King Drew, and ask to see the Book of Legends. It will reveal to you the whereabouts of the four crystals, the location of the masters' resting place and a way to save our world from the evil Shadow Master, Borago.' Morgana's eyes barely blinked at this point. It was as though she had momentarily frozen.

'The Shadow Master? Who is he?' Rose asked.

'Borago was once a pirate king, before he stole the Orbicular Rock from the last Gnome King', said Morgana in a trance. 'He forged his blood with the powerful rock and now rules the southern realm of Anaconda.' Morgana got up slowly from her seat and turned away. Her hands locked against her heart, she carried on. 'All the beasts there bow down and obey him. Only you can retrieve the Orbicular Rock, thus taking away his power and preventing an evil rule.'

Morgana walked up to Rose and placed a gentle hand on her shoulder.

'As the next Crystal Master, Rose, you still have a lot to learn, but it is my duty to guide you.' The Fairy Queen repositioned herself on the chair and looked into her pupil's eyes with fondness. 'So, you will need some help from the Lightworkers.'

'Lightworkers?'

'Those appointed by God on this earth to help you in your quest. Therefore, your first task is to find the warrior who will help you fight the beasts; the second is to seek out the teacher, who will give you knowledge and enlightenment.' Morgana ended by pointing to Noble; the dark blaze on his forehead now started to shine like sunlight on a silver coin. 'And you have already met your guide, who will escort you on your journey. Once you have found both warrior and teacher, you may start your quest in the Neve Realm, to the north.'

All at once, like an apparition, Morgana turned away from Rose and floated back into the tree's trunk.

'Wait, how will I know? Morgana?' Rose asked, breathing quickly and desperately feeling the trunk for an opening. One minute she was leading a sheltered life of nobility, the next she was given the huge task of saving the world!

'Trust your instincts and know this—you will be guided every step of the way. I have faith in you, Rose.' Morgana's voice faded into the hollow of the tree.

Instantly, the circle of large stones sank back underground and Rose was free to go, feeling a little overwhelmed, but determined to see the quest through. The clouds turned a darker shade of grey, and it began to rain heavily. Rose and her guiding horse made haste for Vervain once more. The torrential downpour was relentless, causing poor visibility and a risk of slipping for Noble, but he soldiered on at a cautious pace through the sodden ground and waterlogged plains. The ride home seemed to last forever; Rose found she had to grasp the reins ever tighter, her mind reeling with all the information, while rehearsing her lines for the king. At last the castle came into sight. As soon as they passed under the portcullis, Rose slid off her horse and dashed inside, as though her life depended on it.

'I wish to speak with the king!' Rose blurted. She had made a dramatic entrance into the Great Hall, dripping wet from head to toe, her hair sticking to her face.

There were gasps and gawps from the Royal Court, who were whispering out of curiosity, all eyes fixed on the surprise guest. The gathering was for the arrival of the Van Sprouts. By now Rose didn't care what anyone thought, the puzzle of her life was being pieced together and she needed answers. Flora sat next to the queen, still posing nervously as Rose. For a moment the only thing that could be heard was Rose's heaving breath, as the Court turned to their king for a response. King Yarrow stood to attention.

'State your name', he said firmly; echoing faintly throughout the expansive hall.

'I am, L-Lady Rose, Your Grace', she answered through chattering teeth, the cold now seeping through to her bones. The crystal around Rose's neck flickered with light.

'Rose', the king murmured; identifying her by the crystal pendant, he hurried over as she held on to his arms, cold, wet and exhausted.

In the meantime, the court turned to Flora, who by now had a gleam of perspiration. Sir Dill confronted Flora, pointing his sword at her in a threatening manner. The colour had completely drained from Flora's face and her mouth was too dry to speak; the one saving grace was the bottle of potion she kept in a small drawstring bag around her wrist. Flora quickly took the bottle out and drank from it. Everyone in the hall gasped in horror to see the magical transformation. Some of the court proclaimed that black magic was afoot and heckled Flora, yelling 'She is a witch!'

'Forgive me Your Grace', Flora said with her head hung low.

'Your Grace, Flora is not to blame. It was my idea', Rose murmured, her eyes half closed.

The King knew he had to think fast as the court grew more troubled. He handed Rose carefully to his queen and Flora, and they supported the drenched maiden up to her bedchamber.

'My lords and ladies, I give you my word that I will resolve this matter', the king vowed, hand on heart. 'But for now, everyone bar Sir Dill and Prince Burdock, must leave the hall at once', the king commanded. 'And please, not a word of this outside the court.'

The perplexed courtiers obeyed their trusted king, and collectively vacated the Great Hall, though whispering and in shock. Sir Dill and Prince Burdock were left standing side by side.

'Father, how did you know which Rose was telling the truth?' Rose wasn't the only one looking for answers.

Before the king could answer his inquisitive son, the queen rushed back into the hall.

'My king, might I have a quiet word with you', the queen said breathless from rushing down the spiral staircase.

King Yarrow took Aveena to one side.

'What is it?' he asked.

'Yarrow, Rose knows who she really is. Morgana met with her in the Whispering Wood', the queen confided closely to her king.

'I see.' King Yarrow looked across at his son, eagerly awaiting news, and at Sir Dill, who stood with the prince, also keen to know more.

'Aveena, if this is true, then she will need all our support.' He then walked briskly to where the gallant men stood.

The king began briefing his son and knight as to who Rose really was and how, as the prophet, she must be protected at all cost—for the future of the world depended upon their loyal service and discretion. The two men gave their word to the king and enough was said for now.

For the remainder of that day, Rose rested in her bedchamber. Evening soon fell.

'Flora, I need to speak with the king, but I fear he is avoiding me', the princess said from her bed, as a frantic Flora entered the room.

'I have word, milady, that the king will meet with you tomorrow; now, you should rest.' Her ever faithful maid tucked in the bedsheets and took her dinner plate, before leaving the room. Rose stared into the honey-like flame of the candle beside her bed. In no time at all, she drifted from the thoughts of the day into peaceful sleep.

At breakfast the next day, there was an uncomfortable silence. Seated at the table were Rose, the king, queen and Prince Burdock; very little eye contact between them. Then, the king motioned with his hand to a nearby guard. The guard marched over to where the king sat at the head of the table and bowed forward; the king spoke quietly into the guard's ear. Without hesitation, the guard speedily marched in the direction of the doors. Rose didn't have much of an appetite and pushed a blackberry around her plate with a finger. In her mind there was so much to talk about and she kept going over the details, so as not to forget.

'I have summoned Sir Dill to meet with us in a moment, at the Place-of-Arms', the king announced casually, as he finished his last morsel of bread and butter.

'There we can discuss yesterday's events, in private.'

After their meal, the king led them all into a private room at the back of the castle; this was the Place-of-Arms, a large room, where the king usually assembled his council before going into battle. The party, including Flora, sat round a huge circular stone table, sited at the centre of the room.

'Lady Rose, please explain to the council how you swapped roles with Flora and disappeared without an escort', King Yarrow asked in an authoritative tone.

Rose paused for a moment, as the council directed their attention to her. Flora clasped her hands in support and the queen smiled gently. Rose drew in a deep and began to recount events. She continued in great detail as to how the mission would save Pangaea from a future of evil rule that would span across the realms, if the Shadow Master, Borago, was not stopped.

'My first task is to find the warrior who will help fight, and then I must find the teacher who will instil in me wisdom and knowledge. I was told to start my search in the Neve realm, so I have decided to go north with Noble as my guide.'

'Indeed', the king said twirling the end of his beard. 'It will be quite a challenge for you.' King Yarrow leaned in closer, his palms on the table. 'I also know, Morgana would not expect you to go alone or unprepared.'

'Your Grace, I would be most honoured to accompany Lady Rose', Sir Dill spoke up.

'I also would like to assist on such a noble quest', Prince Burdock added faithfully.

'I am grateful to you both for offering, but first, as my ward, we must train Rose properly in the art of sword fighting', said the king firmly. 'When I think you are ready, Rose, then your quest may begin', the king advised. 'We will commence at dawn and meet here every day, at the same time. No one in this room must ever speak of this mission, or it could leak to the enemy. Sir Dill, you will train Rose as you train your men, no exceptions.'

'Consider it done, Your Grace', Sir Dill said, saluting with a nod and hand on heart.

'Flora, while I do not fully approve of your questionable behaviour', the king stressed, walking slowly towards her, 'I understand the reason and will overlook it just this once, but in future all serious decisions must be put to me first.' He then continued in a gentler tone. 'Now, please see to it that Rose is properly attired for the training and her all-encompassing journey.'

'Yes Your Grace, thank you', Flora said, feeling her eyes well up. She was very fond of Rose, having cared for her since infancy.

'I am ready to do whatever it takes, Your Grace', Rose said fervently, her shoulders back and standing before her king.

'I have no doubt, which is why you have been chosen', he expressed in admiration.

After this, King Yarrow declared the meeting over and all normal activities were resumed within the castle.

For the next couple of weeks Rose endured a tough regime of early starts, lifting large stones and trail-running, come rain or shine. Sir Dill pushed and Rose willingly soldiered on. All she could think about was the cause; over the coming days, Rose learnt to grow in mind and body.

As part of her training, the sword fighting would be conducted every day in the Place-of-Arms.

'Here, take this sword, my lady', Sir Dill said, as he handed her a wooden training sword. 'Remember to use all of you to guide it; your aim is to deflect, not block; to dodge and strike hard.' Sir Dill demonstrated a few moves with another training sword. 'Become one with your weapon. A true swordsman fights with nobility and skill, as well as strength.'

Initially, Rose learnt the basic stance and movements of sword fighting. Sir Dill was impressed at how quickly she picked it up, and in the days that followed, they moved on to real steel blades.

'Now, show no mercy', Sir Dill ordered, standing strong before her with his sword at the ready.

The First Knight's strikes were unremitting, but Rose kept her guard and studied his every move. The clash of blades caused sparks to fly; a surge of energy coursed through her veins, as never before. Intuitively, she knew where the next blade would strike, and at one point smashed Sir Dill's sword to the ground. With time, Rose became more powerful, as her crystal illuminated during the training. It was at that moment that Sir Dill gave his esteemed student a satisfied nod. After Rose's accomplishments were reported to His Majesty, the king was then satisfied with Rose's progress and the training was deemed complete.

King Yarrow summoned the gentry involved in this mission, back to the Place-of-Arms to finalise Rose's preparation.

The king sombrely stood at the ancient round table and paused for a moment, as members took their seats.

'It is time', he announced.

The day he feared had finally come, his ward was no longer under his protection, but destined to go on and do great deeds. The king stalked over to a large pennant emblazoned with the coat-of-arms, hanging from one of the walls, and unhooked it with a long wooden prop. The pennant was guarding a closely kept secret, one which no one—not even the queen—had knowledge of. The exposed wall featured a stone carving of a bearded man's face, its mouth a dark hole. King Yarrow passed his hand through the cavity of the mouth and stretched his arm, now elbow deep. Everyone watched in wonder; none had witnessed this before. Eventually, the king drew out a long, leather sheath. He slid the sheath off to reveal a craftsman's dream of a sword. This was no ordinary weapon.

'Members of the court, I give you the Renaissance Sword, forged by the God Omnio and handed down to every king whoever ruled over Vervain.' King Yarrow went to where Rose was seated. 'It is an honour to now pass it on to you', he announced, gently placing it across the palms of her hands. King Yarrow stepped back, smiling down like a proud father at a celebratory ceremony.

Rose was stunned. Her face reflected the shine from the ornate gold handle and steel blade-edge. There was an engraving along the blade, and Rose read it aloud:

'In God I trust with this sword I will thrust into the enemy's heart.'

No sooner said, than an intense humming vibration came from the hallowed blade, and it began to levitate a few inches above Rose's hands, then lowered back down to signify their union. The council were all agog.

'Remember, this is a powerful weapon', the king continued. 'It can only be used in the fight against evil.'

Next, the king gave Rose the map of Pangaea which was held in a long ivory casket at the centre of the round table. Before concluding, the king spoke to his precious ward, not just as a king, but as a father.

'I hold you in the highest regard, my lady, and you will always have a home here at Vervain Castle. I am at your service.' The gracious king dropped to one knee before her and all those present in the room humbly followed suit.

'Thank you, all of you', Rose said a little choked-up. 'I must leave soon, but the majesty of this moment will forever remain in my heart.' And so,

Lady Rose calmly exited the room, to prepare herself for the long road ahead.

Under a cloudy sky, the castle of Vervain bid farewell to its fair lady, who sat astride her horse outside the main entrance. Accompanying Rose were Sir Dill and Prince Burdock, ready to set off on their journey. Rose was informally dressed in a white tunic laced at the front, a brown leather waistcoat and a pair of knee-high leather boots, over olive coloured woollen trousers. Over all, she wore a long, dark blue, velvet hooded cloak. The Renaissance Sword was strapped to her side in its leather sheath. Queen Aveena handed Rose a bag full of coins to buy provisions, then kissed her sweetly on the hand, too emotional for words.

'May God be with you all', the king said, an arm around his tearful wife.

As Rose inhaled deeply, she escaped to the pages of her mind and reflected upon her inner strength to help carry out this duty to mankind, before instructing Noble to lead the way.

Chapter Eight—The Eyes of a Raven

The next night, at 'The Old Boot' ale house in the market town of Vervain, someone was telling a familiar tale.

'And in she bursts, like a drowned rat. It was...(burp) shocking, I can tell ya; you see, Flora was not Flora, and Lady Rose was not...(hiccup),' described young Eric, in an uncomprehending manner, waving his arms around dramatically, causing ale to spill from his tankard and completely missing his overactive mouth.

'Ah, get away with ya, such nonsense!' laughed the portly publican, who was equally lubricated.

'I'm telling ya! Then, she tells the king that she's Lady Rose, and the stone, thing, starts to glow!' Eric drivelled on, while his friends thought his story was highly entertaining.

Eric was one of the servants from Vervain Castle and he was trying to impress his friends and fancy, by revealing a few secrets from within the castle grounds. Little did he know, someone else in the pub also stretched a keen ear to his tale. Arcadio, the leader of the Mumbala Bandits, sat alone in a shady corner close to Eric. He watched the young man who was entirely unaware, and listened attentively to every word while stroking his pet raven and puffing slowly on a long thin pipe. As the evening drew to a close, Eric staggered from the pub, too inebriated to notice that the sinister bandit was following him. Like a shadow moving in, Arcadio crept behind the young lad; he quickened his pace and grabbed his victim by the shoulders. The brains behind the bandits proceeded to press Eric roughly up against a tree, holding a dagger to his throat. Eric, a mere twig of a lad, stood rigid with fear. The black raven flew off to alert the rest of the bandits, who were camped nearby in the Flower Forest. Arcadio yanked the headscarf from his head and scrunched it into Eric's mouth. By now Eric felt less than merry and was trembling with fear.

'It seems you have some valuable information for me, so you are going to come quietly, or die?', Arcadio growled in his deep exotic accent. Eric's eyes bulged, his cries muffled by the scarf, as Arcadio threw him over his horse and returned to base camp. So far, the bandits had pillaged their way up the centre of the Fatum realm, desperately combing for clues as to Rose's whereabouts. They were congregated in front of a campfire when Arcadio made his return. Two of the bandits dragged Eric from the horse, pushed him to his knees on the ground, and wrapped a long rope around his body.

'Are you sure he knows? He looks like a pathetic worm', Jazarus scoffed, always hostile, standing like an overfed lord with a bottle of wine in one hand and sword in the other.

The bandits jeered at Jazarus' comment. Next, Darius, the more muscular one, held Eric's head up by the hair, while he was questioned by Arcadio, who circled like a prowling wolf.

'Now, I want to know where the Lady Rose is', he said, ripping the scarf out of Eric's mouth.

Suddenly the Flower Forest's fruitfulness darkened to a shady scene of interrogation.

'A' right, a' right, I'll tell ya everything, just don't kill me or tell the king', Eric blurted at lightning speed. 'She used to live at Vervain castle, but now she's gone!'

'Gone where?' Arcadio drilled, pressing the side of his dagger against Eric's cheek.

'I don't know, I swear it!' Eric's eyebrows lifted as beads of perspiration rolled down his face.

'Let me try.' Ramses, Darius's equally well-built brother, stepped forward with a menacing look. He jabbed Eric in the stomach with his pint-sized fist.

'I—don't—know.' Eric coughed while clutching his midriff.

'You're lying!' Arcadio struck Eric's face with the back of his hand. Darius let go of Eric's hair and the helpless lad fell to the ground like a sack of potatoes.

'I think he's telling the truth, Arcadio', Jazarus said, taking another swig from his bottle and belching self-importantly.

'Even so, he knows too much.' Arcadio never admitted defeat and with no hesitation stuck the knife in the innocent lad's back. There was an eerie silence. Eric was no more.

'Get rid of him', Arcadio ordered coldly, as he wiped the blood from his blade on the pitiful servant's shirt-front.

Darius fumbled through Eric's clothes but, finding nothing, dragged the body further into the deep, dark wood, before dumping it for wild beasts to feast on.

'We will ride due north at sunrise, she cannot be far', Arcadio added.

A while later, Arcadio contacted his master with the aid of a magic spyglass, which each villain received from Borago before departing Anaconda. He held the brass and leather tube to his eye, then turned the front lens halfway. Seconds later, Borago was visible through the mini telescope; at the same time Arcadio appeared to him like an apparition in mid-air.

'What is the news, Arcadio?' Borago asked, switching his attention away from local girl Azria, who was dutifully massaging his feet with spice-scented Brahmi oil.

'Master, I have information on the girl', he divulged. 'Her name is Lady Rose of Vervain and she is headed due north. We will hunt her down at dawn.'

'Good', Borago said with a sinister grin. 'Keep me informed and make sure you bring her to me alive.' And with a wave of his staff the vision instantly disappeared.

All the while, the Shadow Master's work-force were well on their way to baring the different realms of Pangaea. The Centaurs had charged their way through towns and villages up to northern Airlastua and were now invading the neighbouring realm of Sirenuse. Captain Nine-tails and his scabby crew were meanwhile drifting at leisure on the ocean, mooring at islands to search for clues; the only thing that kept the putrid pirate king interested in this fight, was gold.

For now, Rose and company were headed for the village of Dandagra, north of Fatum. A lot of the king's soldiers were recruited from there, so it seemed an obvious place to start their search for the warrior. Afterwards, they could continue travelling north to the Neve realm. Once the hilly road was behind them, the rest of the ride was scenic and pleasant. As they passed fields of wheat and flowering meadows, farmers would stop to wave them 'good day.' With favourable weather, the long and winding day was coming to a close when they approached Dandagra, tired and hungry.

On entering the village in the lowering sun, the regal three were greeted with a mass of flowers cascading from hanging baskets and window boxes, beautifully decorating the buildings, while the streets were lined with flower-filled wooden barrels. Maidens wearing fresh floral garlands on their heads, waved pigmented ribbons to welcome visitors to Dandagra. The festivities were in honour of Floral Day, and as it ended, the villagers gathered on the green for a scrumptious feast of pork hock and vegetable soup cooked in big black cauldrons over wood-fires. On a band-stand, positioned centrally on the green, a group of musicians played on wooden piped instruments, including a little old man, who, hunched on a wooden stool, pumped and pressed a concertina with so much enthusiasm that he almost lost his balance! Another older man strummed energetically on an oval shaped guitar called a lute; all together, they created a collective sound of jovial rhythm. The locals jigged along to the lively tempo with rosy cheeks and big smiles, as dusk crept in. There were trestle tables on the green, bright with candle-lit lanterns, where an array of home cooked food was served up. Opposite the green, Rose and the others noticed a queue of rowdy looking men waiting to go inside the local public house, called 'The Travellers Arms', attached to an inn. Some were flexing their muscles and speaking in a profane manner, and as Rose, Sir Dill and Prince Burdock walked over, a clamour of sounds came from within.

'No one must know who we are, Rose', Prince Burdock stated, as he guarded her closely.

'Rest assured milady, you are safe with us', Sir Dill asserted, noticing her worried glance towards the suspicious-looking group of men. 'I will seek shelter for us at this inn for the night.'

Sir Dill went inside the inn to enquire about rooms. Next door in the ale house, the cause of the uproar became more apparent; it was an arm wrestling tournament and the winner would receive one gold coin, which the contenders placed on the table at the start of every match. It was a timeless tradition and, if successful, one could earn a tidy sum. After booking their rooms for the night, Sir Dill marched back over to the party on the green where Rose and the prince stood enjoying some culinary delights.

Chapter Nine—The Warrior

That evening, Rose lay restively in bed, wide awake and listening to all the merriment coming from the festivities outside. She so wanted to partake in the frivolity. 'I have been sheltered all my life; well, no more', she thought. 'Time for my adventure to truly begin.'

So Rose put on her robe and hood, crept past Sir Dill's and the prince's rooms, then hurried down the stairs and out to the village green.

She weaved her way through the happy crowd, feeling nervous and excited.

'Come back for a dance 'ave ya, well c'mon then shake a leg and 'ave some fun!' an old fishwife said, full of the joys of mead, blocking Rose's path.

The plump woman pushed Rose with a heavy hand into the arms of her burly son who stood close by. He towered over her small frame with a victorious smile, as though he'd won first prize. Rose felt uncomfortable and tried to detach herself from his clammy clutches, but he swung her around like a rag doll to the brisk music. Her hood slipped off; the distressed maiden scanned the crowd of locals for assistance. Unbeknown to Rose, someone among the crowd was watching. Thankfully the music stopped playing and Rose blew out a breath of relief. It was about to begin again, when a stranger interrupted the burly man's advances.

'I will take it from here, thank you George', the stranger said, boldly taking Rose by the arm and leading her hurriedly away, leaving the sturdy young man to work out what just happened.

'It's you', Rose said, recognising him immediately. The friendly, familiar face belonged to Gallium.

Once the dim man realised that his name was not in fact George, he chased after them.

'Oi, come back 'ere, she's mine!' the man protested, charging through the crowd like a troll on a hunt.

Gallium sensed 'George' was not going to give up easily.

'Wait here, I can help you', he stressed, seating Rose on a wooden bench outside the inn and turning quickly to face the angry brute.

Gallium drew his sword and, before the man could retaliate, had the tip of the blade within an inch of his face.

'I have no desire to harm you, but I have been looking everywhere for this one. She's trouble, if you know what I mean', Gallium boasted with a wink, hoping to appeal to the stranger's better nature.

By now the crowds were gathering. Rose sat anxiously, while the man's mother stood beside him, arms folded and with a scarlet face that clearly read: I've got my eye on you.

At this point, Rose really wished she had brought her sword too.

'What 'bout an arm wrestle?' someone yelled from the crowd.

Gallium and the man both agreed to an arm wrestle. They all made their way into The Travellers Arms. The smell of sweat and stale beer was enough to put an ogre off. In the cramped surroundings, the two contenders assumed their positions, elbows on the table and opposite hands gripped tight. The lump of a landlord pushed his way past the ale-addled crowd to commence proceedings.

'Right then, the rules are', he began, towering over them with sweaty armpits, 'no lifting elbows, no standing, no two-hand gripping and no spitting or biting. Gentlemen, are you ready?' The contenders nodded in accord. 'Three, two, one, wrestle!' he said, ringing a hand bell to start the proceedings.

The noise from the spectators nearly raised the roof, as the competition started at an even pace. Not long in, Gallium started to show signs of struggle. The opponent's mother was screaming like a possessed woman for her son to try harder. Rose felt obliged to observe from the back of the room, while Gallium fought hard for her freedom. The contenders, cheeks puffed and lips tight, continued trying to force each other's fists to the table. Gallium currently had the advantage; the man's fist was but a hog's breath away from the table top, as it trembled under pressure. Unfortunately, with a quick reverse-slam he lost to the lug—but it was not over yet. Rose felt she had to do something; instantly, she crawled through the dense forest of the patrons' legs, and, once free of the crowd, ran to get help from Sir Dill and Prince Burdock.

This time the fair lady rushed up the inn stairs as fast as she could, her heart pumping ferociously.

'Sir Dill, Burdock, wake up, wake up, please!' She pounded loudly on their doors. Both answered in no time at all. 'I need your help, grab your swords and follow me, I will explain en route.'

The gallant men could see Rose was anxious and did as asked.

When all three reached the pub, Gallium had already fought his way outside, using his trusted steel. His relentless foe pursued him, after grabbing an axe from above the fireplace in the ale house. Using his sword, Gallium flicked the axe from the enraged simpleton's hand, causing it to somersault through the air and land in a door just above a spectator's head. Without a moment's thought,

Gallium then punched the big lug right between the eyes, dropping him to the ground. Resting one foot on his bulging belly, Gallium pressed his sword to his opponent's throat.

'Now, you will let us go', Gallium said in between breaths. 'Or suffer the consequences'. This time, Gallium meant business.

The burly brute admitted defeat and lay stunned, blood leaching from his nose. Everyone cheered Gallium, hailing him the champion.

'My lords, he is the warrior; I feel certain of it', Rose whispered to the others, from a front row advantage.

Gallium swept over to Rose and apologised once again.

'I seem to be making a habit of compromising your safety. Allow me to introduce myself. I am Gallium McLarty', he said formally, with a bow of his head. 'I see you have company.'

Sir Dill and Prince Burdock stood either side of Rose, studying Gallium suspiciously, not yet convinced of his worth.

'Greetings, I am Rose, these are my loyal defenders.' Rose leaned in towards Gallium. 'Gallium we need your help; is there somewhere we can talk in private?' Rose asked discreetly.

Intrigued, Gallium sensed there was something different about this young lady, and led them over to the horse trough where his black stallion Ironbark was tied.

'The best place I know is where we first met', he suggested, 'Come to my tree house when it is first light. Do you remember the way?' Gallium asked, mounting Ironbark.

'Even if I can't, my horse Noble will remember', Rose confirmed.

'Very well, until tomorrow. Gentlemen', he deferred, before riding off by the light of the moon.

'How can you be sure you can trust this man?' asked Prince Burdock doubtfully, still watching the confident stranger ride away.

'When I first met him, he had the chance to kill or harm me, but instead he let me go', Rose retorted.

'We are here to assist you, my lady you can be sure of that', Sir Dill concluded diligently.

Prince Burdock however, still had reservations.

'I know it sounds absurd, but I have a good feeling about this. Now I am rather tired, so good night to you both and thank you.' With that, Rose strode to the inn with her guards in tow, neither one making further comment.

Chapter Ten—Dark Times

At the dawning of the sun, Rose and friends set off to the Flower Forest. The air was cool and the morning fog was lifting, unveiling a long, mildewed road ahead. While on their way, the two black beady eyes of Arcadio's raven identified Rose and her crystal, as it flew low over them. With a loud triumphant squawk, it returned to the bandits' hideout. Rose and her companions left Dandagra far behind, much later reaching the fringes of the Flower Forest. The horses reduced their speed to a trot. The wondrous deep that awaited them appeared still and calm. Suddenly, without warning, a cloud of smoke exploded on the ground beside Sir Dill, and his horse reared. They were under siege by the Bandits of Mumbala! Arcadio had given orders to attack and kidnap the girl.

'Go! Into the forest! Seek Gallium and wait there!' Prince Burdock ordered Rose. 'We will defend from here!'

Rose did not hesitate a moment longer and Noble galloped like never before. The prince made a quick turn towards the enemy, ready with sword and shield. The smoke bombs kept coming, catapulted by Darius and Ramses, the brittle balls of magical charcoal making it near impossible to see. Bravely, the gallant men rode through the grey haze, charging towards the two bandits.

Believing Rose to be the Illuminata, Arcadio went after her doggedly, with Jazarus lagging behind. Through the undergrowth they rode at tremendous speed, Rose ducking to avoid every low branch. She pulled her sword from its sheath and tried to hack away at the offending foliage, but it was all too difficult to hold the reins at the same time.

While the royal escorts battled on the outskirts of the forest, Arcadio followed the trail of slashed branches and hoof prints. Terrifyingly, he caught up with Lady Rose. Galloping alongside her, Arcadio reached out with one hand to grab Her Ladyship's reins, when an arrow suddenly pierced his outstretched hand! The wounded bandit lost his balance and fell to the ground. A shaky, relieved Rose instructed Noble to slow down. Once stationary, she dismounted and looked up to see Gallium. Arcadio sat up, growling like a wounded bear; Gallium restricted his movements with another arrow aimed directly at him.

'Who sent you?' Gallium demanded.

'I will tell you nothing; you will have to kill me first. Argh!' Arcadio pulled the arrow out of the back of his hand and was getting tentatively to his feet, when in came another threat.

'Look out!' Gallium yelled at Rose, as Jazarus came galloping towards them. Gallium drew his bow, but Noble, wanting to defend Rose, kicked up his front hooves and obstructed the line of fire. Jazarus's horse bucked to a halt. Rose turned to see Jazarus's arm stretched out to grab her, and instinctively swung her sword, slicing his hand clean off! It fell to the ground, pulverised.

Jazarus rode off, whimpering like a dog, while, in the midst of the drama, Arcadio mounted his horse and escaped after Jazarus. Gallium hastened over to Rose who appeared frozen with shock at the terrible act she had just committed. She stared at the bloodstained sword still clasped in her trembling hands.

'My lady, are you all right?' Gallium enquired.

Rose did not move or answer; her face looked pale and haunted. Gallium prised the sword from her fingers and cleaned the blood off with a handful of fallen leaves.

'I've never fought for anything in my life before. I suppose I'd better get used to it now', Rose said, a slight quiver in her voice.

Gallium handed back her sword as she continued to stare at the patch of dust.

'It's not something you get used too, it's about surviving. We should leave immediately; follow me.' Gallium helped Rose back onto her horse and led the way on Ironbark.

Rose couldn't help but notice how accustomed Gallium was to finding his way around the dense forest—until she noticed that there were large crosses and X-marks carved into the trunks of some trees, indicating which direction to take. She cleverly deciphered that a cross meant turn left and an X meant turn right; a single vertical line meant go straight ahead. Eventually Rose spotted Gallium's tree house and shortly they dismounted from their horses.

'You will be safe here', Gallium assured her and held open the makeshift door to his abode, to let her in.

'Sir Dill and Prince Burdock will come for me soon,' she hoped, entering the tree house.

As Rose sat down on the small, low bed, Gallium noticed the scratches on her arms and face.

'I have water to clean your wounds.' No sooner had Gallium said it, than Rose closed her eyes, took a deep breath and, with the crystal pendant glowing, her cuts closed and healed completely. The young man observed with astonishment, his eyebrows raised.

'Who are you?' Gallium asked in wonder.

'Please, sit down and let me explain', Rose began, primed for her lengthy story. 'My name is Lady Rose of Vervain. My subjects and I are on a very important mission', Rose continued, explaining how she came to be the Illuminata. 'Pangaea's existence is being threatened by an evil ruler, the Shadow Master.'

'The Shadow Master? I can't say I've heard of him', he said, looking intently at her, curious to know more.

'I was told to look for two noteworthy people to help with my quest—the warrior and the teacher. I believe...' she said. '...you are the warrior who can help me in this fight.'

Gallium looked away for a moment. He slowly got up onto his feet.

'I'm afraid I can't help you, for I have a quest of my own.' He then proceeded to tell his tragic tale. 'And Borago took my father away from me. I haven't seen him for almost twenty years.' He finished with a heavy heart.

'Borago, you say?' Rose's face lit up with excitement.

'You've heard of him?'

'He is the Shadow Master, the one who wants my very soul, so he can rule over...' She sighed and placed her head in her hands. It had been a long day. Gallium crouched down to her level, and with his dark, hollowed eyes looked directly at her.

'If he is the same man who took my father, then I want to be the one to kill him', Gallium asserted frankly, as he got up and stood by the entrance of the tree. 'Now, you rest awhile and I'll just be outside preparing food and a fire.'

'You mean you will accompany me?' Rose perked up immediately.

Gallium gave a pleasing smile.

'Yes, I will come with you.' Then he stepped out of the tree house.

Later that day, inside the castle gates of Vervain, Sir Dill carried a severely wounded Prince Burdock into the Great Hall. The dutiful knight laid the bleeding young prince at the king's feet. The queen rushed over to him with bated breath, fearing the worst, but his moans were reassuring.

'My son', Queen Aveena uttered, pressing her hand tenderly to his cheek. 'We must move him to his bedchamber at once', she said, hurrying the guards to remove Prince Burdock to his quarters. King Yarrow looked attentively to Sir Dill for answers.

'Your Grace, we came under attack from four bandits outside the entrance to the Flower Forest. The prince and I fought two of the men', recounted the fatigued Sir Dill, with blood on his hands, a few minor cuts to the arms and blackened by soot from the bombs. 'The other two bandits went in pursuit of the Lady Rose.'

Concerned, the king suggested they continue their discussion in the Place-of-Arms. After entering the room, the king closed the door then turned to Sir Dill and said,

'What of the Lady Rose now?'

'The Lady Rose fled to the warrior's location in the forest, for safety', Sir Dill explained, 'I felt it important to return the injured prince to Vervain.'

The king patrolled the floor, fingers ruffling his short beard, deep in thought. 'Have you met this warrior?'

'Yes, he saved her from another man's advances only last night. We were on our way to meet with him and discuss the mission, when the attack happened', Sir Dill said, wilting with exhaustion. 'Lady Rose is certain he is the warrior and knows of his location, as she has visited him before.'

'Did you kill the bandits?'

'Only the two who fought us, but I witnessed the other two fleeing in the direction of Dandagra. Prince Burdock was attacked by a demonic raven. It swooped down from the sky unexpectedly, its unusually HUGE claws outstretched.' With hooked fingers, the knight mimicked the bird's feet. 'They appeared to grow right before our eyes! It ripped into the back of the prince like something possessed, even piercing his chainmail', he continued, drawing breath. 'I retaliated, trying to avoid striking the prince; I eventually cut off a claw and the bird retreated.'

'You brought my son home, alive, I could not ask for more', King Yarrow commended Sir Dill; holding the knight firmly by the shoulders. 'These are indeed dark times', he muttered, standing before the portraits of his forefathers. 'As for Lady Rose, I feel confident she is with the warrior. Rest now and at first light we will journey to the Flower Forest.' The king swiftly exited the room and headed off to visit his injured son.

Inside Prince Burdock's chamber, Flora assisted the local physician in applying a herbal dressing to the wounds on the prince's back. His shredded, blood-stained tunic was still on the floor. Queen Aveena sat on a wooden stool beside the bed, cradling her son's hand. The physician assured the king that the young prince, though badly scarred, would recover.

As night fell once more, back at Dandagra Arcadio was demanding that the innkeeper fetch a barber-surgeon. When the local medicine man eventually arrived, he found Jazarus lying on a bed, weak from loss of blood. The barber-surgeon assessed his wounds and promptly prepared for surgery: a leather strap was placed between Jazarus' teeth to bite off the pain, and an iron rod, red-hot from a metal bucket of coals, was used to cauterise the severed wrist. Arcadio and the innkeeper pinned him down with all their strength; Jazarus let out a huge, growling cry as the smell of burning flesh and blood filled the room. The pain was all too much; Jazarus passed out. The barber-surgeon then dressed Arcadio's wounded hand and his pet raven's stick of a leg, before accepting payment and departing.

Later that night at the inn, while Jazarus slept off his painful ordeal, Arcadio attempted again to contact his master through the spyglass.

'Master, I have good news on the location of the Illuminata.' He paused, nervously tapping his finger around the spyglass.

'Well, have you captured her yet?' Borago interrogated.

'Regrettably no, but she is somewhere in a nearby forest', he added, holding his breath for a second.

'What use is that to me?' Borago roared, raising his voice so that the spyglass fractured under the pressure.

'My lord, I will not fail you. I know exactly where she is going', Arcadio bluffed.

'I will give you until the next sunset to find her, or suffer the consequences.' Borago abruptly ended the discussion, while Arcadio's spyglass grew increasingly hot, leaving distinct marks around his eye and fingertips. The bandit quickly flung it from his grip and sat blowing cool air on his burning skin, while contemplating his fate.

'Raven, I need you to find that girl and report back to me. Go.' Arcadio released his trusty bird out the bedroom window—and sat back to wait.

The delicious smell of freshly cooked rabbit was wafting from the campfire through the Flower Forest as the two new-found friends sat together for a well-deserved meal. With an absent look on her face and hardly tucking in to eat, Rose was still hoping her two guards would show up.

'I know it's not much my lady, but it's fresh', Gallium said humbly, offering Rose a small roast leg to eat.

'I'm sorry, it's just I really hoped Sir Dill and Prince Burdock would have arrived by now', Rose said concerned, pausing for a moment with the cooked meat hanging from her loose grip. 'How did you come to be living in this forest?' she asked, changing the subject.

'After I fled from the ship, I travelled from village to village looking for clues about my father's disappearance, but my small means eventually ran out', Gallium's voice deepened, turning his head away from Rose and staring into the fire. 'I came across this forest on my travels when I encountered a couple of angry horse thieves.'

Rose listened attentively, with her head tilted, taking small bites of the delicious roasted meat.

'I watched as the thieves threw a large net over Ironbark from up a tree; my horse slowly fell to the ground tangled in the mesh. One thug wrestled with Ironbark's head while the other beat him into submission with a stick...I fired arrows at them', Gallium confessed still looking intently at the climbing flames. 'One man fled with an injured shoulder, but the other one died.' He rubbed his hands together and concluded:

'I'm not proud of this, but you must understand it was never going to be an amicable encounter.' Gallium lay back with his hands behind his head and observed the evening sky. 'It was the first time I ever killed a man.'

Rose felt Gallium's pain; she wondered what else this lonely soul had endured. Throwing the thin bone from her meat into the fire, Rose sat admiring the silver crescent moon, slowly coming into view through the fragmented clouds.

Yet again, they were spied upon by the evil raven of Arcadio; the smoke from the open fire led the bird straight to them. He squawked contently all the way back to his owner.

'It must be lonely out here', Rose said to Gallium, who threw another small branch onto the fire.

'You call it lonely, I call it free; and what I can't buy, I hunt.' He handed the last morsel to Rose and lit a candle from his satchel. 'You know, my lady, it's strange, but I had a feeling we'd meet again', he said with a warm smile. Then Gallium passed the candle to Rose. 'Here, you can have my bed; I will sleep on the floor.'

'You are most kind. Please call me Rose', she said from the heart, before entering the tree house.

The nocturnal noises kept Rose awake for a long while as she went over the day's events in her mind. A feeling of change was certainly taking place and Rose wondered if she'd ever see anyone from Vervain again. Once Rose was asleep, Gallium lay beside her on the floor, thinking the day had all been a bit surreal.

The next morning, Gallium awoke to find that the previous day had not been a dream at all, and started to believe in Rose's quest. As the dawn danced upon her face through the gaps in the tree;

he thought that, of all the treasures in the world he'd seen, none was more beautiful than she.

Chapter Eleven—The Teacher

Gallium rushed back to the tree house with the berries and fruit he had just picked for breakfast; he had no idea Rose was conversing with Noble.

'All will be well, my lady', the loyal white stallion assured her.

'I trust you slept well, Rose; here I picked these', Gallium said, offering Rose the pile of berries, and an apple he took from his satchel.

'Thank you', she said, graciously accepting the offering then taking a seat on the moss covered ground and a bite from the crisp apple.

'We will need to leave shortly and head north as you mentioned', Gallium suggested.

'Well', Rose responded in between munching, 'I'm still concerned about the welfare of Sir Dill and Prince Burdock.' She looked desperately past the trees, hoping to catch a glimpse of them.

'I don't think we should wait another moment', Gallium stressed again.

'Are you actually suggesting we leave without them?' Rose responded, horrified at the thought of abandoning her family.

'I'm merely highlighting the dangerous circumstances we are in', Gallium said, somewhat defensively.

'I will not leave without knowing whether they are safe!' Rose erupted, as her emotions got the better of her and she threw the remainder of the apple on the ashes of the fire.

'If we are to join forces, we must agree on a plan', Gallium retaliated and stood firmly in front of Rose. 'It is far too dangerous for us to stay in one place for long periods of time, especially with the enemy ready to pounce.' He pointed into the distance. 'I have ridden to the edge of the forest from where you came, and have seen no sign of your prince or the knight', he said spitting out a few irritating pips and swallowing water from his leather bottle. 'My guess is they have returned home safely and those bandits, two of whom I found dead, are under the command of Borago, and will stop at nothing to capture you.'

There followed an uncomfortable silence; then Noble stepped forward, the blaze on his forehead shimmering as he spoke to Rose.

'My lady', he began and lightly tapped his hoof on the ground.

'What's he doing?' Gallium asked, stepping back to make way for the magical horse.

'One moment, Noble', Rose said politely. 'Gallium, he is speaking to me; that is, we communicate through thought', Rose explained to the dumbfounded man. 'Please continue, Noble', she said sweetly.

'I believe Gallium is right, the prince and Sir Dill have returned safely to Vervain', the spirited stallion concluded.

'That is most reassuring, Noble, thank you.' Rose proceeded to take out the map of Pangaea from her satchel to study it with Gallium.

'You can understand your horse?' Gallium interrupted, lightly scratching the side of his head.

'Yes, it's a gift we share from birth', she answered modestly as she studied the map.

'My lady, I can lead the way', the valiant horse spoke again.

'Noble says he can lead us there', she said, rolling up the map and replacing it in her satchel. 'Gallium, you were right, and if I am to succeed in this quest, then we must agree on a plan.'

'Was that an apology, my lady?' Gallium teased, with his arms folded.

'Yes; now can we please prepare to leave?' Rose fluttered her hands in frustration.

Gallium, sensing her anxiety, decided to cease his taunts.

'All right, the Neve realm it is.' Gallium strode into his tree house and began collecting his few possessions. Once the horses were loaded with blankets and belongings, he took one last look back at his lowly dwelling; after many years of training and careful planning, he never imagined his prayers would be answered by a Rose.

Sometime after Rose and Gallium's departure, King Yarrow and his escort trotted into the Flower Forest. Once there, the king got off his horse and inspected the area, when he spotted a piece of torn material hooked to a thorny branch. It came from Rose's robe and he recognised it immediately.

'This is the way, men', the king said confidently, as he jumped back on his horse.

The royal party hastened deeper into the forest, following the trail of crushed flowers and hoof prints, clearly signs of a chase; a short while later they found the tree house.

Sir Dill dismounted from his horse and crouched low to examine the ground.

'Your Grace, this fire may only be a day old', he reported, poking it around with a stick. Sir Dill then looked inside the tree house. 'It appears to be vacant, Your Majesty.'

Suddenly there was a rumble from deep within the forest; a crescendo of pounding hooves was heading in their direction. It was Arcadio and Jazarus, led by the raven. They came to a sudden halt, face-to-face with the king and his men. Arcadio, realising the

91

odds were not in their favour, whistled to his freakish bird to attack, while he and Jazarus made their escape.

'Sire, look out!' Sir Dill quickly mounted his horse and galloped forward, drawing his sword to defend the king from the evil raven's claw.

'Dulich and Birch—after those men!' the king instructed two of his soldiers, while vigorously fending off the evil bird with his sword and nearly toppling off his horse in the process; but, the raven moved swiftly.

The king's soldiers gave chase, until the dense forest slowed the bandits down enough to enable an attack. Jazarus, with only one hand, soon lost his portly balance trying to wield his sword, and fell hard onto the ground. Arcadio, now surrounded, was forced off his horse. Immediately each bandit was tied by the hands, flung belly over saddle, and led by the reins back to the king. Sir Dill was still defending the king from the deadly bird: swoop after swoop, it lunged with its relentless claw. Just then, a shining object hurtled through the air, decapitating the raven. Finally, the evil black bird was dead! King Yarrow looked round to see who he had to thank.

'Your Grace, you are safe now', Morgana said, emerging from a tree like a beautiful butterfly from a chrysalis.

The flying object was her silver crown; it had changed into a sharp metal disc to slice off the bird's head.

'Rose has found the warrior; you need not worry about her', she told them in a soft voice. 'You must return to Vervain until the time comes to do battle.' And with that, Morgana reached out with her hand drawing the crown to her like a magnet, and placed it on her head, before vanishing like fine mist.

King Yarrow did indeed return to Vervain unharmed. His two prisoners were placed in the underground dungeons of the castle, pending further action. He reported back to his concerned wife; both could now relax: so far, so good.

The following day at breakfast, a pimply-looking prison guard rushed into the Great Hall, like a scurrying rat. He huffed and bowed low before the king.

'Sire, it's regarding the prisoners! Come quickly!' he declared frantically, squinting as a rare ray of sunlight streamed in through the windows.

King Yarrow and his first knight followed the guard, marching down some steep steps to the dungeons. It was dark and damp, with a stale lingering odour like wet dog. Most of the time the dungeons were vacant, but occasionally a corrupt citizen or traveller would be detained there. A worrisome thrashing and squealing sound was coming from the cells. The first cell they inspected was Arcadio's. To the king's horror, the bandit was gone, apart from the torn remnants of his clothes. In his place was an angry wild boar. Jazarus had met with the same fate. The demented boars were trying to break through the iron bars by charging repeatedly at them.

'This is the work of dark magic', the king retorted, backing away from the cells. 'We must not speak of it to anyone. Sir Dill, I order you to put these poor creatures out of their misery, and dispose of them by tonight.'

Sir Dill bowed his head at King Yarrow's orders. The king returned to court and immediately arranged an official meeting with his council.

All the while, back at his lair, the Shadow Master grew restless. Expecting the job to be done properly this time, he contacted Taurus, who was hanging out in the Sirenuse realm awaiting further instructions.

'It seems the Illuminata is headed for the Neve realm; you must seek her out there, and Taurus, I'm counting on you to complete the mission', Borago stated seriously.

'Consider it done, master', Taurus replied.

The very next day, beneath a glaring sun, Borago stood on his huge obsidian balcony addressing his mass of misfits—an army of beasts and villains, including the Rock Men from the Moora Desert and the Lyrons from the deepest mountain caves. These wild, black sabretoothed cat-like beasts, stood the height of two centaurs, with huge spikes down the length of their bony tails.

'My trusted followers! Victory is nigh, but not until we strike down our enemies', the Shadow Master's voice grew louder. 'And when the time comes, we will take all the glory!' he proclaimed, standing quite still. An ear-splitting response echoed from the mass, in accordance with the speech; pledging their complete allegiance to the Shadow Master.

Several days had passed since Rose and Gallium had left the Flower Forest, going from village to village in search of answers.

'We should head for Tregonia', Gallium advised, studying the map. 'It's a village in Neve.'

'All right, but I pray we find the teacher soon', Rose said, brushing Noble's mane with her cold hand.

'Sadly I cannot lead you directly to the teacher my lady, but I feel we are close', Noble stated.

'I am grateful to you, Noble, and I hold onto hope', Rose said. 'Noble thinks we are on the right track', she told Gallium.

'I still can't get used to that', Gallium muttered to himself. 'Good, Tregonia it is then', he called back.

After trekking for some time, Rose and Gallium noticed the road merge from sodden soil to a fringe of frost. Further along, the road became even icier, until eventually they were surrounded by a wintry wilderness. The two seekers had evidently arrived in the Neve realm. A distant hoot from a snowy owl echoed in the expansive air; a blanket of snow carpeted the ground for miles and the bare trees were pure white, twinkling in the sun. Truly, it was a magical sight. For a while Gallium and Rose encountered no one, as they ventured north-east to Tregonia. Rose was now wrapped in her thick robe in an attempt to keep warm, while Gallium was shrouded in the woollen blanket normally used on his bed. Their breath was visible in the cold air, their fingers turning blue on the reins. On the clear horizon ahead were the majestic Mystic Mountains, made up of blue-black rock and capped with more snow.

'Look Gallium, over there.' Rose had spotted a white fox under a group of trees nearby. Gallium noticed something strange about the creature and wanted to take a closer look. He got off his horse, sinking almost ankle deep into the snow, and crept up behind it. The fox appeared to be on its hind legs, muttering under its breath.

'Ha! Here's your little fox, my lady', Gallium laughed, as he caught the creature by one leg and dangled it upside down.

'Hey, let me go, by golly!' it cried and wriggled.

What had appeared at first to be a fox, was in fact a Neve goblin. Not the prettiest of creatures or the friendliest, with its pointy ears, thorny teeth and two black dots for eyes. He was wearing a full-length fox's fur, including the head which acted as a hood. Gallium dropped the goblin into a deep pile of snow.

'You, sir, are a fink!' the goblin scowled, dusting off the snow with his long thin fingers.

Surprised and inquisitive, Rose too jumped down from her horse and went to rescue the poor goblin from further humiliation.

'I do apologise for my friend's rudeness', she said, glaring at Gallium, who still thought it was all highly amusing. 'We thought you were a real fox! What is your name?' she asked, studying him curiously; after all, she had never met a goblin before.

'My name, dear lady, is Tomleo', he said grumpily, adjusting his fox-fur over his shoulders. 'My master will be wondering where I am, by golly', he continued and picked up the acorns that had fallen out of his basket. The fidgety fellow had been collecting—or stealing—them from the squirrels, for his master.

'Perhaps we could give you a ride...' Rose suggested, politely.

'Or, we could just keep you as our slave', Gallium interrupted. 'You know, fetch our firewood, groom our horses, polish my boots...'

'I will do no such thing, by golly!' Tomleo protested, stomping around even harder until he had turned red with rage, nearly dropping all the nuts again.

Gallium laughed even more at the easily agitated little critter. Rose took Gallium to one side for a quiet word.

'I really don't think you're helping, Gallium', she said through gritted teeth, with her arms folded.

'Probably not, but it is amusing', he said, blowing onto his hands and rubbing them together for warmth.

'He might know something', Rose insisted. She started to think Gallium was being a little immature.

'Like what? He's a goblin, for pity's sake; rude and annoying', Gallium added.

Rose huffed and rolled her eyes.

'Fine, I was just trying to lighten the mood.'

They both look round to see the goblin was gone; Tomleo had fled and was almost out of sight, his large flat feet helping him race across the deep snow without sinking. Rose and Gallium agreed to let him go and continued on their long journey, not saying much. Unbeknown to them, a fearful threat was on its way.

That day, Taurus and his handful of centaurs entered the Neve realm from the east, which borders the Sirenuse realm. The Shadow Master was guiding them with some limited help from the two witches. The centaurs had prepared for the north winds by stealing warm clothes, such as fur waistcoats, from innocent civilians along the way. In fact, there was no end to their trail of pillage and destruction, as they trampled through village after village, seizing whatever they wanted.

Cold and hungry, Rose asked Noble to show them the fastest route to the village of Tregonia. Her obliging horse nodded, kicked up his heels, and ploughed his way through the snow, closely followed by Gallium on Ironbark. After a short time, a hamlet of wooden huts came into view; smoke from the village fire pits could be seen swirling through the air. The Tregonians were a generation of hunter-gatherers, a proud clan, and a race to be reckoned with.

'I feel certain we will find some answers here, Gallium', Rose said, with a sudden burst of excitement.

'I hope so too, but it might be best if I do the talking. We may not be welcomed with open arms, so be on your guard', he replied.

Finally they reached the village of Tregonia, where the air was dry, crisp and cool. They walked their horses to a wooden post and tethered them there. Gallium began to scour the area. There wasn't a soul to be seen, except for a few farm animals held in large cast iron cages that had spear heads welded onto them, pointing out in all directions. Outside every hut was a burning fire pit next to a pile of wooden batons that were wrapped in rags at one end. The only sounds were the crackling fires and the faint whistling of the wind.

Suddenly, there came a deep masculine voice from behind.

'Who are you and what do you want?'

Rose and Gallium spun round to see a tall, well-built Tregonian. He had long auburn hair, matted and twisted; a patterned sash wound around his body over wolf-skin clothing, and a few telling scars showed about his person. With the stance of an experienced warrior, he grasped a long spear and looked suspiciously at the unexpected visitors.

'I am Gallium and this is Lady Rose of Vervain; we come in peace. We have been guided to your humble village as part of a very important quest', Gallium explained, while laying his sword slowly on the ground and raising his hands in the air.

'I am Lenorc MacBain, fifth generation and leader of the Tregonians', Lenorc said proudly, his chin and chest thrust out. He kept his spear firmly in hand, never taking his eyes off them.

'Master, it's him, by golly! He's to blame for my tardiness.' A rasping voice came from the ground. It was Tomleo; he pointed his long knobbly finger at

Gallium as he cowered at the feet of his master, Lenorc.

'Hush, Tomleo', Lenorc said, kicking him lightly to one side. Tomleo gave a feeble 'ouch' and scurried back into one of the huts.

Gallium forced a sheepish smile at the leader. 'It was all a bit of fun, really', he said.

'Please, sir, may we stay awhile and rest?' Rose interjected, now shivering with cold.

The firm but fair leader, hearing of Rose's kindness from his faithful goblin, felt she and Gallium were telling the truth. Just then, Lenorc's head jerked round towards the distant Mystic Mountains as a haunting howl split the air.

'Aye, you best follow me now, and bring your horses—they can go in the stable with mine, it's too dangerous out here.' The stable was situated next to Lenorc's home. 'Come', he said, 'and meet my family.'

Gallium and Rose eagerly followed Lenorc to his organic home. Rose noticed a few wondering eyes peering from the other huts, but she wasn't afraid of the locals' curiosity. Outside the front door of Lenorc's hut was a stack of chopped wood and an axe still wedged in a tree stump. Inside, there were fur-skins on the floor and woollen blankets on the beds, but what caught Gallium's eye was the bundle of arrows and spears up against the wall by the entrance. It was as though the Tregonians were ready for war.

'Miram, you'd better prepare food for two more', Lenorc told his meek wife, who was busy kneading some dough.

'Well, who do we have here?' Miram beamed, rubbing the flour off her hands on her apron. 'We never have visitors; at least, not the friendly kind.' She paused, her expression rather wan.

99

Noticing his wife's absent stare, Lenorc took over and introduced their three young sons who were sitting at the table. They were equally pasty of complexion and had their father's fiery tinted hair.

'Come sit, I'll pour you a hot brew', Miram said sweetly, as she fetched a ladle.

'Thank you', Rose said, her teeth chattering. 'I'm Rose and this is my friend Gallium.'

'Lovely to meet you both, here, this will warm your hearts', Miram said, carefully ladling a wooden cup of her invigorating home brew. It smelt strongly of herbs and sweet honey, and sure enough, after a couple of sips, Rose could feel herself warming up from the inside.

'Why do you have so much weaponry?' Gallium enquired bluntly.

Lenorc took in a deep breath and began to explain how the Tregonians lived each day in fear of the mountain wolves—savage dogs that not only sought out their livestock but their people.

'You fight wolves every day?' Gallium said, exhausted just thinking about it.

'No, but you never know when they will be back, nor how many.' Lenorc spoke calmly in between slurps of warm brew. 'We have learnt to live close together and always be on our guard', he added. 'The fire pits outside are lit at all times, ready to ignite our torches to use as weapons. Wolves cower at the sight of fire and that is when we throw our spears into their very hearts.' He banged a fist on the table to conclude, and Rose sprung out of her seat, almost spilling her drink.

The entire evening was spent conversing and eating. Rose explained who she was and about their mission.

'But first we have to find the teacher, except, I know not who or where', Rose concluded woefully.

Lenorc's wife Miram had been cooking up a fine stew and the smell was sharpening their hunger. Tomleo was drooling in the corner of the room. The stew was served up with some freshly baked bread, truly the best meal in a long time. The travellers tucked in straight away.

'Ah, this is good!' Gallium exclaimed, chomping and slurping.

'I don't know of any teacher, but I do know of a story from not long ago; a wizard by the name of Malachi, who lived in the Mystic Mountains, used to visit our village to help heal the sick with his herbal remedies', Lenorc told them, chewing ferociously while chatting. 'But then, one day, he mysteriously disappeared. Some say the wolves took him.' He stopped for another gulp of home brew.

At his words, Rose felt a brief tingling sensation all over her body.

'Gallium, I feel Malachi could be the teacher', she whispered. 'We should search for him in the morning, up in the Mystic Mountains.'

Gallium nearly choked on his food at the thought of it, and accidentally kicked Tomleo, who was hiding under the table collecting the scraps that his master and family randomly dropped for him. Tomleo yelped and scuttled into a corner of the room, hugging a lump of bread.

'Are you sure? We don't even know if he's still alive.' Gallium looked bug-eyed at Lenorc for back up.

'Aye, you might fall victim too, my lady', Lenorc advised. 'It's too risky.'

'I did not come this far to give up now—and I was told to follow my instincts', Rose affirmed in a

101

controlled voice. 'Malachi is the teacher, I just know it.' She was now literally glowing with confidence.

'Fine, my lady', Lenorc said, exasperated. 'But I'll only take you as far as the lake at the foot of the mountains.'

Rose looked victorious as she smiled to herself, while Gallium raised his eyebrows and continued eating like it was probably going to be his last meal.

That night, Rose and Gallium sheltered at the home of the MacBains and, in the morning after breakfast, the family equipped the two for the cold road ahead. Kind Miram provided Rose and Gallium with two spare wolf-skin waistcoats and an extra woollen blanket for the cold evenings, as well as a small hessian sack with home-made bread and cheese. Lenorc, true to his word, escorted them on horseback as far as Lake Lunga. Looking around, Rose realised the enormity of this mission, but kept faith, holding tight to Noble's reins. The only sound was the gentle north wind brushing the frosty ground with a faint tinkling. Lenorc had brought along some firewood, and advised them to build a huge fire, in case of wolves.

'I must leave you here and return to my people', the loyal leader said.

'Thank you Lenorc, you have been most helpful', Rose said graciously.

'Good luck', Lenorc responded, bowed his head to Rose and galloped away immediately.

Chapter Twelve—Cold Encounters

Galloping towards the Mystic Mountains across the icy plains, the Centaurs built up tremendous speed with every powerful stride, rapidly gaining on Rose and Gallium.

The sky began to darken over the glacial land, as the day drew to a close. Gallium busied himself preparing a shelter and safe place to rest for the night near the edge of Lake Lunga. With his sword, he cut low thin branches off a fir tree, and laid them on the ground for a mattress, before placing their blankets on top. Ironbark and Noble lay either side of them, a perfect warm shield. They spent most of the day gathering firewood; strips of dry bark, pine needles, branches and twigs from the nearby woodland.

'I hope you are not mad at me for dragging you out to such a miserable place', Rose said, trying to get comfortable on her bed by wrapping the extra blanket round her already cloaked body.

'This was never going to be an easy task, but at least I'm in good company. Now get some rest.' Gallium smiled, admiring her courage and kindness.

The two intrepid travellers were not long asleep, when the incantation of a lady's voice whispered from across the lake:

'Whoever dares to cross these waters, gold will be their prize, for only the brave can reach the other side.'

Gallium woke with a dreamy expression, and listened for a moment, then, as if by force, he trudged to the edge of the lake. Fortunately, Rose heard him stirring and saw the warrior about to step onto the slippery frozen water.

'Gallium, no, it is dangerous!' Rose knew she had to act fast, and instinctively threw a large snowball at his head. It was a direct hit and he tumbled to the ground.

'Argh, what just happened?' he said, slightly dazed and rubbing his head.

Their horses also woke up with the commotion and followed Rose over to the lake.

'I had to stop you Gallium, you seemed to be in a trance', Rose said, and crouched down beside him, making sure he was all right.

At that moment, from across the lake, a hypnotic, translucent figure glided up to the water's edge and presented herself. She appeared serene; made up of water and light. Her white hair glowed like strands of moonbeams and moved freely as if underwater. Her eyes were a frosty blue colour and, around her neck, she wore a necklace of clear quartz crystals not attached by any obvious links.

'Why do you enter my domain?' the lady spoke calmly.

'We are on an important mission to save Pangaea from an evil ruler.' Rose announced.

The White Lady's eyes sparkled at the sight of Rose's crystal pendant.

'Who are you?' the White Lady asked, swooping in closer.

'I am Lady Rose of Vervain, and this is Gallium the warrior.' Rose stood bravely before her, as Gallium stepped forward more cautiously. 'We are seeking the teacher, the one who will lead us to the Gnome Kingdom of Jurien. It is vital we find him.'

'I am the White Lady Alba and keeper of this realm', she said authoritatively, while hovering an inch from the ground. 'Only the Illuminata has the power to open the gateway between our world and that of the Gnomes.'

'With respect—this is the Illuminata', Gallium interjected, trying to avoid her gaze, for fear of entrapment.

'As the Illuminata, I wish to know where we can find the teacher.' Rose was not backing down.

Silence fell, and then to Gallium and Rose's amazement, the White Lady Alba's eyes shimmered intensely as her necklace unfastened itself. Suspended in mid-air, the crystals formed a cluster which shone a radiant light. The cluster of light shot into the night sky, and stopped at a pivotal point above the Mystic Mountains.

'Follow the Northern Star', Lady Alba instructed, pointing to the brilliant cluster. 'When you reach the spot, the star will reveal all, but be on your guard, for danger lurks in these parts', she cautioned, and then like a mermaid's spirit, dived back into the frozen waters of Lake Lunga.

Rose and Gallium didn't say a word until they had returned to their resting spot. A fog started to work its way dreamily from the foot of the mountain across the plains.

'If I may make a suggestion', Gallium said, lightly scratching his ever increasing facial hair.

'Please do.' Rose slumped back down onto her makeshift bed.

'We should take turns to rest; I can keep watch first.'

'I disagree', Rose said leaning in closer.

'I thought you might', Gallium said shaking his head. 'It isn't safe to travel this late at night.'

'We must not lose sight of the star', she insisted. 'It's our only hope of finding the teacher.'

'Do you truly believe we are on the right path?' he pressed, wriggling under his blanket to keep warm. 'I mean, how can you be sure this 'ghost' of a woman isn't luring us to our death!'

Rose paused, knowing full well that she had to convince Gallium in order to keep him on board. So she turned to Noble for assistance.

'Noble, can you guide us safely to the star?' she asked,

'Yes I can, my lady'

'He said...'

'Let me guess; he said 'yes.' Gallium let out a sigh; he could see the look of desperation on her face. Removing his blanket, he slowly got to his feet. 'Very well, you're right, as usual', he said, and proceeded to load the horses for the next expedition. It wasn't long before they were ready to travel once more.

The light of the moon showed the path, which still at times became obscured by fog. Thorny bushes forced them to divert along the way. Up the rugged mountainside they rode, the rocky terrain at times leading them very close to the edge. Loose stones disturbed by the horses' hooves rolled down the precipice, echoing eerily. Rose tried not to look down, holding her breath and gripping tightly to Noble.

'Have no fear, my lady, I will get you there safely', Noble promised.

Further ahead, Gallium noticed moving figures silhouetted in the mist. Stepping out from the drifting mist into the moonlight, the shadowy figures were exposed. It was Taurus and a few of his centaurs.

'Greetings, Your Highness, we meet at last', the Shadow Master announced, appearing in the form of a hologram presented by Taurus through a spyglass.

106

'So, you are Borago, why do you not come for me in person? Are you afraid?' Rose asked.

'Why do all the work myself, when I have 'dogs' to do it for me?' the Shadow Master answered coldly. 'I suggest you come quietly, for the sake of your companions.'

'Rose, refrain, I would rather die than yield to a murderer!' Gallium's outburst caused even the horses to stir. 'Where's my father, you blackguard?'

'Taurus, seize them', Borago commanded, before disappearing like a retractable beam into thin air.

The centaurs surrounded them, advancing slowly with a very large net. The only escape was down the side of the mountain; a worse fate, guaranteed. Gallium endeavoured to protect his lady, slicing off the end of a centaur's spear with his sword, but they were hopelessly outnumbered. Another centaur hurled a large mace at the brave warrior's sword smashing it from his hand, while a third launched meteor hammers at the legs of the horses. Then the centaurs threw the net over the lot of them. Ironbark and Noble whinnied as their legs became entangled by the iron balls and chains, forcing them to the ground. The centaurs pinned down the edges of the net with their spears and Rose, Gallium and their horses were firmly trapped.

The two prisoners rolled off their horses and lay face down, side by side, encased in the net and unable to move. Rose looked at Gallium but dared not say a word, as the centaurs circled them, laughing victoriously.

'Rose I'm going...' But before Gallium could finish his sentence, more trouble arrived.

From out of the darkness, a flash of fur leapt into the air and landed on a centaur's back. It was one of the savage mountain wolves Lenorc had warned them about! As it bit into the centaur's neck, five more attacked the others. The wolves' surprise onslaught had rendered the centaurs helpless, immobilised by their vicious fangs and claws. Taurus was the only one that got away, galloping as fast as he could, back down the mountain. Amid all the commotion, the warrior reached for his steel dagger, pulled it from its sheath and started cutting away at the net.

'Put your head down Rose and lie very still', Gallium advised, while slicing through the mesh.

The centaurs' cries echoed through the open night sky, but were soon silenced by the merciless predators, and they bled to death, staining the snow around them a bright crimson. Rose cringed, her hands covering her ears and her eyes shut tight. Soon came the calm after the storm. While the wolves feasted on the flesh of the centaurs, a larger one, with a silver-grey coat and a white crest on its head, prowled among the corpses. He appeared to be the pack leader. He moved in closer to Rose. Paralysed with fear, she felt his warm sickly breath on her face as he sniffed.

'This one is different, I can smell it', the wolf leader snarled and turned to face the ravenous pack.

'Gallium, I can hear his thoughts', she whispered, slowly removing her hands from her head and turning it to look at the wolf. 'I will attempt to communicate', she said fearlessly.

'Are you mad? They will eat us alive', he barked, grabbing her by the wrist. Rose took no notice.

'Trust me', she said.

Gallium mapped her eyes for faith, eventually releasing his hold. Wriggling her way out from under the ripped net, she took a deep breath and spoke through thought. With a low growl, the pack leader padded paw by paw towards the heroine, his strange brown eyes fixed on the shiny crystal pendant. Gallium had also broken free from the net, and now stood beside Rose ready to defend her, but the horses remained immobilised.

'Do not be alarmed, we come in peace.' Rose remained composed and gathered her thoughts.

'I have no care for friends, unless you are the one who can lift my curse', the wolf snarled in a deep rough voice.

'What curse would that be?' Rose asked, with an ear closer to him.

'The one the Shadow Master has placed upon me. I was once human like you, and now I am forced to live this lonely savage life.' The wolf hung his head in shame and anger.

The hairs on the back of Rose's neck prickled.

'Are you...Malachi?' she asked, her eyes widening.

The wolf quickly raised his head and howled sorrowfully. Borago had cursed Malachi using the Orbicular Rock, afraid of the threat he presented.

Rose felt compassion for this poor creature. Kneeling down and staring deeper into his eyes, she sensed his feelings.

'Forgive me, I have not heard that name in a long time but enough, for in a moment these hungry beasts will turn on you', Malachi warned, as they snarled, teeth bared and dripping with bloody saliva from their jaws.

Gallium swung his sword above his head, ready to strike.

'No, Gallium!' Rose interjected by standing between the two. 'It's the teacher. It's Malachi.'

'How can you be certain?' But once again, Gallium obeyed her command and slowly lowered his sword.

'He told me the Shadow Master cursed him. Let me speak to him.'

'All right, but hurry; the others might not be as friendly', Gallium stressed, eyeballing the rest of the wolves.

Rose proceeded to speak out loud so all could hear.

'Malachi, I am Rose, the Illuminata', she said with intense emotion, and glowed with a strange light.

All at once the other wolves left their eating and cowered down before her.

'Could this be true?' The teacher, extending his neck towards her, sniffed deeply.

'I want to help transform you back to your former self', she said, hoping to discover a way.

'My lady, alas my magic spells do not work, believe me I have tried', he said. 'However, as the Illuminata you have the power of thought. First imagine a way, and then truly believe it, and finally you will know', Malachi advised wisely.

'I will do my best.' Rose turned to Gallium to explain what needed to be done, but Gallium was trying to get the horses back onto their feet. He looked very concerned.

'Ironbark has hurt his leg', Gallium said, feeling a tender spot on Ironbark's lower leg. 'If he does not get up, he will die.' There was a tremor in his voice.

'Allow me to help.' Rose knelt down and placed her cold hands on the injured leg, praying that she could use her crystal on the poor animal. Within moments, Ironbark was up on all hooves, cured.

'What a relief—thank you, Rose', Gallium said, patting his stallion comfortingly.

At this point, the other wolves suddenly slunk back into the undergrowth of the mountain, as though miraculously tamed.

Rose looked to the night sky for inspiration; she remembered what Alba had said about the Northern Star.

'Malachi, the White Lady Alba advised us to follow the Northern Star as it would have answers', she proclaimed, pointing to it. 'I believe it can help transform you. We should go right away.'

Malachi raised his head to face the star and pondered for a moment.

'The star appears to be positioned above Jarrah point. It is a sacred stone table said to be the birth place of the Orbicular Rock. I can lead us there.'

And so, in the dead of night, they all set off further up the mountain, towards the Northern Star.

Chapter Thirteen—Two Worlds

Collide

'Yarrow...Yarrow...', Morgana whispered, appearing as a vision in the king's dream. 'You seem troubled, my liege, but you need not be. Rose is well and has found the teacher.' The beautiful fairy queen swirled like colourful air in his dream state. 'Rest now and I will call again.'

The queen, who lay next to her king, heard his lament and woke him up gently.

'My dear, was it a bad dream?' she asked, stroking his forehead. The king sat up in bed and explained the dream to his dear wife.

'Oh, thank God she is safe', Queen Aveena breathed a sigh of relief.

'I fear there is still much to conquer, but now sleep, my dearest.'

The queen nestled her head on his chest and soon drifted back to sleep; unlike King Yarrow who lay awake, wondering what darkness was yet to come.

Meanwhile, Malachi was escorting the others to Jarrah point. It was once a monumental rock, split open by a lightning bolt from God. Now all that remained was a huge stone slab, surrounded by the broken rubble. Even though the sun was due to rise at any moment, temperatures were still icy, as Malachi the wolf positioned himself on the large flat stone, directly below the Northern Star.

'I feel strange', Rose murmured, glowing all over as the star's beam shone down on her.

'Remember, just believe', Malachi voiced, standing quite still.

Instinctively, Rose placed her hands on the wolf's head and closed her eyes. In doing so, she imagined the creature turning back into human form, believing it would be so. As she did this, she felt a strong surge of energy passing from her to Malachi. Gallium watched with the horses from a short distance, eagerly anticipating the transformation. Rose's crystal pendant emitted a pink stream of light, encasing the wolf completely; Gallium had to raise his arm to shield his eyes from the brightness. After a short time the light softened, and with a flash the star plummeted back into Lake Lunga. All was calm and dimly lit, as Rose regained her normal self, slowly opening her eyes and hoping the curse had been lifted. Gallium marched over to where she stood.

The two of them examined the stone table; the wolf was gone. Lying before them in a fetal position was a middle-aged man, naked and somewhat stunned from his ordeal. Gallium rushed over to Ironbark, took a spare tunic, men's stockings and a blanket from the saddle, and offered them to Malachi. Rose kept her gaze high, but couldn't help noticing some markings on the wizard's forehead— symbols of some kind which gave him an aura of mystery; and he still had the white crest against his dark hair. Rose respectfully continued to look away while Malachi clothed himself, shivering from the cold.

'Thank you, you truly are the Illuminata!' Malachi said, elated by the whole experience. 'How may I assist you, my lady?' he added and dropped down on one knee.

'I was told by the fairy Queen Morgana that you could help us find the Kingdom of Jurien', Rose said, helping him up.

'I can do better than that; my true home is with the Gnomes of Jurien, my lady.'

'Thank you, Malachi', Rose said, her face brimming with delight. 'Oh, I almost forgot: this is Gallium the warrior; he will be accompanying us on this quest.'

'It's an honour, Malachi', Gallium said offering a firm handshake. 'Rose, I think we should rest here for a bit. I'll build a fire.' No sooner had Gallium suggested it than Malachi, uttering strange words, magically created from his open palm a fireball, and blew it on a small shrub. He had lit the perfect fire.

Gallium felt a little stifled by the wizard's intervention, but was grateful nonetheless, and the three companions lay down for a while to recover, even though the dawn was upon them.

'Malachi, may I know what the markings on your forehead are?' Rose asked, with a yawn.

'I will explain once we get to Jurien, my lady', Malachi said with a smile. 'Each day now is a lesson for you; with that knowledge come the answers.' That said, he picked up a couple of pine cones and transfigured them with a spell, forming a pair of fur boots. Slipping his feet contently into the boots, he sat crossed-legged, hands on his knees and closed his eyes.

'What is he doing?' Gallium whispered curiously.

'I'm not sure, but I am exhausted', Rose said, lying tightly wrapped in her blanket and facing the cobalt sky. In no time at all she fell asleep.

At the opposite end of their world, there came a clinking sound from the entrance of the Anaconda realm, at the bridge of Bloodwood Gorge. It was the work of Mumbala's masonry craftsmen, who were sculpting a likeness of Borago from blocks of sandstone. These were carried by the Rock Men and piled on top of each other, equating to a hundred men high, for all to admire when daring to enter the Shadow Master's domain. Borago sat astride his golden gryphon's back, posing for the sculptors. As he did so, they chiselled away at the stone, perched on wooden platforms held together by scaffolds. With a 'heave-ho' and a 'clink-clink' these talented artisans soldiered on in the sweltering heat, despite having already lost a fellow sculptor, who had fallen off the monument to his death—all in the name of Borago's supremacy.

Suddenly, a figure appeared from nowhere. It was Borago's general, Taurus, pausing in the north to rest and inform his master by spyglass again.

'My lord, I have news', Taurus said, a little out of breath.

'Go on', Borago listened attentively.

'After capturing the Illuminata, we came under attack by the mountain wolves. My centaurs are now dead and I only just escaped with my life. I cannot be sure if the girl lives.' Taurus lowered his gaze fearing his master's furious reaction. The spyglass became increasingly warm in his hand.

'I would curse you, but I still have further use of you', the Shadow Master's voice reverberated. 'I will consult the witches about the Illuminata. Now, make your return to Anaconda, Castro will carry you back the rest of the way.' Taurus absented himself and flew with the aid of Castro, back to his lair.

Inside the Mercury Well chamber, the news was not entirely good.

'The Illuminata is very much alive, master, and she has help in the form of a warrior and a wizard', Hemmatia relayed.

'Malachi! Damn you', Borago despaired, pounding his fist on the edge of the well. 'What must I do to be rid of you.'

'It seems the Illuminata undid the curse', Marelda said, glass-eyed and twirling her haggish hair with a rather scaly finger.

The Shadow Master's eyes were darting around the room, as he searched desperately for inspiration. He needed a plan, and quick. 'I will win this war, mark my words', he concluded, promptly leaving the room to think further.

The day was well under way when Malachi gently woke Rose with a nudge. 'Lady Rose, it's time. We must find the gate before nightfall.'

Gallium was already awake and began to prepare the horses. Rose got up slowly with a yawn and a stretch.

'Malachi, is it far to Jurien?' she asked, picking up her things.

'It is a fair walk, but not too long', Malachi responded, rubbing his hands.

'Here, take my horse', Gallium offered politely. 'I can ride with Rose.'

'Most noble of you, sir.'

Malachi introduced himself first to Ironbark, then respectfully mounted the horse and, in fair weather, led them down to the base of the mountain. After a short while, they reached a nearby wood.

The flora in these parts were not as dense as further up the mountain. A gentle breeze rustled the bushes and the sharp sound of a screech owl could be heard from overhead. A perfect blend of scented pine trees and cool crisp air filled their nostrils. The pace was slowing down and Malachi dismounted Ironbark.

'The horses cannot pass through the kingdom of Jurien, they will have to remain here', Malachi told them. 'It is quite safe.'

After that, Malachi escorted Rose and Gallium to a rope bridge suspended high above a torrent. Rose tried not to look down through the wooden slats and with each step the bridge swayed. Gallium followed close behind her. Together they took gradual steps. Rose soon adopted a steady pace and began to find the whole experience less daunting, until a huge flock of birds flew low across the bridge causing them to sway a little wildly. Rose caught her breath, her heart beating as fast as a tiny bird's.

'It's all right, I have you', Gallium said, one hand holding on to the rope bridge, while the other arm supported Rose around her waist. As soon as the bridge had stabilised he respectfully let her go. Rose had never felt safer than in that moment; a little giddy, she continued across.

Once they reached the other side, Malachi led them forward through more wood. Eventually they arrived at a clearing and came to a pause in their journey.

'We have arrived', the wizard said, staring at the ground in front of him, with a smile that could shame a crescent moon. The ground was completely covered with snow. Rose and Gallium looked at each other in bewilderment; they couldn't see anything except more white trees and more snow. Malachi closed his eyes and spoke some ancient words,

'Apri port Jurientus.'

A slight quake came from under their feet, as the snow began to melt from a central point. Soon the ground resembled a watery whirlpool. The wizard saw the concerned looks on their faces.

'Stand back; it will be all right', he assured them.

Gallium was about to climb a tree to safety, when suddenly the water started to drain away, as though a plug was being pulled from the centre of the ground. A large stone-carved pedestal came up from the earth, and on it, surrounded by four columns was a beautiful golden harp, with steps up one side.

'This is the Harp of Truth', the wizard proclaimed, walking over to it with a show of hand. 'It is the gateway to the underground Kingdom of Jurien.' Malachi returned to Rose and took her gently by the hand. 'And you my lady, to prove you are the Illuminata, must unlock it.'

'But how?' she said, as the shine of the gold reflected in her eyes.

'Play it and see.'

Gallium gave her a reassuring nod. Carefully, Rose proceeded to climb the few stony steps. On reaching the top, the Illuminata sat on a carved stone stool, drew a deep breath and began playing a gentle piece of music on the harp, her fingers gliding fluidly across the strings. The two men were captivated by her performance; the warrior even smoothed the hair on the back of his neck with his fingers. Rose closed her eyes, at one with the harp; together they shone. Suddenly, the pedestal started revolving very slowly, corkscrewing back into the earth with a loud grinding noise.

'Hop on, Gallium', Malachi called, jumping on a step.

Gallium didn't hesitate to follow.

When the harp was deep underground, it stopped turning and their heads flicked up to see that the entrance was now corked by the stone slab, perched on its columns. Rose ceased playing and there was a brief silence. They had arrived at a hollow, deep in the ground, surprisingly lit by magical, jewel-encrusted torches lining the walls.

'That was amazing', Gallium said, ruffling his hair with his fingertips and leaping off the step.

Rose held her pendant closely as she also stepped down. Malachi, already ahead, signalled for them to follow him.

'You did well, my lady. Now, let us continue', said the wizard.

Up ahead was an opening in a stony wall. One by one, they stepped through it, to be faced with a narrow staircase lit by more of the enchanted golden torches. Gallium was last in, keeping guard at all times with one hand on his sword and occasionally checking over his shoulder. Rose, however, boldly followed the wizard. There must have been at least a hundred steep steps down, moist from the cool conditions. As they neared the bottom of the steps, they saw a little wooden boat moored by the mouth of a very narrow. dimly-lit tunnel.

'Climb in, it will take us to Jurien', Malachi instructed calmly.

'Here, let me help you', Gallium said, offering Rose a hand.

The wizard sat in the bow and spoke more strange words under his breath,

'Sali lento barcus.'

With a little magic, the boat began to move over the water and through the dark, wet tunnel. With their heads almost touching the ceiling, there wasn't much for the group to see. Every so often, the boat drifted past an alcove lit by more jewel encrusted torches. A drop of water seeping through the porous rock landed on Gallium's nose, and Rose giggled. She lightly traced her fingers above her head, over the smooth wet rock; it felt cool to the touch. After a little

119

while, looking straight ahead, they saw a light—the end of the tunnel.

They were now in a very large area of chiselled rock. In the foreground there stood a small figure of a man, wearing a pointy hat. The oarless boat moored itself to one side, letting all three passengers off. Not much taller than a boy, the little man was in fact a gnome. He had a rosy complexion, black hair and a matching long beard.

'Malachi, my friend!' The gnome gave Malachi a huge, child-like hug. 'You have returned at last!' he celebrated. 'The king predicted your return.'

'Too long my friend; I bring special visitors.'

The cheery chap observed Rose and Gallium with delight.

'Welcome to the Kingdom of Jurien. I am Alfredo, King Drew's assistant.' Alfredo had a unique form of greeting, tapping his head with his hand, once, then placing the same hand to heart, before joining his hands, with a bow. 'Please, step this way. His Majesty has been waiting', he continued, hurrying ahead with a skip and a hop.

The three companions kept up with the happy little man and stepped through another opening in a wall, revealing an immense limestone cave which appeared to go on for ever. Poking out from every surface were sparkling crystal stalagmites and stalactites. Rose and Gallium admired the cool crystal surroundings and, surprisingly, a small hot spring at its centre, mildly bubbling away. The water was a striking clear turquoise blue. As they ventured along, Rose noticed the stalagmites became similar in shape.

'Alfredo, what are these rocks?' asked Rose, observing a pattern.

The gnome's gleeful expression morphed into a forlorn one.

'Alas, these are former kings, who have left our world', he said, clasping his hands and staring at the rock formations.

'I am sorry', Rose said, walking past the erect tombs.

They continued over a small wooden, hump-back bridge, underneath which flowed a pure shallow stream. The waterbed was covered with millions of tiny, sparkling, clear crystals. Before long, Rose and company came to a cave wall; it was coarse but even. Here Alfredo took off his pointy hat and pulled out a short, white crystal wand. The jolly gnome inserted the wand through a tiny hole in the cave wall, to reveal a door, magically outlined by a strong light from inside. The stencil-edged door opened inwards, and Alfredo led the way into another enormous cave. This time, the guests stopped in their tracks, eyes wide and heads swivelling, to admire their new surroundings. All around was an eclectic mixture of sparkle and colour, from every precious stone imaginable. The faint sound of folk whistling came from cavities dotted about the cave walls. Nailed to the walls were hundreds of pulleys bearing empty sacks.

'I must be dreaming, for I have never seen such riches', Gallium whispered to himself, slack-jawed and looking up at the enormous mounds of precious gems.

It soon became apparent that this was the secret treasure Captain Nine-tails had been searching for all those years. Gallium grinned to himself; if only the captain could see him now, he thought. He sneakily slipped a few of the abundant crystals into his pocket.

In between the mounds of gems, was a sandstone path leading to a smooth, transparent emerald throne. Seated comfortably on it was the Gnome King Drew, his wrinkled faced lit up by a gummy smile. He had long hair as white as snow and a long, straggly beard. On the hem of his decorative long robe, Rose noted the same markings as the ones on Malachi's forehead—a star, a dragon's head, a fish and a flower. Behind King Drew was another huge door, this time made of solid gold, shining with a warm glow.

Alfredo scuttled over to a white crystal bowl on the ground, big enough to bath a baby and half-filled with spring water. He knelt down and, using a short wooden baton, clinked the side of the font lightly, and then ran the side of the baton along its edge to create a high-pitched vibration. The sound was so strong, it caused the water's surface to dance.

King Drew continued to sit quietly, observing the guests with a clueless expression. A few seconds later, a stomping of feet came from inside the pigeon holes of the cave walls and out pattered a colony of gnomes, merrily filling sacks with crystals dug from deep within the cave. In turn, they lowered the sacks to the ground with the pulleys, where other gnomes emptied them, either wooden buckets or wheelbarrows. Afterwards, they congregated in front of the king, some zip-lining their way down, or using rope ladders, shuffling and bustling, eventually coming together on the sandstone floor.

'Silence, Juriens!' Alfredo blasted through a large hollow wooden cone. He then gave his royal elder a tap on the shoulder.

'Hem, ah yes, welcome, to the Kingdom of Jurien', King Drew said slowly. 'I am King Drew...' The king's head flopped forwards and he began to snore, the sound muffled by his beard.

Alfredo poked him in the arm with the wooden baton to wake him up. King Drew snorted and said, 'Oh, where was I?' and looked quizzically at his faithful assistant, Alfredo.

'The guests, Sire', Alfredo whispered politely in his ear.

'Oh this is painful', Gallium muttered and stepped forward. 'With respect...' but before he could say another word, he was astutely interrupted by Malachi.

'If you please, King Drew, this is the prophet Illuminata and this is the warrior, Gallium', the wizard divulged diplomatically. 'The time has come to retrieve the sacred crystals and bring back the Crystal Masters.'

King Drew's eyes lit up, and, smiling into his rosy cheeks, he signalled with his wrinkly hand for Rose to step forward.

'I know who you are my child, I have been waiting for you and...', once again a nudge from Alfredo was required. 'Err, let me see; as for you, young Gallium', he said pointing shakily at the warrior, 'I knew your father, Captain Aiden McLarty.' The king stared into the distance, nodded off again, and Alfredo continued to patiently poke the ageing monarch. 'What was that?' the king snorted.

'You knew my father?' Gallium was keen to hear more, and he edged closer to the Gnome King.

'Oh yes. Your father died protecting our secret, this is why you have been chosen', he said, leaning forward with a cough. 'Hem, I have no doubt that you are just as brave.'

Gallium pondered this for a moment, touching the smooth gems inside his pocket.

'So this is the kingdom he served', Gallium said in surprise. He had always known that his father was a great man, but not to what extent.

Rickety King Drew beckoned Alfredo for some assistance. Alfredo lent an ear to his superior.

'It is time', the king spoke.

Alfredo nodded, picking up the cone and addressing all present.

'Gnomes of Jurien, I present the Illuminata! The time for hiding in fear is at an end', he paused for breath, as his message resounded throughout the great cave. 'The God Omnio has answered our calling. Let us consult the book.'

The gnomes all cheered and hailed the Illuminata, throwing their pointy hats in the air. The book Alfredo was referring to, was the Book of Legends.

'Please step this way', Malachi directed Rose and Gallium. He showed them to the arched golden door towering above them. It had no key hole or handle; instead, etched on it was a rose bush, spiralling to the top.

'Apri port oro.' Using another spell, Malachi unlocked the golden door. Instantly, it opened outward from the centre. King Drew and Alfredo stepped through first, closely followed by Malachi and his guests, and once all inside the wizard chanted another spell to close the door. This time, the entrance was not to another cave, or a tunnel, but to a room. At first all was dark, but a single flame from the wizard's forefinger lit a multitude of strategically-placed candles. In the large round room was a wooden book case that curved halfway round.

It was filled with a plethora of leather-bound books and a collection of colourful tonics in tiny glass bottles. It smelt like an ancient library; there was even a large inglenook fireplace containing a black cauldron, full of some kind of green sludge. The room had an expansive ceiling representing the night sky, studded with diamonds like pin-prick stars, twinkling brightly. At the centre of the room was a rectangular desk covered with notes of sorts, a peacock-feather quill, and an alembic used for distilling the essence of liquids. Immediately to the left was an iron spiral staircase, leading to an open-plan bedroom. Carved into the wooden handrail were small, gargoyle heads apparently in a slumberous state. After a moment or two, a smoky black cat stepped casually down the staircase, and wandered over to Malachi, purring contently, while rubbing its body against his leg.

'Horatio, my furry friend! I've missed you.' Malachi crouched low to stroke the smooth fur of his pet and then stood back up. 'Welcome to my home; it's thanks to you my lady that I have returned. Now, would you please excuse me for a moment?'

The wizard went upstairs to change into his own clothes. As he did so, each gargoyle head came to life momentarily and spoke.

'Welcome back sir.'

'Good to see you sir', they expressed in high tones.

The Gnome King sat on an armchair to rest his ageing body, Alfredo by his side. In the meantime, Gallium couldn't help but touch everything in sight, and nearly dropped a large jar of pickled newts. He quickly placed it back on the mantelpiece. Rose wandered around the room examining each interesting item and randomly studying the various book spines; titles such as 'Healing with Herbs', 'Mind, Body and Soul' and 'Potions and Tonics', all simply signed 'M.' Astonishingly, a frog leapt from between two books, one of which was aptly titled 'Amphibians.' It jumped onto the desk and into the

125

cauldron, whereupon a bubble of sludge rose to the surface and burst, loudly sounding the frog's last croak.

Chapter Fourteen—The Book of Legends

Before long, Malachi returned wearing a long wizard's robe in jade green with a gold trim. He stalked over to the inglenook; hanging above the mantel was a painting. For a moment, he stood admiring the picture of a little rowing boat against a background of a small island, with a mass of palm trees under a clear, blue sky.

'Are you seeing what I'm seeing?' the gobsmacked warrior said to Rose.

'It looks as if the water in the painting is moving', Rose replied, equally astonished.

All at once, Malachi reached into it and grabbed an object from the boat as it moored on the beach, pulling out something rectangular wrapped in a blue velvet cloth.

'Herewith is the answer to all our problems', Malachi said, placing the object on his desk for everyone to gather round and see. 'I give you the Book of Legends, inscribed by our first-ever Gnome King, and narrated by the God Omnio,' Malachi said, unwrapping the book to show its detailed leather cover with handcrafted inscriptions.

'Your forehead has exactly the same symbols', Gallium remarked.

The four symbols were indeed the same as Malachi's. A star, then a dragon's head, followed by a fish and lastly an unfolding flower. Embossed onto the cover below these, was a hand print.

'Correct, young warrior; I was born with these markings', Malachi said, taking a seat on his elaborately carved wooden chair.

'So, how did you get the markings?' Rose asked confidently, feeling the time was right.

'The day I was born, my mother died. Our people, believing I was a bad omen because of my birthmarks, forced my father to abandon me in a dry well', Malachi sighed and continued his tale.

'From the beginning of time, it was the secret gateway to Jurien; that is, until the Shadow Master condemned one of our gnome kings to death', he said, looking hypnotically into the flame of a candle burning on his desk. 'Therefore, in order to prevent the Shadow Master discovering our secret world, the ancient passage was destroyed.'

'What happened to your people?' Rose enquired.

'They were never seen again; but, the gnomes found me and cared for me to this day', Malachi observed with a smile as his king softly snored. 'They taught me spells and how to harness my gift.' The wizard deftly demonstrated each one using his hands. 'Fire.' A ball of fire rose from his palm and hovered there. 'Water.' He rotated the other wrist to show a ball of water levitating above his palm. 'Air.' He did the same again, exchanging palms, to show a mini tornado. 'And earth', he concluded, releasing dry soil from his fingers to the floor.

'Why did Borago curse you?' Rose queried. She felt a deep empathy for Malachi, relating somewhat to his life.

'The Shadow Master saw me as a threat, and since I would not reveal the whereabouts of Jurien to him, he cursed me to a savage life.'

'Could you not have put a spell on him?' Gallium tested, he too wanting to know more.

'You have no idea how powerful the Orbicular Rock is', the wizard said in a shaky voice. 'After all, it is how Borago came to be the Shadow Master, ruler of chaos and conjurer of curses.' Then the wizard, looking down at the book said, 'Observe.'

What followed next was simply magical: Malachi pressed his palm against the hand print on the book cover, causing the symbols along the top to illuminate all at once, and the book was unlocked. The wizard opened the intricate cover to reveal the first page. As he did so, the book let out a deep exhalation, as though awakened after a long sleep. Rose and Gallium witnessed this marvel with bated breath. On the first page, in black ink, was an account of Pangaea, and on the next page, the map of Pangaea, visually displayed as a three-dimensional hologram. Everyone (except the Gnome King Drew who was still sleeping) absorbed this monumental moment.

'Please.' Malachi signalled for Rose to sit in his chair.

Her hands slightly clammy with excitement, and eager to discover more, she lightly moistened her lips with her tongue and read aloud:

'...a place where the mind is at peace, the soul is pure and the heart is grateful' is how the Introduction ended. 'I don't understand; why do you need me when you have the answers already in this book?' Rose asked.

'My dear child, you are as precious as that gem around your neck', King Drew piped up from his slumber. 'In time you will see just how powerful you can be.' The crotchety king's head fell forward sleepily once more.

'My lady, please continue to read', Malachi said patiently.

Rose went on to reveal the prophecy of the Illuminata. It read:

'Only she who is born of the fifth crystal can find the teacher and the warrior, to assist in lifting the curses, retrieving the four sacred crystals of Pangaea, and bringing back the masters to end the evil rule.'

Feeling the thin corner of the ancient page, Rose carefully turned to the next. From the top, the page showed a drawing of the first symbol, a star; the outline shimmering realistically. The passage under it read:

'The first crystal belongs to the Crystal Master, Lapis Lazuli. It lies in the frozen waters of Lake Lunga, located in the Neve realm.' Rose took a breath and continued to the next text, under a drawing of a dragon's head.

'The second crystal belongs to the Crystal Master, Amazonite. It hangs around the neck of the Purple Dragon, inside the Aurora Mountains of the Airlastua realm.'

The dragon-head symbol breathed a tiny puff of smoke from the page, causing Rose to look nervously at Malachi, before proceeding to the following page.

'The third crystal, a pearl, belongs to the Crystal Master, Perlana. There, in the deepest waters of the Sirenuse realm, you will find a silver fish with a pearl for an eye.' The fish symbol began to swim on the spot, creating ripples across the page. Rose trembled slightly.

Running her eyes halfway down the page, she saw a drawing of a flower, which appeared to blossom animatedly.

'The fourth crystal belongs to the Crystal Master, Zincite, and is found at the Cliff of Promise', she read, 'in the Fatum realm. The lotus flower will open

130

only for the chosen one; within its silky smooth petals, is the crystal.'

At this point, Rose's mouth felt tacky, as she struggled to swallow in between talking, and Malachi noticed this. He drew a cup of water from a wooden bucket of never-ending supply.

'The sooner we find these crystals', Gallium interrupted, eager at the prospect of being the warrior, 'the sooner we will be rid of our enemy.'

'All in good time, Gallium; first I must pack the book for our journey', Malachi said, closing it. 'It will be our reference and guide.'

The others watched closely as Malachi wrapped the book in the original cloth and placed it back into the painting. The boat within the painting returned to its mooring at the island's shore. Then Malachi took the canvas out of the wooden frame and rolled it up, using a length of string to tie it closed.

'There, now we can transport the Book of Legends safely and no one will know', the wizard concluded.

'It is time, it is time', the Gnome King announced, uttering the same spell to re-open the golden door and hobbling out of the room with the aid of Alfredo.

Chapter Fifteen—The Battle of

Bloodwood Gorge

After sending Castro to carry Taurus speedily back to Anaconda, Borago was able to continue with his fiendish plans.

'Taurus, the time has come to take matters into my own hands.' The dark lord paced the stone floor in front of his fireplace, slightly hunched in thought. 'If the prophet cannot be brought to me, then I will have to go to her', Borago declared, drinking the last drop of wine from a golden goblet, before tossing it into the fireplace. Magically, it combusted to display a scorching vision of his bandit crew, who were chanting the Shadow Master's name, and waiting in the wings to wreak havoc.

'But first, we must destroy the Illuminata's allies; go and assemble my blood-thirsty army. We head north at sunrise, starting in the Fatum realm', he commanded.

That same evening, Borago dismissed the entertainers of Mumbala (excluding Azria, who had become his personal servant), while Taurus was left to prepare the men and the weaponry.

With the dawn of battle looming, King Yarrow dreamed another message from Morgana, warning him of the imminent threat from the Shadow Master.

'My king, you must head to the borders of Anaconda and stop this monstrous army from spreading into the other realms', Morgana pronounced, before fading into the distance like a drifting cloud.

The king immediately sat up in bed and woke his loving wife with a gentle pat on her shoulder.

'Aveena, I have been summoned.'

The queen rolled over to face him.

'Summoned?' She blinked and stared at him with concern.

'Yes; Morgana requests I take an army to...Bloodwood Gorge.'

'I see', Aveena said now fully alert, realising full well that was the divide between their realm and that of the 'beasts' of Anaconda. 'When is this...to happen?' The queen couldn't quite bring herself to say the word 'battle'. She considered it a fearful word with dark connotations.

'I'm afraid that I must leave immediately; we are to surprise the enemy with a sudden attack at dawn', the king replied, and without a moment to waste, he hastily got out of bed.

'I understand', the queen said, sombrely pulling back the bedsheets and rising out of bed.

The king turned away to avoid his loyal wife's worried face and proceeded to his robes.

'My love, would you not consider the help of my brother? He could...' The queen was silenced by the king.

'No, I won't hear of it.'

'But his army could join with ours', she added quickly.

'Have you forgotten how he forbade our marriage,'. the king twisted towards her, 'on account that you were betrothed to another with greater wealth?'

'He may think differently, under the circumstances.'

'It would be in vain. Remember, we are banished from his kingdom.' He recoiled, catching a glimpse of his own disapproving look in the mirror, but continued, 'I will not grovel to such a king.'

'Forgive me, it was but a thought', the queen said, assisting him with his robe.

'I know you mean well, but I can do this', King Yarrow said, hugging his beautiful wife, as though it was their last.

Word had reached the king's gentry via Sir Dill, ordering the entire Vervain army of a thousand men to be ready within the hour. Once congregated, like a sea of lit torches, the brave soldiers rode imperially out of their homeland, leaving behind anxious loved ones. They stood by the wayside, tearfully and praying for the safe return of them all—sons of mothers, husbands of wives, fathers of children.

The king and Sir Dill were at the forefront, bravely leading the army across muddy fields, dense woodland, and gushing brooks, occasionally in torrential rain, and only stopping for moments at a time. The king knew they had to arrive before sunrise if they were to prevent Borago reaching Fatum, and beyond. Lighting the way was the moon with some help from their oil-burning torches.

Hours passed and the climate gradually changed to drier conditions. Sir Dill raced on in front to assess a suitable location for the attack to take place, while the king kept his army to a trot.

'Your Grace', Sir Dill said, reporting back moments later. 'I have been as far as the hills up ahead; if we ride beyond the hills, we will risk our exposure.'

'Very well, we will take refuge at the brow of the hill, until our enemy is in sight', the king ordered. 'Instruct the men to douse their torches, we cannot risk being seen.'

'At once, Your Grace.'

There, the gallant army lay low, taking turns among them to keep watch. King Yarrow had no idea what they were up against, but he had every faith in God and his men to carry out their duty. The monarch felt moved to a deep sense of pride, looking over his shoulder at the rows of men, who devotedly awaited their king's command.

The morning was fast approaching, and up in the Mercury Mountains, Borago was preparing for battle, totally unaware that his journey may be cut short. Azria devotedly assisted her master, placing an unsightly metal helmet on his head. It was smooth, with eyelets to see out of, and had a tattoo resembling his own engraved on it.

'Master, I have gathered your army and they await your command.' Taurus directed the Shadow Master onto the balcony to address his followers. Below him was a collection of Lyrons baring their gigantic sabre teeth, and being ridden by the Bandits of Mumbala. Towering at the rear were the Rock Men banging their fists together and, on the frontline, the centaurs grouped with all manner of weapons— spears, spiked metal clubs, and axes.

'Citizens of Anaconda, as your leader and your salvation, I command you to fight against the ones who would have us destroyed', Borago spoke in a stentorian voice, raising his staff. 'Today we ride north to seek and eliminate. Are you with me?'

He received a mighty roar in answer, some simply shouting 'Aye' in agreement. Amid the cacophony, Castro flew down, landing majestically on top of a battlement, and waited for his master. The Shadow Master was to lead the entire army, flying on his gryphon.

At the edge of Anaconda, as usual there wasn't a cloud in the sky and the sun was up in full force. Sir

Dill and his men began to feel the effects of the heat underneath their heavy armour. At the same time, Borago and his villainous mass were now at the start of the bridge. He and Castro flew ahead, only to be unexpectedly hindered by the bright sun reflecting off their adversaries' shields and armour. Castro shrieked loudly at the abnormally fierce glare that caused him to momentarily lose his sight. Borago couldn't identify the troops below, but felt deeply suspicious. Regaining control of his mutant bird, he directed Castro down to the ground. The Shadow Master dismounted from his winged beast, as Taurus quickly came to his aid with a Lyron for his master to ride the rest of the way. Borago climbed onto the back of the wild feline creature.

'Something's wrong, Taurus', the Shadow Master said, squinting as he scanned the distant hills for clues. 'We must proceed with caution, as I fear we are not alone.'

His army soon caught up from behind, and were halfway across Bloodwood Gorge.

Over the ridge, King Yarrow and his men had heard the loud shriek, and witnessed the tumble of the mighty bird.

'Your Grace, what was that?' Sir Dill asked turning to the king.

'That, Sir Dill, was our signal to launch the attack.' King Yarrow spurred his horse on to the top of the hill.

'My brothers-in-arms', the king pronounced. 'Now is the time to rise and defend our lands.' Then came a clattering of swords and armoury, as the soldiers stood to attention, then mounted their horses, ready to follow their king.

'LET THE BATTLE COMMENCE!' King Yarrow bellowed at the top of his lungs, charging down the other side of the hill towards the bridge, closely followed by his army.

The arid, sun-baked terrain showed jagged cracks that spread with every pounding hoof. The thunderous noise of man and beast became increasingly deafening, as the two armies closed in on each another.

By now, the army of Vervain was clearly visible to the evil eyes of the Shadow Master. Veins of fury protruded from his neck as he witnessed the threatening display of military mass. Quickly, the Shadow Master gave his order to strike back. The ferocious feline carrying Borago waded to one side, as his master hurried the league of assassins to the other side of the bridge.

Soon, the Lyrons had claimed their first victims; pouncing on the soldiers of Vervain, their claws gripping tightly and their oversized teeth effortlessly penetrating their armour. Close by were the Rock Men, using their club-sized fists to knock down the soldiers of Vervain, just as if they were hundreds of skittles. Others were being squished underfoot as they tried to run away. The Centaurs were swift with their spears and axes, waving them around like twirling batons before launching them at the enemy.

Soon a merciless fight was underway. Blood squirted from lacerated arteries, leaving a scarlet stain that stretched from the hillside down to the bridge, marking the severity of the battle. An hour in, the temperature suddenly soared, curdling the gut-spilling bodies and creating a lingering stench of death. Vultures circled high above ready to devour the unfortunate. The courageous troops of Vervain kept up morale by shouting 'For Pangaea!'—but in vain. Sir Dill fought his way over to speak with the king.

'Your Grace, the heat is proving too much for the men, plus the enemy is strong', he said, fending off another centaur by plunging his sword through the half-man's torso.

King Yarrow, fighting for his own life, had to agree. How would they conquer such a force? With another centaur down, the king pulled away, galloping halfway up the hill, and in total distress called out to the Fairy Queen, Morgana.

'Morgana! Why have you sent us here like lambs to the slaughter?!' he shouted, with his chest heaving and sweat pouring from his head.

The fairy queen soon responded in a clear and concise voice.

'Courage Yarrow, all is not lost. Unite your men, and use your shields in the direction of the enemy and the sun. Now go.'

The king responded immediately, charging back down to re-join his men. After updating Sir Dill and his son with the plan, he ordered the remaining soldiers to withdraw: 'Comrades of Vervain, we must draw back! Draw back!'

Sir Dill and Prince Burdock led the soldiers, with their king, to the other side of the hill.

The Shadow Master's army, believing the cowardly Vervains were retreating, ceased for a moment, gathering at the bottom of the hill like hypnotised fools, awaiting orders. Their general, Taurus, galloped back to where his master stood by the bridge.

In that time, the king had regrouped his army on the brow of the hill, momentarily out of sight of the enemy.

'Sir Dill, deploy your archers as discussed', King Yarrow ordered, 'and when the infantry and cavalry are in place, I will give the final command.'

The gallant knight rode to the top of the hill and called to his men.

'Archers, form a line!' Sir Dill instructed.

Within minutes, the synchronised soldiers formed a long line, doubling up in areas and wedging their arrows in the ground, ready to pick up and draw.

In the meantime, Taurus, arriving to meet his master ,asked:

'My lord, what will you have us do now?'

'We go after them', the Shadow Master commanded coldly. 'Look!' He jabbed his finger in the direction of the Vervain army.

'Lock!' From the front line Sir Dill gave the command to take aim.

The king knew that attacking from any height meant the Vervains had an advantage.

Taurus charged back to his army, calling to attack. The monstrous bunch clambered, ran, and galloped their way up the dry stony hill to fight.

'Draw!' Was the next instruction given by Sir Dill to the archers. The tension was mounting as the taut wooden arrows were drawn back into position.

'Loose!'

The Archers released their metal-tipped arrows to the heavens, and down they whistled like a shower of deadly splinters, piercing the enemy in seconds— some through the head or neck, even an eye.

'Infantry, take up your position!' Prince Burdock was already preparing his infantry to storm over the brow and form a blockade.

Looking like a long metallic wall, the soldiers of Vervain were packed together, and behind them, led by King Yarrow, was the cavalry with swords at the ready.

'At my command!' the king yelled, tilting his shield up towards the hellish sun. 'Shields in front!'

As one, the Vervain army held up their shields to the sun's rays, angled slightly towards the foe. The reflected light was agonisingly bright, and, with a little magic from Morgana, the rays' potency intensified, blinding every bandit and beast in sight and sending them into a frenzy. The mad mob ran back in the direction from which they had come; literally, the blind leading the blind! Unable to see, one group of Lyrons attacked each other, and the Rock Men crumbled into mounds of rubble from the heat of the reflected rays. Most of the centaurs were left stumbling over corpses, crying in pain while they covered their eyes, while Lyrons and bandits who, misjudging their position, fell to their deaths in the deep gorge.

Once the dust settled and silence fell, King Yarrow and Vervains' heroes looked on with sadness at the travesty caused to their fellow brethren.

'Let us not forget the true courage shown today, God bless these souls, as we bring back hope to our people', the king expressed with deep sentiment.

The tired, brave heroes returned to Vervain with heads held high. The battle was won—for now, at least.

Chapter Sixteen—The First Task

Following a restful night's sleep, Malachi, Rose and Gallium returned to their horses. Malachi observed his horse Dewdrop, standing with Noble and Ironbark. The three newly formed companions were on their way to see the White Lady Alba. It was mid-afternoon in the dry, but freezing conditions as they approached the edge of Lake Lunga.

'My lady, I think it best you call to her first', Malachi advised wisely.

Rose got down from her horse and walked confidently over to the side of the lake. Feeling brave and composed, she spoke: 'Lady Alba, we have come for the crystal of Lapis Lazuli,' her breath escaping from her mouth like mist.

Everyone's eyes swept the horizon for the delicate figure. Almost instantly, from across the body of water, Alba appeared, floating towards them in a daydream.

'Who seeks this priceless stone?' her soft voice resounded across the wilderness, tinkling every icicle hanging from tree and bush.

Gallium, not wanting to take any chances, stood alongside Rose.

'It is I, the Illuminata. We have found the Book of Legends, and it has led us here to claim the first crystal.'

The White Lady moved in closer to Rose; they were almost nose to nose. Rose stood motionless, holding her breath for a few seconds.

'It IS you', Lady Alba said, convinced and moved back a little. 'I cannot give you the crystal', she said looking down.

'Why not?' Rose asked.

'I have been cursed into guarding it, but you have my permission to cross the icy lake and attempt to take it from beneath the ice.' Alba pointed to where the crystal glowed at the centre of the lake, and then like an ice sculpture melting in the sun, she dissolved back into the water. Only her voice could be heard, saying, 'Beware and tread with care.'

'Allow me, my lady', Gallium said, eagerly preparing himself for the challenge by removing his heavy outer garments.

'What about using a spell?' Rose said, turning to Malachi.

'I'm afraid my spells, as I have experienced, do not work on these powerful curses.'

Rose took in a breath.

'Very well, but do be careful', she responded.

Gallium, standing by the edge of the lake, took a moment to study his options. He decided to distribute his weight evenly across the ice by lying face down, thereby minimising the risk of cracking. On his stomach, the warrior used his hands and forearms to pull his body across the cold, slippery surface, but it was too difficult to grasp. Changing tactics, he decided to use his dagger to speed things along, by digging its point into the ice and dragging his body across. Repeating this sequence, he drew closer and closer to the glowing gem beneath the icy crust. His hands soon grew numb from the cold, and he struggled to keep his grip. He had gone a fair way, when suddenly, fine cracks in the ice started to map an outline, making Gallium feel a little uneasy; his breath shortened and his entire body grew very cold. He lay uncomfortably still, planning the next move. Rose gasped at the sound of every fracture made in the ice. The crystal was almost within reach.

'Malachi, shouldn't we do something?' she asked, nervously biting her bottom lip, and rubbing her hands together for warmth.

Malachi was about to answer when the ice shattered into a million pieces, and Gallium fell into the freezing water.

'Gallium!' Rose cried, almost launching herself after him, but Malachi grabbed hold of her arm.

'My lady, it's far too dangerous!'

For a brief moment nothing happened, then like a human cannon ball, Gallium shot out of the water, and fell hard onto the snowy ground beside the others. He was pale, drenched—and unconscious. Ironbark trotted over and licked his master's face, but he didn't move. Malachi felt his neck for a pulse and put an ear to his chest, listening for a heartbeat. Rose, also deeply concerned, rubbed Gallium's cold hands.

'He's alive, but only just. Quickly, my lady, use your crystal to heal him', the wizard instructed, fetching a blanket and rolling it to cushion Gallium's head.

Rose did not hesitate and, with a deep breath, closed her eyes and imagined Gallium alive. The Illuminata placed her hands on his chest and concentrated hard. The pink gem stone began to glow brighter than ever before. Slowly, Gallium regained consciousness, spluttering and gasping for air. Then he unclenched his other hand, letting go of an object. It was the crystal Lapis Lazuli!

'You did it!' Malachi exclaimed, holding the stone up to his face. It was beautiful, predominantly dark blue with shimmering gold flecks. 'My lady, the stone has a narrow hole for you to thread it on your chain.'

143

'Very well', Rose said, taking the crystal, and like thread through a needle, the first crystal was caught up.

Meantime, the wizard had magically started a cheerful fire to keep them warm.

'How did you capture the crystal?' Rose asked Gallium, as she helped him sit up, wrapping the blanket around him.

'Last thing I remember', Gallium recalled through chattering teeth, 'I grabbed the star as I sank to the bottom, paralysed by the freezing temperatures. And then, nothing', he said, hugging himself dry, very relieved to have made it alive.

Malachi became distracted by something in the distance; it was the White Lady. She waved at the wizard before plunging back in the water. Malachi suspected she had something to do with saving Gallium from drowning.

The next morning the three travellers were equipped to set off in search of the second crystal, when Gallium strolled up to Rose, who stood in a daydream patting her horse.

'Rose, I must thank you for saving my life', he said.

'You're welcome, although I did feel partly responsible for your state', she replied. 'You could have died.'

'You needn't worry about me', Gallium stressed with a smile. 'I have lived dangerously all my life.'

Malachi called them over. The three sat huddled around another fire, admiring the pages of the Book of Legends.

'So, the second crystal is to be found in the Airlastua realm, inside the Aurora Mountains', he said, closing the book. 'As luck would have it, I know the way to Airlastua, therefore I'm more than happy to lead us there.' Malachi placed the book once more in the enchanted painting and climbed on his horse.

'Thank you Malachi', Rose said.

'I for one, can't wait for warmer weather', Gallium said, hugging his body.

With their belongings packed and courage to drive them, they went off in the direction of warmer climes.

Chapter Seventeen—'Shiver me timbers!'

Overwhelmed by his unexpected defeat, the Shadow Master was consulting the Witches of the Well as to the whereabouts of Captain Nine-tails Johnson, the Captain having failed a couple of times to respond by spyglass. Armed with information from the witches, the Shadow Master climbed onto his golden gryphon and flew in the direction of Port Oreon, on the east coast of Anaconda. Castro flew high for some time, before touching down at the centre of this forsaken harbour town, a haven for pirates, bandits and suchlike to commune while squandering their wealth on liquor and other indulgences. Port Oreon was also notorious for recruiting sea crewmembers, and the nearby coves were a perfect location to secretly stash a pirate's treasure.

When Castro landed on the waterfront, creating a huge gust of wind with his wings, a local drunk ran away in fear, and in blind panic jumped off a pier. Borago slid down the wing of Castro, his staff in tow, landing deftly on his feet. Close by, other inebriated privateers were just as stunned by the Shadow Master's earth-trembling arrival, immediately recognising him as their dark lord. Afraid, they made way like hunched fools, as he walked past. Borago marched on, scanning the area suspiciously. In frustration, he grabbed a local man by the scruff of his neck.

'Where is Captain Nine-tails?' he demanded gruffly.

The insignificant sailor unsteadily pointed his dirty finger in the direction of 'The Pretty Polly', one of the local ale houses (and not named after the feathered kind).

The Shadow Master prowled over to the entrance of the pub, and with one powerful kick at the door with his heavy booted foot, made a dramatic entrance. He was seething with anger and wanted everyone to know it.

'Trembling Teresa!' the chubby landlord exclaimed from behind the bar, dropping a bottle of rum onto the floor, while a young wench screamed the cobwebs away from a corner.

'Where is Captain Nine-tails Johnson?' roared Borago.

For a brief moment there was a stunned silence.

'I'm over here…my lord. Havin' a bad day, are we?' Captain Nine-tails mocked from a dark corner, taking another glug of his favourite ale, before pushing a dishevelled maid off his lap and casually rising from a wooden bench. The bench creaked, relieved of its heavy occupant.

'I want a word with you, Johnson', Borago avowed, stomping off to a more private room at the back of the pub.

Unimpressed, the captain spat on the floor and grudgingly followed. The two men sat down at a small table in the dusty, poorly lit room. Borago noticed Captain Nine-tails wasn't wearing his spyglass.

'I specifically said I would send for you when needed. Why do you not wear the spyglass?' he interrogated Johnson.

'So, I hear you lost the battle', the captain belched, placing his heavy feet casually on the table, almost tipping it over, and barely able to move in such cramped conditions.

'I merely encountered a temporary setback, that is all', Borago said, his brows inverted with a deep crease, trying really hard not to lose his temper, as he pulverised the table's disused candle in his clenched fist.

'I'm warning you, Johnson, do not cross me.'

'Oh pipe down, what in all things gold do you want?' the captain said, examining his black fingernail.

'This is what needs to happen', the Shadow Master began, his elbows on the table and fingers interlaced. 'We will sail together and track the Illuminata.' Carefully he took a green crystal ball from the pocket of his long coat. 'And this is going to help us.'

'My thirst be for gold, and that's all!' the captain protested, flailing his arms. 'For years I've been searchin' for this so-called kingdom of treasure you promised me!' Johnson rose to his feet, eyes locked on Borago. 'And my men won't hang around for nothin' neither.'

'This is why we both need that girl alive', Borago said smugly, rubbing his chin and sinking back into the chair. 'She has seen the treasure, and knows exactly where it is.' He showed Captain Nine-tails a vision of the gems of Jurien, from inside the crystal ball.

The captain's pupils dilated at the sparkling sight, and he sat back down in awe.

'Find the girl; get the treasure', Borago whispered, grabbing a dagger from his belt, and stabbing it into the old wooden table, thus snapping Nine-tails out of his trance. 'So—are you in?'

The captain slowly rose to his feet, at the same time coming to a decision. 'All right, I'm in but the crew will answer only to me...and we'll need a down payment.' The two powerful, despicable men sealed the deal with a firm hand shake.

'Done', Borago agreed. They concluded by leaning across the table at one another, eyeball to eyeball.

At this point, the Shadow Master roughly sheathed his dagger, exiting the room with an air of authority and leaving Captain Nine-tails muttering rebelliously.

Later that day, the Shadow Master rejoined Captain Nine-tails aboard the ship Exodus, and set course for the Triton Sea from the south.

Chapter Eighteen—The Second Task

In the northern part of the Airlastua realm, the sun peeped occasionally from behind puffy grey clouds. The ground was lush and green, and quite muddy in areas. After a couple of days' travelling, Rose, Gallium and Malachi arrived at the nearby town of Terrera, north of the Aurora Mountains. It was a tired-looking old place, still sodden from heavy rainfall. They entered the town at a solemn pace, Some local children greeted the three visitors, waving excitedly, but mostly, the children appeared unwell; a pale-faced boy was hobbling on crutches, yet another young girl had a rasping cough and, scratching at her throat, seemed desperate to attract Rose's attention; their worried mothers hurried them back indoors.

'Hello', Rose said, waving at the locals, but there was no reciprocation.

Then Malachi noticed a large wooden board nailed to a post at the side of the road. On it was some lettering painted in dark red, which read:

'WARNING! Sorcerers, witches, beasts and black magic are not welcome here!'

This understandably made the wizard feel a little nervous. Malachi quickly pulled a headscarf from his pocket and wrapped it around his head, covering the birthmarks. He also removed his robe and packed it away. Saying nothing to his companions, he elected to lead the way on foot over to a nearby inn. The locals appeared unsettled, as they scurried to their dwellings. Some of the windows of the small houses were boarded-up, and a few of the front doors showed signs of forced entry, their wooden panels dented. Hanging high above the centre of the town was an unusual gilded clock, which showed no sign of working, judging from its motionless, rusty cogs. Mounted on a tower overrun with ivy, this old clock had two faces. One represented the direction of the sun, indicating when day turns to night; just below it, a slightly smaller face displayed the four seasons, at its centre a gold compass. Visible at the top of the tower through an arch, was an enormous bell.

All at once a woman's mournful cry was heard coming from inside one of the houses that stood in a row along the main street.

'My baby!' the young woman cried. 'Please Doctor Maurice, save him!' She fell to her knees at the front door, sobbing uncontrollably and tugging at the doctor's leg.

Unimpressed, the doctor prised his leg free. A grey man with scraggly overgrown hair, he supported his thin lanky frame by leaning on a walking stick.

'Marzia, go to your baby before it's too late', he said numbingly.

At this, Rose felt compelled to help and headed to the woman's house.

'My lady, they mustn't know who you really are', Malachi uttered, standing before her and blocking the path.

'But I cannot stand by idly, knowing what I know', Rose argued, with clear compassion.

The doctor proceeded to feebly escort the mournful mother back inside the house.

'I'm sorry, I cannot allow it', Malachi insisted, nudging his head discreetly towards the sign for her to read. 'Not to mention risking our mission. Now, if you'll excuse me.' The wise wizard dismissed the conversation by casually stepping inside the inn.

Rose was left standing in front of the sign, her mouth slightly agape.

'Malachi's right, it's too risky', Gallium said, standing behind her and tenderly putting his hand on her shoulder. 'We're just trying to protect you.'

Rose let out a huge sigh.

'What about protecting the people of Pangaea', Rose said, swivelling round to face him. 'What about that poor innocent child.' Her eyes were now wet with emotion. 'I feel I ought to do something.'

'Fate will decide, as always', Gallium said, and went to fetch their belongings from the horses.

'The inn has a room for each of us, my lady; we can stay the night', Malachi said, and went to assist Gallium with their things.

'Very well, I will pray for hope', Rose expressed, while quietly thinking to herself, ' this doesn't end here.'

Later that evening, Gallium sat on the window-seat of his room at the inn, reading his father's diary, occasionally lifting his eyes to the window in between accounts. Unbeknown to him, a familiar hooded figure turned up at the door of Marzia's house. It was Rose. Not one to give up, she had sneaked out of the inn, alone. She knocked on the door gently. Moments later, an eye blinked through a peephole in the door.

'Who goes there?' Marzia said, still blinking.

'Please, don't be afraid; I would like to help you and your child', Rose said sincerely, clasping her hands together.

To Rose's delight, the bolt of the door was scraped back and fingers wrapped around the edge of the door, slowly pulling it open and revealing a head, nervously peering from behind.

A perplexed Marzia was looking her up and down.

'Who are you?'

'Someone who cares', Rose answered.

Marzia's reddened eyes stared intently at Rose's face; she sensed a kindness in her smile, and allowed her to enter. The front door led directly into the small but cosy main living area, where a low fire burnt in the little fireplace. The baby was in an oak crib by a window, struggling to breathe and red with fever.

'He is dying', Marzia said with a tremble in her voice. 'I have no money to give you, but I would sell my soul to Helidor himself to save him.' Marzia picked up the tot and hugged him close.

'I do not require money, or your soul', Rose said, resting her hand on Marzia.

'Are you an angel or...a witch?' Marzia asked staring into the fireplace.

'I am neither, but I can help if you will let me.' Rose stroked the baby's forehead; he felt very warm.

In desperation, Marzia accepted her kind offer with a nod.

'My name is Marzia', she said smiling meekly.

'I am Rose. Where is the rest of your family?' Rose asked, glancing out of the window.

Marzia's eyes welled as she tried to suppress her sorrow.

'My husband died a short while ago, at the hands of the centaurs', Marzia said, anxiously pacing the floor and cradling her baby.

'The centaurs were here?' Rose asked, alarmed.

'Yes, they...they tried to take me away, but Reno, he...', Marzia responded, swallowing the lump in her throat. 'I ran and hid in the tower, until they left, just like he told me to.'

'You poor dear', Rose said despondently; she couldn't help feeling partly responsible for Marzia's misfortune.

'Now I'm forced to witness this', Marzia wept, embracing her baby.

'I am sorry for your loss, but I promise you this, your son will live', Rose said confidently, rubbing Marzia lightly on the back to comfort her. 'Now, do you have fresh water to drink?' Rose looked around the dimly lit room for a pail or something.

'It's over there.' Marzia pointed to a wooden pail with a ladle, on the floor beneath the window.

Rose poured some water into a tin cup and brought it over to Marzia.

'There, rest now Marzia', Rose said softly, passing the cup and settling the forsaken women into a rocking chair. 'I will keep watch over you both tonight.'

Marzia, exhausted by the whole ordeal, soon fell sound asleep, still holding her dying boy.

Rose carefully picked up the baby, took in a deep breath and placed her hand on the baby's forehead.

'There, there, little one', Rose whispered softly, caressing his tiny forehead with her thumb.

The Illuminata was all aglow; so too was the infant. As the light could be seen from outside the window, someone witnessed the miraculous event.

It was the doctor on his way home after a tipple at the tavern down the road. Rubbing his eyes in disbelief, he looked again to see Rose performing the wondrous act.

Moments later, he knocked loudly at Marzia's door. The pounding could be heard up and down the street.

'Open the door!' he exclaimed. 'I know she's in there!'

Stunned by this outburst, Rose immediately placed the infant in his crib.

'That sounds like...the doctor.' Marzia woke in a daze, and slowly rose to her feet. 'It must be urgent.' Marzia thought it best to open the door, before he knocked it down.

Rose hesitated, as she stood in a corner, pondering her next move. She couldn't see another way out of the house. Holding her breath, she froze.

The doctor forced his way past Marzia, hobbling with his stick.

'Who are you?' he protested, swaying slightly.

Rose stuttered.

'Answer me!' the enraged medic said.

'She is not your concern!' a stern voice answered from the doorway. It was Gallium.

'She is a witch I tell you, I saw it with my own eyes.' The doctor shook his walking stick in Rose's direction, exclaiming, 'I will have you arrested!' as he backed away from Gallium, who moved in closer. Marzia crouched down next to the crib, rocking it gently.

'She is not a witch, you old fool', Gallium responded, trying not to frighten Marzia, who was whispering comforting words to her child.

'It's your kind who took my wife Isabelle', the old doctor continued sorrowfully, clutching his stick.

'Look', Gallium was now almost pressed against the doctor, towering over the cranky old man. 'You've been drinking', he said, sniffing the intoxicating fumes on his breath.

'Like a selfless martyr, she sacrificed herself for this wretched town', the doctor whimpered pitifully.

'Sir, please, I do pity you, but you are sadly mistaken', Rose voiced, feeling his pain. 'I am but a simple nursemaid, trying to help.'

The doctor was too consumed by his loss to notice anyone.

'Let's go', Gallium said, holding out his hand to Rose.

'I bid you all goodnight.' And with that, she promptly left with Gallium, returning to the inn across the road.

'We will see about that', the doctor muttered, leaving the house and hobbling down the street.

'Rose, forgive me but, what were you thinking?' Gallium said, ruffling his hair, and trying not to cause a scene as they marched up the stairs of the inn.

'I did what I thought to be right and I have no regrets.' Rose stopped at once to face her warrior on the landing. 'By morning, that baby will be cured', she added confidently, before entering her room.

Meanwhile, trouble was brewing on board the ship Exodus, which had now made its way to the middle of the ocean. Captain Nine-tails Johnson and the Shadow Master Borago sat at the table in the captain's cabin. Flinders was standing by the door, awaiting orders. At the centre of the table was the emerald crystal ball and a sack of gold, all worth a small fortune.

'I call upon the Witches of the Well', Borago commanded.

A green mist began to grow and swirl from within the globe, followed by the usual cackling and giggling.

'Oh, it's been a long time since I was on a ship, master', Marelda said with her face pressed against the clear ball.

'What is thy bidding, master?' Hemmatia asked, as she too, gradually appeared.

'You will tell me where I can find the Illuminata.'

'She is not far from these waters, somewhere in the realm of Sirenuse, but we cannot give an exact...'

'Yes, I know, because of her cussed crystal', Borago interrupted with a grunt.

'My advice would be to...', Hemmatia began.

'Hunt her down, yes, great idea sister', Marelda piped up dimly.

Hemmatia cast a sticky spell on her impertinent sister, temporarily sealing Marelda's mouth shut, before continuing.

'First, you must use the curse of a thousand deaths; it will seek her out like prey', Hemmatia suggested. 'Head for the coast of Sirenuse and release the curse on the shores of Coral Bay.'

'But I need her alive! Besides, I had planned to use the curse during battle', Borago said.

'The curse is at your command, my lord', Hemmatia said, reassuringly. 'But hurry, the Illuminata does not stay in one place for long.'

The two hags disappeared like smoke, deep within the crystal ball.

The pirate king Johnson, listening to every word, was still none the wiser.

'Captain, I have work to do, I will return in a few days', Borago instructed, grabbing his staff and going up on deck.

'Cracking cannons! But we've just set sail', Captain Nine-tails said, waving his arms around so vigorously that he struck a fellow pirate, while pursuing Borago.

'I have wasted enough time here, the curse of a thousand deaths must be performed', Borago said, whistling for his gryphon. 'You have your first sack of gold, now stick to the bargain.'

'Mr Flinders, chart a course for Port Oreon!' the captain barked, rubbing his face in frustration. 'What's this curse then?'

'You will see', Borago said, as the magnificent winged monster picked up his master with its giant claw, and flew in the direction of his lair.

Later that night, back in the town of Terrera, the local inn was visited by the Doctor and the Mayor of the town, together with a couple of guards. The doctor had reported Rose to the authorities, claiming her to be a witch. The men stormed into her room uninvited, and dragged her by the arms out on to the street.

'Let me go!' Rose yelled, trying to free herself from the guards, who were tying her hands behind her back. They pushed her to the green and proceeded to fasten her to a post opposite the clock tower.

Gallium had woken up to hear Rose's distress, and without hesitation rushed to her rescue, sword in hand. Hidden among the crowd, the warrior sneaked up behind one of the guards, and pressed his blade to the man's throat.

The shocked guard dared not yell or move, as the edge of the sword was pushed firmly against his skin.

'Release the lady, or this guard will die', Gallium demanded.

The gathered civilians froze, awaiting the Mayor's orders.

'Oh dear now, well, you see, I'm afraid I cannot do that, this...woman... is a witch', the Mayor said, shuffling backwards as he read from a scroll. 'And according to our laws, err, where is it...ah yes: she must be burnt at the stake.'

The nimble-looking mayor seemed keen to avoid any confrontation, hiding behind his subjects, while at the same time, insisting that rules are rules.

Suddenly, a gong was banged from somewhere among the crowd, grabbing everyone's attention. The crowd parted to reveal Malachi, holding a bronze gong. Opting for a more diplomatic approach, the wizard walked calmly past the citizens and stood the other side of Rose.

'Citizens of Terrera, this woman is not a witch!' Malachi proclaimed. 'She is our salvation!' he then whispered to Rose: 'You must reveal who you are or there will be serious consequences.'

Gallium quickly released the guard and ran over to join Rose and Malachi.

'Prove it!' remarked a local man and everyone else agreed.

'People of Terrera, you live in fear and I understand why', Rose said, grimacing as her wrists rubbed against the post. 'But I am not your enemy, the enemy is someone truly wicked', Rose confessed.

'Why should we believe you?' the mayor asked pompously, shadowed by a couple of his guards. 'Why, our very own doctor saw you using black magic', he said, stepping back and ushering his guards to restrain the wizard and the warrior.

'What, that drunken old fool?' Gallium exclaimed, looking daggers in the direction of the mad medic.

The mob crept closer with fire-lit torches and vacant expressions, as though brainwashed.

'Gallium, hold!' Malachi shouted, as he waited for the right moment to act. 'My lady, show them who you are!'

Closing her eyes, Rose took in the biggest breath and summoned all her might.

'I, am the Illuminataaa!' her voice reverberated throughout the town, so much so, that the bell in the tower gave a loud BONG! and the cogs of the old clock began to turn once more. The people, amazed by her powerful presence, recoiled like frightened children.

'Mercy, mercy!' they cried, crouching on the ground like worms.

The dawn was creeping up, and just at that moment, Marzia came rushing excitedly from her house, clutching her baby.

'It's true, she is innocent!' Marzia declared, hurrying over to stand in front of Rose and facing the people. 'She has saved my son! I for one, am eternally grateful.' Her healthy baby gurgled happily in her arms.

The Terrerians all gathered in awe around Marzia, and Gallium seized the opportunity to cut Rose free from her bindings.

The doctor felt a wave of panic, and while his kinsfolk were preoccupied, hobbled away as fast as he could, avoiding any further embarrassment. The disillusioned mayor stepped up immediately to speak with Rose and the others.

'Forgive me, my lady', the Mayor said red-faced and genuflecting. 'People of Terrera, our prayers have been answered and we must be thankful for this special lady.'

The townsfolk rejoiced at the announcement and soon retired contently to their homes.

Following the turbulent night, the three guests were offered a room each at the mayor's château behind the clock tower. It was there that Rose and her friends briefed the Mayor on their vital mission. The following morning, the Mayor invited a few of Terrera's very sick to his huge white house, where the Illuminata took a short time away from her cause to heal the suffering civilians. Later that day, the Illuminata, the wizard and the warrior said their goodbyes and left for the Airlastua realm.

All the while, the Shadow Master was well on his way to creating the most deadly curse yet, the main ingredient being—the souls of the damned.

'Taurus, I need just a few more victims; bring me more scum to sacrifice', the Shadow Master ordered from the edge of the Magma Pit, blood dripping from the tip of his dagger.

'As you wish my lord; I will gather a small army and leave right away.' And, as the general went to retrieve more murderers, plunderers and disease-riddled criminals (some already captive in the prisons of Mumbala), the grinning Shadow Master returned to his castle for another evening's entertainment.

After an overnight stop, Noble and the other horses and their three riders, galloped for hours to arrive in the Valley of Essence. This was a key location in the Airlastua realm, where the travellers would begin their search for the second crystal. Observing the natural splendour of the place, the three trotted under a glorious sun, turning their faces to embrace the warmth and the sweet floral fragrances floating on the air. The flora on the hillside displayed a colourful selection of every flower and herb countable, in these parts. It truly was a joyous sight. Rising up in the background were the Aurora mountains, carpeted in green and capped with the rainbow-coloured Aurora lights. The air moved constantly, soft as a translucent silk scarf. Running through the valley was the River of Achelous, from its source at the Aurora Falls near the base of the Aurora Mountains, and flowing south through the centre of the next realm, Sirenuse. It was near the mountains, by the river, that Malachi suggested the group rest for the night.

'It's so beautiful', Rose commented, jumping down from her horse, and breathing in the scent from the uncurling flowers. She sat dreamily on an enormous log, but all was not what it seemed.

'I wouldn't sit on that if I were you, my lady' the wizard keenly advised.

'Aah! It's moving', Rose said, as the creature slowly produced two stumpy turtle-like legs on each side of its log-shape body.

'What is it?' Rose said, observing and backing away disconcertedly to join Malachi.

'It's a dorphinian; harmless creatures. They sleep on land and feed from the river', Malachi said, as the sloth-moving thing, with rough textured skin and webbed feet, ambled over to the water's edge, before plummeting to the bottom of the river.

'Oh, and one more thing, my lady', the wizard continued, positioning himself crossed-legged on the ground, 'I would avoid sniffing the dark blue blooms; I used to come here on my travels and collect them for a dream potion.'

'Have you travelled much?' Rose said, picking a few flowers.

'In my younger days, yes, the gnomes advised me to venture out and broaden my mind', Malachi replied.

'How wonderful, I intend to do the same', Rose said, now looking interestingly at Gallium, who was knee-deep in the river.

Holding a spear above his shoulder, with knees slightly bent, and keeping very still, Gallium watched the ripples moving closer as he waited patiently. And then, SPLASH! With a quick jab of the wooden spear he had crafted, he caught a delicious rainbow trout.

'Ha! Now that's a fish', he said, demonstrating the extra-large catch in the air.

The day drew to a close and the three companions sat around another magically lit campfire, Malachi taking this opportunity to study the Book of Legends with Rose and Gallium.

'I say we go in tonight while the Purple Dragon sleeps', Gallium said, flicking twigs into the fire.

'According to legend, the dragon never sleeps, and it never leaves the cave. Its sole purpose is to guard that crystal', Malachi said, closing the book, and replacing it in its safe place.

'Maybe I can speak to it; perhaps if it knows who I am, we may appeal to its better nature', Rose said, staring into the flames in deep thought.

'I admire your theory, my lady' Malachi said, smiling and producing tents for each of them by transfiguring three moderate rocks, with the use of a simple spell. 'Well, the sun has set and my dreams beckon, goodnight to you both.' Malachi retired to his tent for the remainder of the evening.

Gallium sat by the fire, subdued, and watched as the flames danced erratically, with small bursts of ember.

'You seem deep in thought, Gallium. Is something wrong?' Rose asked, as they shared a seat on a smooth, large boulder.

'Nothing of concern, my lady', Gallium replied, pulling 'The Traveller's Book' from his satchel, and flicking through the pages.

'I remember seeing that book in your tree house', Rose said softly and leaned in closer. 'I'd love to hear a story.'

'This used to belong to my father, it's a journal of his voyages across the sea.' Gallium smiled to himself. 'As I recall, once we sailed to the Island of Andromeda. I was but a young boy', he said, trying to find the passage in the hand-sized book.

'Ah, here it is.' Gallium read an excerpt aloud.

'My mission, by order of the king, was to form a friendship with the Andromedas, in order to gain safe passage to the island's most treasured secret, known for its healing powers.'

There was a ruminant pause from the warrior. Leaning in closer, Gallium whispered mysteriously to Rose, 'Unicorns.'

'Ha, how exciting! I've read about them, but to actually see one, it must have been thrilling', she said.

'Yes, yes it was', Gallium said, lightly rubbing the page between his finger and thumb, as he continued to read. 'The Andromedas were a friendly race, and by order of the king, I offered precious gems in exchange for full entry. The deal was sealed.'

'When I was a child, I barely stepped foot outside the castle', Rose said, brushing a stone on the ground with the side of her foot. 'Although, I was taught to swim down at a river—under close supervision, of course.' Sloping against the boulder, Rose sat on the ground, as she admired the screen of stars sheltering them.

'What about your mother? What was she like?' Rose asked, tilting her head.

'Unfortunately, my mother died when I was an infant, but my father told me of her gentle heart and flawless beauty.' Gallium cleared his throat, 'I grew up alongside my father and, after the day he was taken from me, I vowed to find him and take back his ship', he said snapping the book shut.

'But, enough about me, *you* are the most mysterious person I have ever met', the warrior continued, twisting round to face Rose. 'Who are your parents?'

'My home was, is, with the Vervains and my purpose is to complete this mission', Rose answered awkwardly, rolling a pebble in her hand. 'I never knew my real parents.'

Gallium had unintentionally touched upon a sore subject.

'My apologies, Rose.'

'No it's all right, I am just tired', Rose said, slowly getting up. She was still trying to work out the pieces of her life, never mind explaining who she was. 'Until tomorrow, goodnight.' And into her tent she went.

'Goodnight, my lady.'

The search for the Purple Dragon continued at first light, the three galloping north of the River Achelous, past an occasional blossoming tree. The sun-kissed ground soon changed from grass to pebbles, and in no time at all they had a visual on the Aurora Falls, a mighty torrent of water elegantly cascading down the mountainside like a white veil. As they neared, the waterfall's spray lightly misted their faces. Rose, Malachi and Gallium left their horses to one side and continued on foot in search of a way up, or into, the mountain. Gallium ran ahead, keen to be the first to find an opening. Getting close to the rock-face, he searched high and low, even leaning towards the back of the fall to find an entrance of some sort, but there was no visible gap, no entrance—and no clue.

'I can't see an opening anywhere!' he shouted over the noise of the cascade, by now quite saturated and battling to keep his balance on the wet rocks.

'I didn't think it would be an obvious entrance, otherwise the Purple Dragon would escape or, worse, be discovered', Malachi said, confiding in Rose.

'Let me try', Rose said, armed with the Renaissance Sword and walking briskly over to where Gallium stood.

She too looked about for a way in, when something growing up the side of the falls caught her eye. She was strangely drawn to it. It looked like an anemone, about the size of a giant sunflower head and vibrant orange in colour, with moving tentacles. The urge was too great, Lady Rose stretched out her hand to touch it.

'Rose, wait!' Gallium shouted, but it was too late; the woodland plant opened wide in the centre, like a mouth, and as Rose reached out, it sucked her in, swallowing her whole.

Malachi, immediately poising for a spell, was interrupted by Gallium pushing past and diving straight into the mouth of the anemone-like plant.

Seconds later, Gallium landed alongside Rose in a shallow rock pool inside the dimly lit cave. The two were spellbound, for scattered all the way up the cave walls were more of the florescent tentacle plants, identical to the one outside only much smaller. This pretty psychedelic display provided low-level lighting for the cave.

'Are you all right?' Gallium asked, as he helped Rose out of the water.

'Yes, a bit wet that's all', she said, wringing out the ends of her hair and picking up her sword.

'I think I'm getting used to it', he said, emptying his water-filled boots.

'Look, these plants go deep into the cave.' Rose pointed to a narrow cavity in the wall. 'I think this is the way.'

Squeezing through the gap, she found there was just enough room for a human.

'It must be where the dragon lives, I can feel it.' She carried on walking undeterred, Gallium following.

Moments later, they arrived at an entrance leading to another part of the cave. The sound of snorting, puffing and growling was coming from within. Gallium gently pinned Rose against the stone-face wall, wanting to assess the cave before they marched in.

'Wait a moment', he said, quietly.

Having witnessed the rear of a gigantic purple scaly dragon in a confined space, he reported hurriedly back to the princess.

'It is the dragon', he whispered.

'Good, now let me pass', Rose insisted, keen to meet the beast.

Only, Gallium wasn't sure about this; he blocked the path.

'Wait, could you maybe communicate from here, my lady? You know, get better acquainted first', Gallium said, concerned for her safety.

'Really Gallium, you worry too much', Rose said, shaking her head slightly with a half-smile.

'Well, let me see; first you lead me to a pack of hungry wolves, then an angry mob and now a fire-breathing dragon. Yes, I think that qualifies for a little concern', Gallium said ironically, with his hands placed firmly on her shoulders.

'Have a little faith, Gallium', Rose said calmly, before moving him to one side with her arm. 'After all, we are still alive.' She moved forward to step into the cave.

At first the dragon didn't notice that someone was there. Rose drew in a deep breath and began to communicate telepathically.

'I am the prophet Illuminata, and I have come for the crystal you guard', she connected courageously.

'The prophet you say, but the stone is not mine to give away, for it is part of me you see. It controls my destiny', it said in a gritty voice.

'I have no wish to harm you, dragon. Tell me how it must be.'

The dragon shuffled around to face Rose; the marine-green crystal Amazonite looked like a speck of rock hanging from its neck. With its monstrous tail nearly sweeping Rose off the floor and peering down the end of its smoke-filled snout, it spoke to her again through thought.

'If you truly are the chosen one, release the crystal and the curse will be undone.'

Rose had to think this one through quickly. She wanted to help the poor creature, who had been duty-bound for so long, but how? From the smoke seeping out of its nostrils, Gallium naturally suspected that the dragon was about to erupt. Acting in haste and with no regard to their earlier conversation, he decided to take matters into his own hands. The warrior charged into the cave like a wild boar on the loose.

'Gallium, wait!' Rose called anxiously.

The dragon's eyes widened at the sight of Gallium's advance, and tried to swipe him into the cave wall with its tail. The athletic warrior hurdled over the spike-tipped tail. The dragon attempted to squash him once more, with another whack, as it turned to face its offender, but to no avail. It then took in a deep breath and with nostrils lit like two smouldering furnaces, let out massive flames of destruction. At which, Rose instinctively interjected and stood between the beast and her warrior, with the Renaissance Sword acting as a shield. The magical sword created a dome of protection and the flames dispersed into cool steam on impact. Once the flames died, Gallium swiftly launched himself onto the dragon's tail and commenced climbing, holding on to the horns of its back. Nearing the head of the dragon, the warrior stabbed it between the shoulders and held on to the sword with all his might. The beast roared in agony, trying to shake the warrior off, except that the restricted cave left hardly any room for movement.

'Argh! You bring anger and violence!' the dragon cried out to Rose.

'This was not my intention!' Rose said, yelling aloud for all to hear, and terrified of failing the mission.

She watched helplessly from the edge of the chamber, trying to think fast, shuffling her feet and firmly clasping her sword.

Just then, out of nowhere, Malachi appeared carrying a huge bunch of the dark blue flowers that he had been busy collecting outside.

'Dragma verse me!' he said in a piercing voice.

Surprised to hear its name, the dragon jerked its head round. It was about to take another deep, fire-filled breath, when, like a gust of wind, Malachi magically blew the petals into its nostrils. Overcome by the intense perfume, the dragon's eyes rolled back, its eyelids closed, and it came crashing to the ground with a huge thud. It was in such a deep sleep, that each out-breath sounded like waves rolling onto the shore.

'We must act fast', Malachi said to the others.

The wizard tried a frozen spell, to break the chain holding the crystal around the dragon's neck, but it didn't work. The curse had a strong hold.

'As I feared', he said to the others.

'Here, let me try', Gallium said, yanking his sword out of the dragon. Still perched on top of its back, he tried to cut the thin chain, but his blade could not penetrate it.

'Allow me', Rose said, drying her eyes with a sleeve.

Using the Renaissance Sword, the trusted blade cut the metal chain effortlessly, as though it were made of cotton thread. The gem slid off and fell into Rose's hands. There, the perfect stone started to glow, until Rose added it to her collection. The good lady fastened her necklace, relieved another task was complete.

'Wait; the dragon asked me to free it from these walls. How can I do that?' Rose said, seizing Malachi by the sleeve of his robe.

'You already have, my lady. Observe', Malachi said, as all three witnessed the sleeping dragon change into a multi-coloured mist spiralling up and disappearing into the cracks of the cave.

'What just happened?' Gallium asked, rubbing his behind after falling through the mist onto the hard surface.

'It's free now. Quickly, let us return the way we came', the wizard said, taking off.

'Yes, I'm fine by the way', Gallium added, rising swiftly to his feet to run after them.

Arriving back at the entrance of the cave, the three dived back into the anemone, one by one, and lightly rolled onto the gritty ground outside. Looking up at the top of the falls, Rose noticed the Aurora lights forming the shape of a dragon. Later that day, the tired companions slept comfortably under another beautiful starry sky, in close proximity to the mountains, knowing phase two of the mission was over.

Chapter Nineteen—A Stolen Moment

When Gallium woke the next day, he couldn't find Rose in her tent, or anywhere. Malachi was still fast asleep, so he wandered along the river towards the Aurora falls, looking for her. It was a warm, sunny morning and the water looked inviting. A pair of dragonflies chased each other along the surface of the turquoise water, while frogs croaked among the reeds. Strolling along, he heard singing, and surprisingly, found that it was Rose. She was bathing in the crystal-clear waters which pooled at the bottom of the falls. Gallium was about to turn and walk away, feeling the back of his neck uncomfortably, when Rose spied him.

'Good morning Gallium, have you come for a swim too?' she said.

'I could be persuaded', he responded modestly, walking over to where she swam.

Rose smiled up at him, with a glint in her eyes from the sun, as she trod water in her under-tunic.

'The water's lovely and warm.'

'You know, you really shouldn't be wandering off alone', Gallium said, scanning the area.

'It's all right, I have my sword', she said, pointing to it on the bank of the river.

The warrior shrugged his shoulders at her carelessness.

There was a peaceful silence between them; then, looking past Rose, Gallium noticed a much smaller fall on the other side of the pool. It streamed from a

172

jutting rock to create a narrower cascade that splashed onto a huge stone slab.

Gallium took off his boots and shirt and lowered himself into the soft warm water. Gliding through it a short distance, the warrior then hoisted his body on to the cool slab of rock.

Rose decided to follow and swam towards him. While waiting for Rose to catch up, Gallium showered under the spring water, still wearing his olive-green linen trousers, cupping his hands and taking a few mouthfuls from the mini fall.

'Ah, now that's fresh', Gallium said to himself, relaxing his back into the rock-face behind the fall, his arms folded.

Rose clambered onto the stone surface, her undergarments dripping wet and her hair heavy and straight with water. For a moment, an awkward look passed between the two friends. Then Rose began playfully flicking water at Gallium who was less than intimidated.

'You're forgetting I'm already wet', he said unfazed and not even flinching.

At this, Rose stopped teasing him. She stood motionless, her eyes glossy and bottom lip quivering slightly, the only sound that of running water. Transfixed by Rose's beauty, Gallium advanced slowly towards her, and carefully stood before her. The natural shower sprinkled down on the pair. Rose's breath deepened at the sight of his intense gaze, and with one another's palms pressed together, their lips softly met in a lingering kiss.

'Now I have an even greater purpose for ending my quest', Gallium said sincerely in her ear.

'I, I think we should get back.' Rose said, slowly letting go of him. 'Malachi will be wondering where we are.'

'Malachi, yes.'

The captivated pair made their way swiftly back to camp, exchanging glances, not really sure what to make of their stolen moment. They were also completely unaware of prying eyes spying on them from the river.

The River Achelous was vast and extensive, its further reaches flowing into the neighbouring realm of Sirenuse. With a chill, Rose remembered reading about the third crystal—a fish, with a pearl for an eye, which lived at the mouth of the river. Leaving the pleasant Airlastua realm far behind, the brave and noble trio arrived in the Sirenuse realm. Silently, they trotted alongside the running water with its pebbly banks, and still they were followed by inquisitive eyes. Having travelled for a long time, dusk was now upon them, and Malachi suggested they stop to recuperate. As was his habit, he took himself off to a nearby mound, sat down cross-legged and began to meditate.

'Let me guess, my lady, I go and hunt while his weirdness sits on his rump with his eyes shut, again', Gallium said, vigorously pulling out a spear from his saddle.

'In fairness, you are good at it', Rose said flashing him a smile.

The smitten warrior put aside his frustrations and smiled back at Rose.

'All right', he said, strolling off towards the river, pebbles crunching underfoot.

Rose went over and sat on a patch of cool grass next to Malachi.

'The young warrior needs to learn that the mind is more powerful than the sword', Malachi stated in a calm voice, still with eyes closed.

'Oh, you heard', Rose said, blushing.

'When you quieten the mind, you can hear and feel everything, my lady.'

'I suppose he will learn in time, as I hope to', Rose sighed, combing the soft blades of grass between her fingers.

'The secret to being a master is not about mastering others, but mastering your own thoughts', Malachi said, only his mouth moving. 'You are the key to all the undoing, believe in yourself and lead by example.'

'Lead? I can't even control my own emotions', Rose said with a shrug. 'I almost jeopardised the entire mission; no, worse, I almost had us all killed.'

'You saved a soul. I was wrong not to support you', Malachi said humbly.

'And I must learn to listen.' Rose remained on the soft ground, with her chin resting on lifted knees, and watched as in a daydream while Gallium speared fish.

'Your divine order is growing, my lady, and in time you will learn how to use it.'

The wizard came out of his meditative state, conjuring a fireball from one hand, and raising it in mid-air using only the power of his mind.

Rose witnessed his wondrous talent, watching as the fireball was extinguished with a ball of water conjured from Malachi's other hand. The droplets of water gravitated, instantly hydrating the ground.

'Now, let's eat', he said cheerfully, with a loud clap. 'We must keep up our strength.'

Rose followed Malachi to rejoin Gallium, who was busy preparing another fresh catch over the campfire. Malachi, aware of the chemistry between the two young stars, said nothing. As the couple's love was evident, the wizard kept his focus on the cause.

Chapter Twenty—The Curse of a Thousand Deaths

In the depths of the Mercury Mountains, the air was shrouded from the incineration of yet another sacrifice. Taurus had just pushed the one-thousandth off a stone ledge and into the sizzling magma pit. As the final prisoner screamed his last, Borago took from his pocket the ornate silver box that held the red-back spider, which he released into the pit. The curse of a thousand deaths was forged, using an old spell from the witches, as uttered by the Shadow Master.

'What souls lie herewith, unite in strength, and form the curse of a thousand deaths.'

A dark collective spirit echoed the voices of the sacrificed. Making its way from the swirling pit, the curse grew in the form of a smoky, black-hooded figure with a red stripe down its back. It hovered across the floor on a small dark cloud, to where its master stood. It had no visible facial features, apart from a mouth with long white fangs. The Shadow Master circled the evil source, studying it in detail.

'Now, demonstrate your venom', the Shadow Master commanded.

Taurus and the centaurs cautiously distanced themselves, as the curse detected their movements, until it homed in on one of them. The poisonous smoke from the curse's mouth filtered through the air and up the centaur's nose, filling his lungs. The cursed man-horse started coughing uncontrollably, until he was gasping for breath, his hands around his neck in desperation. This was quickly followed by a loss of circulation, rendering the young half-breed paralysed. It was a sudden and ugly death. The remaining centaurs froze with fear at the tragic sight of their comrade, while the Shadow Master coldly applauded his masterpiece.

'Excellent, I will name you Agrimo; I am your master. Return to the box and let us depart on your deadly mission.' Borago, indeed pleased, held open the ornate box and Agrimo hissed his way in, like smoke being sucked into a void.

'Now, I must return to the ship. Taurus, I trust you will take over in my absence and communicate with me when necessary.'

'Yes my lord', Taurus said, saluting.

Once more, Castro gave his master a ride back to the ship Exodus, in fair weather.

From the port of Oreon a while later, came a shout from the crow's nest, 'Captain, it's that bird again!'

Sure enough, the golden gryphon glided down and lightly released the Shadow Master from its clutches onto the deck, before flying off.

Borago marched confidently up to Captain Nine-tails, who secretly grumbled as he couldn't wait to see the last of the menacing lord.

'So, you got it then?' the captain said, with his feet planted heavily.

'I have the curse, yes, and it is ready to be unleashed. Set course for Coral Bay', Borago ordered, before retreating into the captain's cabin.

Inside, he explained to the current pirate king how the curse would be let loose on the shores of the bay to capture Rose, while destroying all else in its path.

'Ooh, I've got to see this', Captain Nine-tails said, twirling the corners of his moustache with his fingers at the thought of the fiendish plan. 'Flinders, set sail for Coral Bay and bring us a feast.'

177

'Yes captain, right away sir, whatever you like', Flinders said, fumbling with the corner of his waistcoat, a part of his original uniform.

'Why are you still here?' the captain barked, kicking Flinders' backside to get a move on.

'Ow! Of course sir.'

The next day, a brilliant sun jewelled the Sirenuse sky as Rose and company journeyed towards Coral Bay.

'Right, Coral Bay is within reach', Malachi said, cutting between the enamoured pair on his horse, pretending he still knew nothing of their affections for one another.

The three friends had been travelling for hours, when the estuary came into sight.

'Wait, over there!' Rose said motioning with her finger at something swimming in the water. 'There it is again!'

What Rose saw were the eyes that had been following them for miles, only now there was a visible head too. It was a mermaid, then another and another. The mermaids swam closer to the water's edge, flipping their scaly fishtails. These alluring beings were the daughters of Achelous, the God of the River, who helped keep the wetlands of Airlastua and Sirenuse fertile.

'Why do you enter our realm?' Teles, one of the mermaids asked suspiciously, with her sisters suspended in the water beside her. She had shimmering golden hair, and like her sisters, could entrance a sailor with just one look.

'We are on a peaceful mission', Rose said, as she got off her horse and hiked over to meet the pretty sisters.

Ligeia, the shy red-headed one, noticed the crystals of Pangaea, and whispered in Teles's ear.

'Who are you?' Teles asked, with penetrating eyes.

'I am the Illuminata; my name is Rose. We seek the crystal of Perlana', Rose said. 'I believe you can help us.'

'My name is Teles, and we are the daughters of the river God, Achelous', she said, as they splashed their tails in delight. 'We can lead you to the crystal, but first, in order to survive in our world, you must transform into a mermaid.'

'Rose, are you sure you can trust these sirens?' Gallium said, at the same time not looking in their eyes. 'Where I come from they have a bad reputation.'

Ligeia gave him a wicked stare, and Molpe, the dark-haired one, stuck out her tongue in offence.

'My lady, with your approval, Gallium and I will observe from a safe distance', the wizard said, also trying to avoid the sea beauties' spellbinding gaze.

'Very well, Malachi', Rose said, holding the gems on her chain. 'Teles, I trust you; tell me what I must do.'

'Molpe, go and fetch the elixir of the river', Teles said. 'Step into the water Rose', she added.

Malachi gave Rose a reassuring nod and she did as Teles instructed.

'Am I the only sane person here?' Gallium addressed everyone out loud.

'Gallium, it's the only way for Rose to retrieve the gem', Malachi asserted keeping guard of the warrior's actions.

Molpe disappeared for a moment, then returned with a miniature solid gold bottle with a silver flip-top lid, and handed it to her sister, Teles.

Rose turned to Gallium and hugged him reassuringly.

'Gallium, I will return', she whispered in his ear.

179

Gallium puffed defiantly. 'And I will wait. Here, take the Renaissance Sword with you', he said pulling the sword from its sheath.

And with her sacred sword, Rose waded into the water.

Molpe and Ligeia assisted Rose by carefully removing her garments and tossing them onto the bank. Malachi and Gallium respectfully turned their backs on the scene. This continued with Teles pouring three drops of liquid pearl on Rose's tongue. For a moment, nothing happened, and then, she lost her balance, and went under. All was calm and silent, except for the warrior, who had briefly looked over his shoulder to check everything was all right. He darted over when he saw Rose gone.

'Rose, are you all right?' Gallium shouted. 'Rose!'

Malachi grabbed him by the shoulder to prevent him swimming in after her. The wizard had no doubt the Illuminata would be fine. Suddenly, like a dolphin, Rose leapt into the air and splashed back down again. She had changed into a magical mermaid, with a tail shimmering like mother-of-pearl and hair like silk, covering her modesty.

'I feel fantastic!' Rose declared, and swam over to Teles, who returned the Renaissance Sword. The Illuminata's appearance was the same, apart from the new scaly fishtail.

'Are you ready, Rose?' Teles asked, leading the way.

'I am.' Rose, swimming down into the depths of the river after Teles, was escorted by Ligeia and Molpe.

The wizard and the warrior waited on the bank, the one more confident than the other.

'Gallium, you needn't worry about Rose. She is stronger than you think', Malachi said, as he made himself comfortable on the ground.

'I care about her, is that such a crime?' Gallium asked openly, a spark in his eye.

'I am aware, and no, it is not a crime, but you must stay focused.' Malachi remained in his usual relaxed pose.

'How can you be so calm at a time like this?' Gallium protested, as he began shaving strips off a piece of driftwood with his dagger.

'I have every faith in the Illuminata and you should too.'

Gallium's frown showed he was having none of it, and continued in frustration to hew the piece of wood with his blade.

Chapter Twenty-One—The Third Task

Rose swam after Teles, who guided the way out to the Triton Sea, at the same time discovering just how different the world was underwater. They passed through a wonderland of sea life, a myriad of yellow Tang fish swimming gracefully past Rose's head, and amazing plant life, which gently swayed with the current, in all shades of green, yellow and blue. Floating by like a dream-creature was a sea dragon, smaller than her hand, with its leafy fins and pointy little dragon face. Looking along the seabed, Rose spotted a blue crab scuttling past a couple of clown fish, in and out of a bright pink anemone. Deeper and deeper the mermaids went into this unknown abyss, the marine life gradually disappearing behind them. Teles came to an abrupt stop, then turned to Rose and spoke telepathically.

'Our journey ends here. Good luck, my lady.'

Quicker than a shark's tail, Teles swam away with her sisters until completely out of sight.

Soon all was darkness, but before Rose had a chance to panic, the Renaissance Sword illuminated, and served as a light. It also felt weightless, not heavy as it did on dry land. After a while, Rose pinpointed something up ahead, evidently a shipwreck lying on the bottom of the ocean. From within the broken vessel, a piercing sonic sound vibrated.

'This is it', thought Rose. She could hear the wise words of Malachi in her head, but how was she going to defeat such a threat in these unnatural conditions?

Meanwhile, Gallium had concerns of his own.

'This doesn't feel right', Gallium said pacing the gravelly ground. 'I should be there protecting her.'

Quietly, Malachi murmured a spell: 'Aqua visioni.'

With his wizard's hands conjuring water in the form of a crystal ball, he beckoned Gallium.

'Observe', Malachi said.

'I see nothing. No wait, it's Rose, and she's alone', Gallium said examining the vision. 'I knew we shouldn't have trusted those sea wenches.'

Malachi, at least, kept the faith, steadying the ball. They kept watching as Rose started to swim closer to the wreck.

'I am the Illuminata and I have come for the pearl; show yourself.'

A sinister voice spoke in her mind. 'The pearl is mine to keep, and yours to weep.' It came from a swordfish lurking within the wreckage.

'I fear you are wrong and I will take the pearl back to its rightful owner', Rose replied.

All at once, a silver flash darted across from within the wreck. Rose's head spun in surprise. The swordfish shot through the rotten wreckage and broke free. It came charging towards Rose, who composed herself and concentrated hard. This large streamlined slayer with its pointed bill, showed no mercy. As the fast-approaching fish drew nearer, Rose summoned all her power from within, before swimming straight up vertically, causing the fish to dart directly under her. As it turned round to launch a second attack, Rose swam for the wreck. The fish was gaining speed, but Rose had a plan; she anchored herself in front of a broken mast and waited. The voice spoke again.

183

'Foolish girl to think you could defeat me. I rule these parts, as you will see,' the fiendish fish declared.

There was a fizz, and a static sound arose from below the wreck. To Rose's horror, up from the deep came several electric eels.

'Right that's it, I'm going after her', Gallium insisted and started removing his boots.

'Gallium, you would not make it there in time, or worse, you would drown', Malachi said, letting the ball of water dissolve through his fingers and marching over to the worried lad.

'You call yourself a wizard!' Gallium yelled pointing out at sea. 'She is going to die!'

'I will not fight you, warrior. This is her task.' Malachi formed another vision, using the same method as before. 'Do you really think I would leave her to die? Come and see for yourself.'

Gallium inhaled deeply, thought about it for a moment and conceded. Somehow he trusted the wizard, despite the situation.

With her sword stretched out in front of her and her back against the mast, Rose was ready to strike. The eels advanced with their sleek electric bodies, but the Renaissance Sword protected Rose by absorbing the currents of energy. The Illuminata suddenly started to glimmer and with one forward lunge of the sword, lightning bolts shot out of it, blasting the eels. The snake-like fish exploded into tiny bits from the surge, and the remains slowly sank to the bottom of the deep, dark ocean. The swordfish, enraged, swam full speed at Rose. At first she held her ground, until, at the last moment she flashed upwards and out of the way, just in time to see the bill of the fish become wedged deep in the mast. Rose did not hesitate a moment longer and sliced the cold-blooded creature in two. She then cut out the pearl from the fish's eye, and turned in the direction from where she had come.

'Yes! Woo-hoo! She made it', Gallium said, leaping in the air with his fist held high. He paused awkwardly, turning to Malachi. 'My apologies Malachi, for not trusting you.'

'I understand', Malachi said forgiving him. 'You see, I sensed the sword would protect her all along.'

When Rose returned to dry land, accompanied by the mermaids, Gallium was on the bank, arms folded and with a smile as big as the crescent moon, relieved to see his lady love.

'You have done well, my lady', Teles commended. 'We must return now to our home under the sea. Your mermaid shape will change back to human, once you are on dry land.'

'Thank you, daughters of Achelous', the Illuminata said, threading the shimmering white pearl on her chain and, with that, the sea princesses flipped and dived back into the water.

Rose was gently lifted out of the river by her warrior.

'I said I would return', Rose said softly.

'And I said I'd wait', Gallium whispered back.

Gallium lowered Her Ladyship onto a blanket to dry. Once wrapped in it, Rose started to morph back into herself; her tail parted down the middle to become legs once more. Gallium quickly passed her clothes to her and both men looked away while she dressed.

'The ocean is a different world, wouldn't you say Rose?' Gallium asked, walking with her to a more comfortable spot, where Malachi had again transfigured three tents.

'Yes, it was a wondrous sight, all the different colourful sea creatures', Rose said excitedly.

'It has its dangers too. The main thing is, you are safe', Gallium said, patting Ironbark, and removing a blanket and spear from the horse's saddle. 'Right, now to prepare a meal fit for a princess.'

Another day almost over, the fellowship of three relaxed for the night under the sparkling Sirenuse sky.

Chapter Twenty-Two—Something

is Coming

'Land ahoy, captain!' a pirate shouted, as the ship Exodus approached the shores of Coral Bay.

'Drop anchor', Captain Nine-tails ordered.

'Drop anchor!' Mr Flinders repeated.

'We'll carry on in a rowing boat from here', the captain said to Borago, who stood straight-faced beside him.

By the light of the distant moon, the captain, Shadow Master and two crewmen rowed across dead calm water, before reaching the shore of Coral Bay. The long sandy bay was deserted and the nocturnal sounds of cicadas could be heard full force. All four members disembarked from the little boat. The Shadow Master positioned himself facing inland towards the palm trees silhouetted high above them. He produced the silver box and released the evil curse; he then spoke clearly, as the Orbicular Rock on his staff glowed.

'Agrimo, heed my command. Go forth and capture the Illuminata; bring her to me alive.'

Within seconds, the dark, deadly mist escaped through the open lid and transformed into the black-hooded hybrid, resembling a shadow on the sands. Borago raised his arm to the captain, signalling to get back in the boat, but one of the crew, curious to see more, went further along the beach. Soon he felt the effects of the cursed smog, and coughed himself to death. Everyone else held their breath and clambered back in the boat.

The voiceless curse, bowing to its master, glided swiftly across the ground, before disappearing into the undergrowth in the dead of night.

'Certain it'll work?' Captain Nine-tails asked, holding firm to the sides of the boat.

'It better', the Shadow Master replied.

Borago and his crew returned to the ship to wait tensely for Agrimo to bring back the girl.

That same warm night, the haunting hoot of an owl came from a nearby wood. Rose relaxed, knowing that today she had excelled herself, and fell fast asleep in her tent. Until, that is, a most peculiar feeling overcame her. Instantly, with her eyes wide open, and slowly rising from her bed, she staggered to Gallium's tent for help.

'Gallium, please wake up', she called desperately.

Gallium rushed out to find Rose bent over and shaking.

'What is it Rose?' Gallium supported her by the arms as she swayed. 'Your eyes are glowing like the moon', he said, raising his eyebrows.

Malachi who was still awake, came out of his tent to investigate.

'My lady, what is it?' he said.

'I have a disturbing feeling', Rose said with a moan. 'Something is coming, and it is not good', she said, holding her stomach.

Gallium lowered Rose to a sitting position and sat beside her.

'We must move from here right away. Gather your things and let us ride north', Malachi instructed while magically undoing the transfiguration spell of the tents with a few words.

'Malachi, she is not fit to ride', Gallium said, now holding Rose in his arms, her head resting on his shoulder. Rose was rapidly weakening, her pendant flickering intermittently.

Malachi looked knowingly to the skies.

'If I am right, then we are all in grave danger. Help Rose onto your horse', Malachi instructed Gallium. 'Noble, you must lead us out of this realm. We must make great speed for the Cliffs of Promise.'

Noble responded with a neigh, while Gallium lifted Rose onto his horse.

Malachi removed the painting with the Book of Legends from his satchel, then handed it to Gallium.

'Guard it well; if anything should happen to me, Rose can return it', the wizard instructed.

Gallium looked unsure, but did as he was asked and put it in his satchel. Noble stood at the front and with a snort, his birth mark shone ever so slightly, as he led them all to safer terrain.

Just as they made their quick exit from the Sirenuse realm, the curse neared their last campsite. Agrimo, sniffing and hissing on the ground, drew in a huge breath and swelled in size, detecting Rose's scent once more. Onward he went, moving faster than the strongest of winds, leaving a continuous trail of black soot in his wake. The curse of a thousand deaths passed through the once-fertile Sirenuse realm, destroying every delicate bloom and leaf, turning the flora a shade of grey. The innocent wildlife also perished, with rabbits not quite making it back into their burrows and birds falling out of trees, suffocated. The striking rainbow fish began to float to the surface of the River Achelous. Even the blameless civilians in their isolated huts nearby, never woke from their sleep.

Noble galloped ahead, closely followed by Gallium and Rose on Ironbark, and Malachi on Dewdrop. Thus they rode for several hours, stopping only to give Rose a sip of water, while not far behind, destruction followed. As they crossed the border into Airlastua, a feeling of despair set in.

'Malachi we need to stop!' Gallium called, clinging on to his beloved.

'What is it?' the wizard said, responding immediately as their horses came to a halt.

'I'm concerned for Rose. We have ridden non-stop and she's still no better.'

'All right, we will seek refuge in the nearby cave of the Aurora Mountains', Malachi said, now leading the way.

By late afternoon they reached the cave to rest. This time, Malachi was able to use a spell to enter, the curse having already been broken. The spell expanded the anemone-like entrance and they walked in quite normally.

'We should be safe here, but we cannot stay for long', Malachi said, ushering them into the mountain.

Mindfully, Gallium lay Rose down on a blanket. Her eyes were losing their shine, as, looking up, she managed to stretch a thin smile.

'Isn't there something you can do?' the worried warrior said, stroking her cheek.

'I realise your concern, but Rose is under some sort of curse', Malachi said, delicately checking her pulse and placing a hand on her forehead. 'Fortunately, the rose quartz is keeping her alive.'

'What did she mean by "something is coming"?' Gallium asked.

'My guess, it's whatever the Shadow Master has unleashed with the powers of the Orbicular Rock. He is capable of conjuring any manner of demonic curse', the wizard said, staring long at the floor, remembering his own dark experience.

'Surely we should stay and fight', Gallium said, with a hint of aggression.

'Not until I can be sure of what it is.' Malachi took the last piece of bread from his satchel and shared it with Gallium. 'We need to keep moving and find more food.'

'There are plenty of villages in the Fatum realm; I should know, I have drunk in most of them', Gallium said, forcing down a bite of the bread.

For a short time, the warrior, the wizard and Rose remained in the cave, while far out at sea, the demon expert was admiring his creation.

'So what does your glass ball tell you?' asked Captain Nine-tails, tearing shreds off a chicken leg with what decaying teeth he had left.

'I spy Agrimo devouring his way through everything in search of her. So far, so good', the Shadow Master said, eyes glued to the green crystal ball.

'All I knows is, this thing better deliver', the captain said, patting his bulbous belly and taking one last slurp of rum, before unleashing an almighty burp.

'Don't worry, I will stay here until it does', Borago said, obsessed with his cause.

'Right, well, I'll leave you to it. I'm off to dream of mermaids massagin' my feet', Captain Nine-tails grinned, staggering to his feet under his excessive weight. 'Keep an eye on his lunacy over there, I don't trust him', he whispered to Flinders, standing guard outside the cabin door.

Eventually, Captain Nine-tails made it into his luxuriously draped four-poster bed situated at one end of the cabin.

The evening had progressed with temperate, cool conditions as the two men and the poorly princess

191

again began riding through the night. Rose slumped over Ironbark, seemingly semi-conscious. Upon entering the Fatum realm, the winds increased and it started to rain heavily.

'Stay with me Rose, stay with me', Gallium whispered to her, holding on tight to keep his lady love secure in her saddle.

A while later, Malachi noticed something solid ahead. He gathered speed and overtook Noble, leading the way towards the mysterious building. It was a longhouse, used by farmers to keep animals in the barn attached at one end, while the people lived at the other end. Malachi jumped down from his horse, his boots squelching as he waded through the mud to investigate the derelict dwelling.

The longhouse was indeed long and very old, but the damp granite walls still stood firm. The remains of the attached barn however, were merely splinters of wood rising out of the ground, surrounded by overgrown grass and binary weed.

'The house appears to be abandoned, probably due to a fire', Malachi reasoned, wiping the dirt-smeared window with the side of his fist and peering in. 'There is no one inside; I suggest we rest here for a short time.'

Gallium agreed; Malachi then tied the horses to a timber post from the burnt-out barn.

'Wait a moment while I repair a few things inside', Malachi said.

Thereupon, he entered the house through the wooden front door, just barely hanging by its hinges to the rotten frame. The main living area was filthy; the few pieces of furniture were smoke damaged and soot covered every surface. What grim cause was there for such wreckage, Malachi wondered.

'Ripero vetri, ripero tet', the wizard spoke, fixing the broken window and part of the roof.

He continued with the restorations.

'Ripero mobil, incendio fuoco.' Finally, throwing bits of broken timber onto the hearth, he magically ignited a roaring fire, blowing fireballs from his hands onto the kindling.

'All right, bring her inside', Malachi said.

Gallium carried his precious Rose and laid her on a blanket by the fireplace. She lay still and damp, murmuring as though suffering from a fever.

'Is she going to die?' Gallium asked, as he knelt beside Rose, holding her hand.

'I cannot say, but she is weakening', Malachi said, attentively looking out of the window, surveying the darkness. 'In my experience, as with most curses, the evil approaching is absorbing Rose's energy. You watch from the window, and alert me if you see anything—anything at all', he stressed.

Gallium did as asked and kept constant watch at the window. Malachi then delicately unfastened Lady Rose's chain and unthreaded the crystals, putting them in his robe pocket, but left the rose quartz in her curled hand.

'What are you going to do with the crystals?' Gallium said, glancing over at the wizard's actions.

'Whatever is out there probably wants the crystals too. Don't worry, I will return them one way or another', he said, before taking up his position by the front door, armed with the Renaissance Sword.

Malachi and Gallium stood and waited, and waited, and then slumped to the floor, neither of them able to stay awake, their eyelids heavy with sleep. All at once, a breeze came whistling through the gaps of the house, waking Gallium. He peered out of the window and couldn't begin to describe what he saw, partly due to the lack of light.

'Malachi, come quickly', Gallium called in a low voice. He pointed to a dark mass close by, outlined by its static energy.

'It is here. *Whatever* happens, you must stay with Rose, do not come outside', Malachi said, gripping Gallium's forearms tightly.

The curse had gained speed by manifesting itself into a large black tornado, violently ripping through everything in its path. The longhouse started to quake, the curse destroying it stone by stone, using its powerful winds like a vacuum to suck in the debris.

'It will kill us all!' Gallium shouted over the noise, covering Rose with his entire body to protect her from the rubble now crashing to the floor.

Without a second thought, Malachi put on his hood, and holding the crystals securely in his hand, rushed out to face Agrimo. At first, the wizard just stood still.

Once the wizard was in its path, the tornado stopped spinning and shrunk down to resume its former image of the hooded menace. Hissing and hovering, its yellow snake-like eyes lit up and it homed in on Malachi. Unexpectedly, it spat out a long thread of spider web, which spun violently around the wizard, cocooning him on the ground. Gallium witnessed the scary scene from the now glassless window, itching to help, but knew he must remain with Rose. At that moment, the curse changed back into the tornado, sucking the poor wizard up into the air and inside its dark void. Momentarily, there came a bang and a clash of thunder. It boomed all around as lightning flashes flared from within the tornado. There appeared to be a surge of energy forcing the spiralling wind to break down. It dispersed with a thousand cries echoing in the night sky, until the black mass dissolved into thin air, to reveal a glowing body upon the ground. It was Malachi.

Chapter Twenty-Three—The Fourth Task

'No!' the Shadow Master's outburst was in sharp response to the vision within the crystal ball. 'You hags said this would work! I ought to banish you both forever!' he blasted, tossing the captain's table to the floor, as the clear green globe rolled off the table and into a corner.

'There is one thing you ought to know', the witches cried at once from within the ball.

'I have heard enough!' Borago bellowed, turning away, his nostrils flaring.

'As you say my lord, but it does concern you greatly', the slender witch said.

Borago drew in a sharp breath, but blew it out long and slow through his prominent nostrils. Once composed, he listened. 'Go on.'

'You have something she needs—the Orbicular Rock', Hemmatia said.

'The Orbicular Rock, interesting', he said, admiring the swirls within the powerful rock.

'It will complete her mission', Marelda added with a coy smile.

'If she wants it, she must come and claim it', Borago said, running a hand over the smoothness of the rock.

'The prophet will come to you eventually, master; you must set a trap', Hemmatia said.

'Very well, I will prepare for her coming and then it is over!' The Shadow Master took the crystal ball, placed it back in his pocket, and made his way up on deck to his ride, which was never far away.

No sooner had Borago exited the cabin quarters, than Mr Flinders came rushing to where the captain lay fast asleep in his bed.

'Captain, sir, he's leaving', Flinders said, reluctantly prodding the overfed belly, as the captain lay on his back snoring loudly.

The hefty pirate king let out a severe snort, and rolling like a barrel to his feet, went in the direction of the dark lord.

'Wait just a midget's moment, what about us?' Captain Nine-tails bellowed at Borago, rubbing his tired eyes.

The Shadow Master turned slowly to address the red-faced pirate.

'May I remind you who gave you a ship and crew?' The Shadow Master was not about to surrender to his minion.

'That may be, but they answer to *me* now, and we wants our gold, see', the captain said, twiddling the end of a braid in his beard. The half-awake crew advanced stealthily as they listened in on the conversation.

'Once I have the girl, you will get your reward, now return to Port Oreon until further notice; that's an order.'

At this point, Castro arrived and airlifted his master. The captain was left stewing on that last comment as he and his scurvy crew of men watched the Shadow Master fade into the distance.

'Lads, at sunrise we return to Port Oreon', Captain Nine-tails Johnson said.

The crew sluggishly dispersed to their dorms, one or two lagging behind.

'Once we get back, I'm off', a scrawny sailor muttered with a wink to a fellow shipmate. 'I heard Beardless Bert needs a crew, and he'll give a down payment too', he concluded, wiping a snotty drip from the end of his nose with the back of his hand, ignorant of the fact that Johnson was right behind them.

'I'll have no mutineers on my ship!' the captain burst, cracking his whip.

The two trembling pirates turned fearfully towards their angry captain. Nine-tails then channelled his rage with another sharp lash of his whip, so hard that it cut the end of the mouthy pirate's bony chin; the rest of the crew froze on the spot.

'Mr Flinders, make them walk the plank and let that be a lesson to you all', he warned.

'Please sir, 'ave mercy!' the first one pleaded, rattling like a bag of bones, while covering his wound with his skeletal hand.

'I had nothin' to do with it, sir', the other fellow begged, down on his knees.

Mr Flinders hesitated at first until he caught sight of his master's glare.

'Knuckles and Patches, tie the mutineers and set up the plank', Mr Flinders said regretfully. He was never meant for a role of injustice, but in a hostile environment such as this, it was do or die.

After the unfortunates had plunged to their doom, crying all the way down, the captain addressed his crew sternly.

'Now, who's next?'

The cowardly lot scurried back to their dorms, not a word passing their scabby lips.

'I thought as much, ha-ha!' the captain laughed his way back to his comfy bed for the remainder of the night.

Daybreak was climbing above the treetops and shining on the mildew-covered ground of the Fatum realm, as Gallium ran to where Malachi lay, pale and cold after the stormy night.

'Malachi, can you hear me?' he called, an ear to his chest, listening for a heartbeat.

The wizard was miraculously still alive, but unconscious.

Gallium took the crystals from Malachi's hand and rushed back inside the longhouse to Rose. He painstakingly inserted the chain through each gem and fastened it around her neck.

'Rose, I hope you can hear me, Malachi is hurt', Gallium said, as the princess gradually regained consciousness. Gallium gave her water to sip, and the crystals began to shine softly.

'I...must...help him', Rose said, attempting to move.

Slowly she pushed against the floor with her forearms, and sat for a moment. Now the curse had been defeated, the Illuminata was coming back.

Gallium draped the blanket over Rose's shoulders and assisted her to her feet, still weak from her ordeal. They walked slowly to where Malachi lay, unmoving. Rose knelt down by his side and closed her eyes to concentrate. Nothing happened.

'No! I WILL save you', she said, clasping her hands.

Taking an even deeper breath, she tried again, focusing and believing with all her might. She placed her cold, clammy hand on the wizard's forehead. After a few more deep breaths, Rose's body started to illuminate with power. The colour slowly re-appeared in Malachi's cheeks, the air filled his lungs, and his eyelids lifted. The wizard had returned.

'Hhh, Rose, I see my plan worked', Malachi said with great effort, barely able to raise his arms.

'I honestly thought you were gone for good', Gallium said, deeply relieved. Despite their differences, they were good friends.

'I am so glad you are well now; what actually happened?' Rose said, having slept through most of the drama.

'Well, it was simple really; by combining the powerful crystals with the power of the Renaissance Sword', Malachi said, taking big breaths as Gallium slowly pulled him up, 'I was able to draw the curse to me like a magnet', he paused. 'And with the help of some magic, the dark force was destroyed', Malachi finished, waggling a finger in his left ear, which was ringing like a bell from the whole ordeal. 'It took all my strength, but I knew you would bring me back, my lady.'

Rose blushed with gratitude.

'The dawn is upon us', Gallium interrupted, looking up at the horizon. 'You should both rest awhile.' Rose and Malachi agreed and re-entered the longhouse to convalesce for most of the morning.

Just then, within the castle walls of Vervain, all ears were attentively tuned to the voice of their troubled king, who was addressing the court from the Great Hall. This included the entire nobility from around the kingdom.

'My loyal subjects, we may have won the Battle at Bloodwood Gorge', King Yarrow said; 'however, the next time the Shadow Master strikes, the clash will be even mightier.' There were gasps at the mere mention of the dark lord's name. The king paused, staring vacantly, while all the court whispered to each other, 'what can we do?' 'Is he listening?' said others. The king was wondering if Rose would ever make it home.

'My king?' Queen Aveena whispered, leaning across from her throne.

'Pardon me, Your Grace, any word from the kingdoms in the other realms?' Lord Montague of Vervain enquired, never one to miss an opportunity to voice his opinions. Montague was a rather flamboyant character, with a theatrical manner and colourful plumes on his wares.

'I have not yet contacted them', King Yarrow said, despondently. 'There has been no time or need.'

'My lords and ladies of the court, has our kingdom not suffered enough, losing some of our finest soldiers?' the impertinent Montague now said, as the court muttered similar sentiments to each other.

'Lord Montague, people of the court, I am grateful for the loan of your guards', the king said. 'Let us not forget, Sir Dill is at present enrolling more men from within Fatum, and I have every faith in the Illuminata's quest.' The king sat back down on his throne.

'Yes, but surely Your Grace, it is as much the fight of the other realms, as it is ours', the meddling lord insisted, turning to the court for backup, like a proud peacock.

'My lord, if you will allow me to finish', the king answered sternly, and rose again to his feet. Lord Montague shrewdly withdrew from further interrogation, by stepping back with a bow. 'As I have explained, the Illuminata—with the help of a warrior and a wizard—will bring back the Crystal Masters of Pangaea', King Yarrow said, taking a great stride forward.

'My lords and ladies, have I ever failed you?'

Most of the court shook their heads in support.

'There is no time to delay, we must unite once more, as the Shadow Master will stop at nothing. He

201

must not prevail!' the king said in a resounding voice.

'Aye, hail King Yarrow, hail King Yarrow', the court agreed as the king seated himself proudly back on his throne, kissing the hand of his beloved wife.

By midday, Rose and Malachi felt as fresh as the first bloom in May. Gallium was attending to the horses, feeding them grass and grooming their manes, when Rose went outside to return the blanket, gently laying it on Gallium's arm.

'Thank you Gallium, for looking after us', she said sweetly.

'Rose, I thought I'd lost you', Gallium said, as he packed the blanket onto Ironbark.

'I don't remember a thing', Rose said. 'When this is all over, I am certain King Yarrow will reward you greatly.'

The couple were serenaded sweetly by the sounds of nature. Gallium put his arm around Rose's waist and pulled her close. He looked deep into her tender eyes.

'I would die a thousand deaths to be near you.' And another melting moment was stolen, as they embraced.

A short while later, Malachi rejoined them, instructing Noble to continue their journey in search of the fourth crystal. Through fields of golden arable lands they rode, the wheat dried by the summer sun, swept against the horse's legs as their hooves pounded the gritty ground. Soon, it began to rain heavily, a downpour that lasted for hours, with the added chill of a merciless wind. Malachi suggested they stop at a local inn for food and shelter, catching sight of their next place of rest up yonder in a town called Mulberry. Here was a tavern, attached to an inn fittingly named 'The Mulberry Bush.' They took lodgings for the night, relishing the chance to dry off in comfort. The ambience of the tavern was that of an informal, friendly establishment, with colourful hand-painted wares, like horseshoes, jugs, tankards, buckets and wooden window shutters, giving a sense of rustic charm. As the three travellers settled down to a well-earned meal, shouts could be heard coming from the kitchen.

'NO! NO! NO! If I've told ya once, I've told ya twice. Give it 'ere.' It was the landlord's short curvy wife, also known as The Cook. She burst out of the kitchen totally exasperated and gripping a wooden spoon, dripping with batter.

'Gwen, put a lid on it, we've got guests!' shouted the hairy, equally stout landlord. This was Gwen's husband, working behind the bar, and grinning crookedly at Rose and company.

'Right, well, ya can take over, I'm off to bed', Gwen squealed, with a disparaging curtsey to her husband, before stomping away.

'I wouldn't like to work for her', Gallium muttered from behind his tankard of beer.

'Quite, but the food is delicious. No offence Gallium, even I was growing tired of fish', Malachi commented, as he took another morsel of hot, crusty meat pie.

'Oh, you haven't offended me, I was tired of cooking it', he said, munching on a chunk of gravy-drenched bread.

The local men in the tavern all appeared short in stature and rather portly, with plump rosy cheeks. They all wore similar belts and braces with brown or green pantaloons and pointy leather shoes on their feet. Some of them were smoking long, thin pipes. The women were of quite similar proportions, and all dressed in flouncy gowns. Later in the evening, the effects of over indulgence sparked off singing and a jig or two.

'Happy little souls, aren't they?' Rose said giggling, as two of them danced around their table.

'So would you be, with ten jugs of ale inside you', Gallium said, with a wry smile, raising his jug as one of them wobbled past.

'Have a jig with us squire', one of the merry little men said, tugging on Gallium's shirt.

'No thank you.' Gallium abruptly pulled away.

'Where's your sense of fun?' Rose said, getting up a little shakily from her seat and joining in the merriment.

Malachi decided the excitement was all too much and happily retired to his room.

'So, what are we celebrating?' Rose hiccupped, as she twirled to the rhythm of the lively musicians, beating on their instruments in the corner of the tavern.

'I haven't a clue', a local man said, chortling and spilling most of his ale down his front. 'We tend to do this most nights, ha-ha (hiccup).'

'What brings you here, milady?' another Mulberrian enquired, now at eye-level with her crystals.

'We are on a mission, shush!' Rose whispered, with a wink and a nudge of her elbow. 'Not a word.'

'What sort of mission?' the curious little man said, shoulder-to-shoulder with the swaying princess.

'I think 'milady' has had quite enough for one night', Gallium said responsibly, taking the jug of ale from Rose's, who didn't put up much of a struggle. Instead, she blew a pathetic raspberry, while Gallium stood with arms folded, unimpressed.

'Oh, all right', Rose said, surrendering with a stomp. 'Goodnight, my funny friends.'

Gallium dutifully escorted the giggling princess to her room, and left her to sleep off the eventful evening.

After a comfortable night's sleep, the prophet, the warrior and the wizard met for a light breakfast in the tavern.

'Must we go so soon?' Rose asked, gently rubbing out the creases in her forehead.

'I think a certain lady has a sore head', Gallium said, smirking.

'I'm fine, really', she said with a sideways glance at Gallium.

'Well we should be off, time waits for no one, my lady', Malachi said.

'You are right. Only, it's been a while since I have had so much fun', Rose sighed, staring down at her plate all forlorn and missing home.

'No doubt you will again', Malachi said, lightly patting her hand.

'I'll go wait by the horses', Gallium said.

The little people of Mulberry followed the princess to her horse.

'You are welcome any time, milady', they said, waving goodbye as the hopeful heroes rode away, with Noble confidently in the lead.

The weather being fine, they rode on for several hours. A chalky incline led them up a steep trail, and they were greeted by a cool westerly breeze on arriving at the Cliffs of Promise. This was the highest coastal point in the Fatum realm. One by one they got off their horses and stood at the jagged edge. The cliff overlooked the wide ocean and was mainly bare rock with the occasional stray root poking out. Fortunately, the morning mist from the sea had lifted making things more visible.

'The flower could be anywhere', Rose said disappointedly, standing with hands on hips at the cliff's edge and surveying the scene.

'Yes, wait a moment, while I consult the Book of Legends', Malachi advised, running back to his horse, to fetch it.

Rose nervously rubbed the precious gems around her neck with her fingers. 'Although, I have a feeling we're close', she confided to Gallium.

There seemed no obvious means of scaling down the wet rocky cliff.

'Well when we do find it, Rose, let me get it', Gallium said, with fists clenched at his sides.

'I'm afraid this is another task for the Illuminata', Malachi advised, while sitting on the ground, paging through the Book of Legends. 'According to the book, my lady, you are the only one who can intuitively discover where the flower of spiritual promise is, and take the crystal from its centre.'

'No! It's too...' Gallium was gently silenced by Rose's finger against his lips. Looking him straight in the eye, she said calmly:

'I must do this.'

Gallium's heart sank and he refrained from saying another word.

Casually walking over to a nearby tree, Malachi placed his palms firmly on its trunk, and concentrating hard, chanted aloud.

'Radico veni e cresci, cresci!'

The earth shook a little and, pushing its way speedily out from under the tree, came a very long root. Gallium and Rose lost their balance and fell forwards onto the ground. The wizard nonchalantly transfigured the elongated root into a rope.

'Rose, this rope will help you reach the flower', Malachi explained, gathering it up. 'Gallium and I will lower you down.'

Rose positioned herself at the edge of the drop, gazing into the depths below the cliff and nervously contemplating the next move. Despite the chill in the air, perspiration appeared on her top lip. Then, the Illuminata caught sight of something to the left of her—a glowing light from down below.

'Over there; what is that?' Rose walked briskly across and stood above the point.

'It must be the flower, I'm certain of it', she said to the others, trying to pin-point its location. 'I need to go down there to discover exactly where it is.'

Malachi gave the princess a nod of approval, and proceeded to hand one end of the rope to the warrior, who then raced over with it to Rose.

'Rose, hold on tight and use your feet to walk down backwards', Gallium advised, tying it around her torso. 'Don't worry, I will keep you steady and safe.'

A gentle wind whistled past their ears, as the wizard fed the rope gradually to Gallium who carefully lowered Rose a little at a time. Feeding the rope further and further, while gripping it tightly, the warrior dug both heels into the ground to anchor his body. The damp sea air and corroding rock made for a slippery surface, so that Rose began losing her footing. Now out of sight, she suddenly ordered Gallium to stop lowering.

'Malachi, hold!' he said. 'I think she has reached it.'

Unbeknown to the men above, something on the rock face was tugging at Rose's hair.

'Stop!' She cried, her voice aimed at someone—or something—else.

'Who goes there?' said a squeaky voice by Rose's ear.

'I am Rose. Let go at once', she ordered, pulling her head away, at the same time trying not to swing out on the rope.

'Rose-let-go-at-once?' another squeaky voice said. 'Do we know a Rose-let-go-at-once, Flint?'

'No, never heard of her, Cobble', came another high-pitched voice.

Gallium soon made out Rose's distress and called to her, but there was no answer. Two, tiny grey sprites had emerged like ghosts from the cliff face. These elfin beings were now poised just above Rose's head. She tried desperately to flick them away with her hand, but they kept leaping about, weaving her hair like ribbon around a Maypole, creating a tangled mess.

'Are you all right Rose?' Gallium shouted once again, arms locked in position, while holding on with white knuckles.

'I will be once I...am...rid...of...these pests', she answered in frustration, failing to swat one. 'Please let me go. I am here to collect the crystal from the flower, it's vital for my mission.'

'Crystal? Only the chosen one can collect the crystal. Ain't that right, Flint?' Cobble said, cheekily swinging from Rose's ear and onto her nose, now hovering eyeball to eyeball.

'But I am the chosen one. I am the Illuminata', Rose pronounced, a little cross-eyed.

'If that's true, you'll first have to guess our real names', Cobble sniggered.

'Yes, that's right. Ha, she'll never guess', Flint said laughing.

'Well, let me think.' Rose paused for thought, what could possibly be their real names? In view of their location and the sprites' dim-wittedness, she posed a question to them.

'Simple, as this is the Cliffs of Promise you are to promise me you'll tell the truth and nothing but, agreed?' Rose said.

'All right', they both answered submissively.

'Good, Flint and Cobble, what are your real names?'

At first they looked oddly at one another, but like bewitched buffoons, they answered.

'Cobblerock' Cobble said, curling the corner of his top lip.

'Flintmine' Flint said, hinging his shoulders to his pointy ears, equally puzzled.

'How did you do that?' Cobble seethed, jumping up and down on her head, not even making a dent.

'Oh no, she's good. She must be the chosen one', Flint said, hanging on the end of an exposed root.

'Enough!' Rose snapped, her voice causing the crystals to glow around her neck, and a slight avalanche of loose rubble to crumble to the depths below. 'Gallium! Swing me closer to the left! I see the flower!' she said calling up to him.

'Hang on, Rose!' Gallium replied turning his head to Malachi. 'I'm going to direct Rose closer to the flower.'

'Err Cobble, I think we'd better let her go', Flint said, nervously biting his non-existing fingernails, as Rose's body completely illuminated.

'I think you're right. Off you go then, Daisy'

In an instant they both untangled Rose's hair and bounced their ghostly bodies back into the cliff's face.

'It's Ro...oh never mind. Ready when you are, Gallium!' she called.

Gallium, crab-stepping to the side, swung Rose slightly to the left.

'Stop! That's it!' Rose said loudly, startling a seagull who was flying in to land.

Inches away from her face, in brilliant splendour, was the pure white lotus flower, its silky petals presently closed. At this point, Rose was able to stand on a ledge, lightening the load on the rope. She focused for a moment, catching her breath. Her hands were white from holding on so tight, and numb with cold.

'Can I make a suggestion?' Cobble asked, poking his stone-faced head out from behind the flower.

'What is it?' Rose rolled her eyes.

'It has been said by our creator, that the chosen one would come one day and take the crystal with a single breath', Cobble declared, arms folded and wearing a smug grin.

'A single breath you say.' Reaching forward with her chin, Rose blew ever so softly on the flower.

One by one the petals slowly unfolded and started sparkling with magic. The dazzling light from the crystal began peeping out as it opened, causing Rose to narrow her eyes and the sprites to turn into a fine dust that blew away with the sea breeze. Once the floral beauty was open, the light dimmed to a soft shine. Carefully, Rose reached into the centre of the lotus and lifted out the crystal. Now, with the stone in her grasp, the flower rapidly withered away. Looking up to the heavens with a sigh of relief, Rose clutched the stone to her chest. The final task was over. Shivering slightly, she called up to Gallium to pull her back to safety.

When Rose finally reached the top and stood on firmer ground, Gallium hugged her close, then rubbed her hands to warm them. Feeling her warrior's hands so chafed from gripping the rope, Rose miraculously healed the abrasions by placing her palm on his, before threading the last crystal.

'Well done, my lady', Malachi said, walking over to her. 'We are on the road to victory! May I suggest we...'

'Home. With respect, I would like to visit my home before facing the final battle.' Rose gave an emotional plea, tears welling in her eyes. Malachi finished his sentence with an agreeable nod.

'You witches vowed the Illuminata would come in search of the rock!' Inside the Mercury Well Chamber, the Shadow Master's patience was running low. 'Well? What do you have to say about that?'

'Master, the road is long and the nights are cold', Marelda said, clutching her bosom.

'What in Hell's fire does that mean?' he said, pounding his fist on the side of the well, creating a slight dent.

'What it means', Hemmatia said, through tight teeth, and peering at her foolish sister, 'is that the girl is making her descent to your kingdom, but it will take a few more days. All we can do is wait.'

'Wait!' The dark lord smoothed his bald head, and let out a big, audible breath. 'Very well, crawl back into your hole; I will be back.'

The Shadow Master vacated the chamber with an air of urgency, apparently having other matters to attend to—the Captain being one of them.

The journey back down to the hills of Vervain would take a couple of days and, as the dry evening set in, the three companions took up residence for the night, once more in Dandagra. Rose's body weighed heavy with exhaustion as she sank into her bed at the inn. Staring at the low-beamed ceiling, she felt an overwhelming sense of contentment; all she could think about was returning home to see her loved ones.

On the road once more, the intrepid princess and company set off at a steady pace. A fine drizzling rain did nothing to dampen Rose's excitement; her spirits stayed high, knowing that soon she would be reunited with her family. After riding non-stop for hours, they saw the old market town of Vervain come into view. The masses of cumulus cloud began to disperse as the sun came shining through to set the perfect scene. Rose beamed at the sight of the villagers rushing to welcome them back home. Word of Lady Rose's homecoming had spread to the Royal Court via Morgana, and King Yarrow declared it a day of festivities. Noble led the procession as people threw flowers and cheered 'God bless ya, milady!' and 'all hail to our heroes.' Chickens were roasting on a spit manned by the local butcher, brimming with pride at his produce, and broth was bubbling in large cast-iron pots over open fires, all in preparation for the evening's celebration. Mouth-watering aromas filled the air.

In the distance, Rose noticed someone familiar. Standing incognito among the people was Morgana, wearing an emerald-green hooded cloak and smiling directly up at Rose.

'You are on your way to greatness, Rose. Keep the faith', Morgana conveyed through telepathy, as she turned and walked away, mysteriously fading into the crowd like a dream.

Eventually, the three travellers arrived at the castle gates of Vervain, where a fanfare was sounded from the battlements as the portcullis rose to let the heroes through. As soon as the three had arrived in the courtyard, Rose's guardians rushed to greet her, and without hesitation, she jumped down from her horse with a thud and ran to hug them.

'It pleases me to see you well, my child', the king said, holding his ward close, while the queen struggled to fight back tears.

Noticing her faithful nursemaid, Flora, hovering in the background, Rose knew that a warm squeeze from her was most certainly in order, too.

'Oh merciful 'eavens', Flora said, wiping a tear from her plump rosy cheek with the corner of her apron.

'Welcome home, Rose', Prince Burdock said with a smile.

'Burdock, you're alive! Thank God', Rose said, giving him a hug. Sir Dill, equally pleased, stood to one side and bowed his head respectfully. 'Sir Dill, it's good to see you well.'

Gallium was slightly more reserved, still astride his horse, but smiling warmly as he watched the exchange of love. His hand brushed his father's sword; how he wished he were somewhere close by...but still, he was pleased for Rose.

'Come, Gallium, Malachi, let me introduce you to my family', Lady Rose said, a skip in her step.

The wizard and the warrior dismounted and followed the Vervains into the Castle.

'Welcome', King Yarrow said. 'The queen and I are greatly indebted to you both for returning our Rose.'

A more sinister scene, however, was set at a cove far away, where the booming voice of a man echoed across the bay of Port Oreon.

'Heave, you lazy lot!' Captain Nine-tails bawled, cracking his whip on a rock, while his crew conveyed bags of loot from another night's pillaging.

'Good evening, gentlemen', the Shadow Master said, literally dropping in from a height, courtesy of Castro, and landing on his feet beside the captain.

'What is it *now*?' Captain Nine-tails demanded, dragging his palm over his face and clutching his beard.

'Is that really any way to greet your master', Borago taunted, closely inspecting a jewel from an open chest.

'I told you we weren't going to hang around forever', the captain said, feeling the braids of his whip.

'Yes, whatever you say; I am here on more important matters.' The Shadow Master circled the captain.

'I need you to hire more men', he said, his tone hostile. 'There will be a battle once I have destroyed the girl.'

'All right, how many men?'

'As many as you can muster.' The Shadow Master stepped up on a boulder, his arms outstretched; holding the rock-topped staff, he addressed the entire crew: 'My fellow mariners, join me in the fight for our freedom, and I WILL reward you richly!'

At that, Borago tossed the large jewel high in the air, and, with a blast from the Orbicular Rock, shattered it into a hundred pieces that showered down like tiny diamonds, into the waiting hands of the crew.

'It'll take time, but all right.' The captain and the Shadow Master shook hands in accord.

Meanwhile, during a lengthy update in the Place-of-Arms regarding the success of the mission so far, the rest of the castle's residents were preparing for a ball in honour of Rose and her guests. That very evening, the table in the Great Hall was laden with culinary delights, while musicians strummed and banged out joyful music from a corner. The Lady Rose, radiant in a deep-red silk gown with golden thread, was led by the king and queen to the head of the great table, followed by a smartly dressed wizard and a not-so-scruffy warrior. Gallium's shabby garb had been replaced by a suit of fine clothes, gifted to him by the king. The whole court observed them curiously, the lords wondering who this so-called warrior and wizard were, while the ladies of the court swooned at their chivalrous presence. One person in particular, Prince Burdock, kept a close eye on the warrior; after all, it had been the prince's job to protect Rose. Gallium and Rose's love seemed to radiate around the room, as they exchanged affectionate glances; even the crystals around her neck shone faintly. The hearty meal concluded with the gentry moving to the centre of the hall, as dancing commenced.

Gallium was about to get up and dance with Rose, when he felt a tap on his shoulder.

'Might I have a word in private?' Prince Burdock requested, signalling with a sideways glance for Gallium to follow him out of the hall. Gallium obeyed and the two honourable men stood in the entrance hall.

'So, Gallium, I hear you were once a pirate', the prince said, standing tall, his hands clasped behind his back. The prince, with his sun-kissed hair, was no arm-wrestler, but tall and brave nonetheless.

'I'm afraid, my lord, you have been misinformed', Gallium said, a little perplexed.

'I see', Prince Burdock said, stepping closer to him. 'My apologies, but you do live in a tree-house, am I right?' he said with a small smile.

215

'Forgive me, my lord, but I fail to see where this conversation is going', Gallium said, making to walk away.

'What about your father? Wasn't he a pirate?' Prince Burdock persisted.

'My father was a good and honest captain', Gallium remarked defensively, leaning forward. 'Under the orders of the Gnome King of Jurien.'

'Look, I'll be frank', Burdock said calmly, showing his hands in submission and looking straight at the warrior. 'I only wish to know if your intentions towards the Lady Rose are honourable; after all, what could you possibly offer her?'

Gallium moved in closer to Burdock, now face to face and undeterred. One of the king's guard, sensing a threat, stalked over to protect the prince.

'With respect, my lord', he said; a slight quake in his voice. 'I care enough to do whatever it takes to help Rose in her quest; you can be assured of that.' At which, Gallium swivelled round and marched straight back to rejoin the festivities. Still, the prince remained unsure, so he ordered the guard to keep a watchful eye on the young warrior.

Chapter Twenty-Four—Sin City

The next day, heads were sore from the mead that had flowed so freely the night before, but hearts were glad—all except one.

'Father, I must speak with you.' It was Prince Burdock, first person to join their majesties for breakfast.

'What is it, Burdock?' King Yarrow said, seated at the head of the table, munching on berries.

'Well, it's about Gallium, the warrior', he began. 'I fear he may have developed feelings for our Lady Rose.'

'Was that not obvious last night?' the king asked. 'I for one am happy for her', he raised his goblet in celebration. 'Strikes me, Gallium has proven his loyalty by protecting Rose.'

'I have to agree, Rose could do far worse', Queen Aveena added, munching daintily on some berries.

'But, he has nothing—no money, no home— he's a mere vagabond!' Burdock declared, springing up from his seat.

'Where does it say in this kingdom that you marry for money?' For a second, the king remembered how harshly Aveena's family had judged him at the time of their courting.

The prince, fearing instantly he may have overstepped the mark, sat back down. 'Forgive me, I simply mean we know nothing about him', he said, staring at his plate.

The king glancing at his wife, was lost for words, shaking his head in disappointment.

'Well, not entirely nothing', the queen said, trying to stay neutral about the whole affair. 'His father was captain of a royal ship.'

'My son, it is Rose's choice', the king said carefully, 'and as the Illuminata, we must honour that.'

'Very well, as you wish, father', Prince Burdock said, bowing his head politely. 'Excuse me, I seem to have lost my appetite.' He hurriedly exited the hall.

'He will come round', the king said to his worried queen. 'His heart's in the right place.'

On the way out of the Great Hall Prince Burdock passed Gallium.

'Good morning, Prince Burdock', Gallium said.

The prince, straight-faced, did not answer, and instead gave a quick nod as he walked on.

'Ah, good morning young Gallium', King Yarrow said with a pleasing smile, offering him a seat at the table. 'I trust you slept well.'

'Indeed, Your Grace', he replied, taking a seat. 'Thank you for your warm hospitality.'

'It is I who should be thanking you for taking such good care of our Rose.' The king leaned closer to Gallium and added, 'She is like the daughter we never had.'

'Your Grace, I want you to know that my feelings towards the Lady Rose are strictly honourable', the warrior said.

The moral declaration was interrupted by the arrival of Rose and Malachi. Everyone then joined in the conversation about the previous night's merriment, when all at once, the doors of the Great Hall blew open and in flew a bright blue wagtail. The bird rapidly changed into Morgana, who befittingly wore a gown of peacock feathers.

'Salutations', she said enchantingly, taking centre stage.

'Queen Morgana, what news do you bring?' King Yarrow asked in a serious tone, rising to his feet.

'I'm afraid time is running out. The crystals must be reunited with their masters.' The fairy queen glided up to the table's edge like a gentle breeze. 'The Shadow Master grows restless; it is only a matter of time before he again wreaks havoc on this innocent land', she said, looking directly at Rose with her sparkling green eyes. 'Rose, you must take back the Orbicular Rock before it's too late, but be warned, the Shadow Master knows you will try to claim it, so journey wisely into his realm of Anaconda.' At the centre of the hall, Morgana's splendid plumage fanned around her shoulders; 'This quest is far from over', she pronounced as, with a swish of her gown, she transformed back into the small vibrant blue bird and flew out the main doors.

The king and company remained silent for a moment. The atmosphere became more sombre, as the ugly truth forced their attention to graver matters.

'The fairy queen is right', the king responded earnestly, pushing his plate away. 'This will be your most challenging journey yet.' He looked at their faces, his eyes glassy.

'I promise to see this quest to the bitter end, Your Grace', Rose proclaimed with a small frown.

'And I', said Gallium, standing up.

'You can count on us, Your Grace', Malachi said, also on his feet.

Later that day in the courtyard, Rose scanned the tranquil sky, releasing a long breath, as she looked inside herself for courage.

'We have enjoyed your visit immensely, Rose', the doting king said. 'Good luck to you all and may God speed.'

'I will return', Rose said, hugging King Yarrow tightly.

'No doubt; now go—and have courage.' Releasing himself from her arms, the king gave orders to raise the portcullis.

As the three rode non-stop due south through the Fatum realm, the wrath of the Shadow Master became increasingly evident. Rose surveyed the burnt down houses and broken mess with a heavy heart. The remains of human bones were scattered on the ground like dry twigs. Trotting ahead, Rose stopped at an abandoned windmill, waiting for her companions to catch up. The old windmill's sails were left bare and broken by the recent fire. The loose iron hinges were all that remained of the entrance door. Intuitively touching the cold stone wall of the mill with her delicate fingertips, Rose sensed that victims had been trapped inside to perish in the inferno. The Illuminata vividly felt the terror and could hear the screams of the innocent civilians. She felt shackled by guilt, since the dark forces had condemned these poor people to their horrible fate, in search of her.

With a quivering lip and eyes screwed shut, leaking out a tear or two, Rose was soon met by the others. As she climbed back onto her faithful horse with an air of determination, Noble let out the loudest neigh.

'Malachi, Gallium; I cannot allow more suffering, nor will I rest until this poison is history', she said, clearing her throat and quickly drying her eyes with her fingers. 'I want to keep riding for as long as the horses can endure.'

'As you wish, my lady', Malachi said, bowing his head. He felt her pain and was ready to serve.

'I agree', Gallium said, looking down at the injustices that had been wrought. 'We ride to the Devil's lair. Yah!'

All three riders urged their horses onwards, through ever changing climes.

After some time, it was clear that their relentless galloping had tired the horses; their nostrils flared and their heads hung low. The air became increasingly warm; looking down from a hill, they saw the ground gradually changed from earthy brown to sun-baked sandstone. Black crows were settling to nest among the twiggy treetops as night drew in. The monstrous statue of the Shadow Master stood silhouetted on the horizon of Bloodwood Gorge, setting the scene for a more sinister leg of their journey. There was a prominent pause between the three travellers.

'Over that bridge is the realm of Anaconda', Malachi said quietly and scanned the area down below. 'We need to find a safe place to rest; follow me.'

As they cautiously ventured into the treacherous realm, the horses' hooves clapped against the stony path of Bloodwood's bridge, echoing down the great ravine. The gorge was dry, deep and cavernous, while the air was tainted by a putrid smell. Staring up at the dark lord's monument, Gallium visualised his nemesis dying in front of him, by the warrior's sword. Malachi led his companions to a single pear-shaped tree growing further away from the gorge, and outlined by the setting sun.

On close inspection, the tree's huge, globular trunk appeared to have a hollow entrance, with enough room to house a few people. Hanging from its thin branches were melon-sized green pods.

Jumping down from her horse, a pensive Rose walked around the impressive tree, running her fingers along its coarse sienna bark. Gallium cut one of the low branches with his sword and then sliced a pod open. Inside was a dry fruit, filled with seeds.

'Witches' warts!' Gallium said, spitting out a mouthful of the fruit and dropping the rest on the ground. 'That was foul.'

'No matter', Malachi said, setting up camp inside the tree's trunk. 'We have enough food and water for a day or two.'

'But we don't know how far until our next stop', Gallium remarked, looking across the dehydrated landscape at the fast-setting sun.

'According to the map in the Book of Legends', Malachi said, studiously leafing with his finger. 'We should reach the City of Mumbala say...no more than half a day's ride?' he estimated.

'I'm quite tired, so if you'll excuse me', Rose said blinking sleepily.

'Yes of course; goodnight my lady.' Malachi went over the map once more. 'Gallium, I suggest we take it in turns to keep watch tonight; I'll stay up first.'

'All right, just nudge me when you're done', Gallium said, taking his sword inside the tree trunk, where all three of them could sleep comfortably.

'Indeed', the wizard said, sitting on a blanket admiring the star-filled sky.

Meanwhile, back inside the Shadow Master's castle, Borago had a peculiar feeling in his stomach.

'She's close, I can sense it', Borago snarled, in front of Taurus with eyes closed and lightly holding his abdomen. Getting up reflectively from his throne and brushing away Azria who was massaging his feet, he again visited the Mercury Well Chamber. Once there the fretful dictator demanded confirmation from the two witches.

'Well, am I right?' he said.

'Yes master, you sensed well. She travels with the same two men and in this direction', Hemmatia said.

'I know, she has a warrior and a wizard', the Shadow Master said in a monotonous tone.

'You must destroy the men, for they could be your undoing', Hemmatia warned, a tremble in her voice.

'Yes, do be careful master', Marelda cautioned.

'Leave it to me', the Shadow Master said, waving the witches back into the well with his staff and turning quickly towards the flight of steps.

With the help of Taurus, the Shadow Master sent word to the corrupt authority of Mumbala, instructing their guards to kill the two men who were travelling with the girl who bears the crystals, but to bring the girl to him alive.

The next morning, after a night of sleep interrupted by unfamiliar nocturnal sounds, Rose noticed Malachi was gone. She found a note on his blanket.

'Gallium', she said, shaking the warrior gently from his deep sleep.

Gallium eventually came round and sat up to find Rose flapping the piece of parchment in his face.

'It's a message from Malachi; he says it is best we separate and make our own way to the City of Mumbala', Rose said, her eyes wide, as she tried to steady her hand holding the note. 'Once we arrive there, Malachi will find us.'

Gallium pulled the note carefully from her hand to read it again, saying:

'I trust his judgement Rose, but I will not leave you. We will go to Mumbala together.'

'I hoped you'd say that', she said, as they stared at one another, hesitantly anticipating the inevitable journey ahead.

'We're in this together', Gallium vowed with a kiss. 'I best go and pack now.'

Soon the enamoured pair were again riding onward, ever guided by Noble.

The heat intensified as the day progressed, and, not far down an arid track edged by the occasional spindly bush, the couple heard ominous whispers.

'Who are you?' Gallium demanded, promptly jumping off Ironbark, his sword ready to defend. 'Show yourselves.'

'Beware, beware', the faint voices cried.

'It sounds like it's coming from down here', Rose said, inclining an ear to the ground to hear better.

'We are the desert sprites of Anaconda. Beware the evil shadow that rules these parts.'

To Rose and Gallium's amazement, these tufts of grass with thin pointy leaves, that were scattered over the dry land, were talking to them. On taking a closer look, Rose could just make out their pixie-like faces through the thin blades of grass. The sprites hopped in closer and closer still, using their roots as feet, repeatedly saying 'Beware!'

'Well, thank you, but...', Rose said politely, only to be cut short as the huddled tussocks ignited, burning instantly to the ground. Rising slowly to her feet a bit bemused, she noticed something familiar about the ashes.

'Look it spells out a word: b-e-w-a-r-e.'

'This is pointless; shall we continue?' Gallium said, hot and bothered, as he put away his sword and straddled his horse once more.

'Agreed', Rose replied, getting back on her horse, unfazed.

Once again into the dry heat and crackling terrain they travelled, trotting by the remains of more animal carcasses, which had fallen prey to the unforgiving sun. The intense heat forced Rose and Gallium to shed bits of clothing, tearing strips with their bare hands to form rags with which to protect their heads and faces. The crows circulated up above, waiting to feast on yet more prey.

Hours later, as the horses dragged their weary hooves across the dusty plains, Rose, missing her home, sang a fairy love song that Flora had sung many times.

'I will love you 'til I die. Say you love me too, until then I will wait, for true love's kiss from you.'

The weakening princess removed a leather pouch from her belt with her sun-scorched fingers and was about to take a sip of water, when out of nowhere, Noble reared in fright, as a rattlesnake startled him under hoof. Rose nearly lost her balance and clung to Noble's mane as the water pouch fell onto the ground.

'Oh no, my water', Rose said, watching helplessly as the last drop dribbled into the dust. The hissing serpent slithered away into a nearby bush.

'Forgive me, my lady', Noble said, snorting wearily and looking down at his now motionless hooves.

Slumping forward onto Noble's neck, Rose felt weak with dehydration. The crows were swooping down from the sky, their cruel claws ready to rip into her flesh. Gallium and Ironbark galloped to her aid, Gallium swinging his sword with such speed that it sent shredded feathers flying. Undeterred by the crows' screeching, he managed to slice off a couple of wings as he rode. The rest of the flock flew away in fright. Noble lowered himself to the ground, so that the warrior could tend to his beloved, when the same snake reappeared. It slithered over to the injured birds, unhinging its jaws to reveal two deadly fangs, before swallowing the ill-fated birds whole. This time,

225

the snake began to grow terrifyingly huge in size. Gallium swivelled round at the sound of its rattle, now the length of a dragon's tail.

'Noble, stay with Rose, and Ironbark, hold steady while I deal with this curse myself.' Gallium opted to battle it out on foot, perspiration trickling down his torso, as he moved in, cautiously assessing where first to strike the reptilian beast. Watching on, Rose tried to regain her strength by using the crystals, but without water to fuel her energy, it didn't work.

The giant serpent plunged suddenly, its fangs narrowly missing the warrior, who jump-rolled to safety and briskly got to his feet. The creature came at him again and again. The heat began to affect Gallium's vision, which was now slightly blurry. The next strike was to be the venomous fiend's last, however, as Gallium stood firm, steadily gripping his sword with both hands, and at that moment the serpent dived at him once more. The warrior stepped forward and dropped to one knee, at the same time driving his sword up into the underside of the snake's head. With a loud cry, the large snake fell dead, its body collapsing on top of the warrior. The settling dust revealed no sound or movement: Rose had passed-out on her horse, while Gallium was covered by the scaly corpse. Ironbark whinnied for his master and slowly, from beneath the dead snake, came a commotion: first, a squelching noise, followed by a wriggling of the reptile's head, and finally, slicing his way out, the warrior Gallium!

Staggering to his feet and catching his breath, he wiped the sticky slime from his face, very much alive. Shaking the gluey mess off his head as much as he could, and trying to gather his thoughts, he quickly retrieved a water pouch from Ironbark, before rushing over to where Rose lay. As Gallium lifted her head in his arms, he noticed that the colour in the pink crystal was fading.

'Rose, you *must* drink.' The warrior carefully poured a trickle of water over her dry, cracked lips. It took a moment for Rose's awareness to return; she continued to drink, blinking a few times. Steadily, the Illuminata and the crystals revived. By sipping more water, and with the help of the crystals, Rose made a quick recovery. Gallium lifted her back onto Noble and the two companions rode off again, much relieved.

'My lady, Mumbala is close by', Noble spoke, as he trotted towards this infamous city of sin.

'Gallium, Noble says Mumbala is near.'

'I think I see it', Gallium said, mapping the horizon. 'We must advance with caution.'

Side by side, they neared Mumbala. A cacophony of sounds rose into the air, accompanied by a burst of pungent aromas. The city's enormous sandstone archway was creepily decorated with severed fingers hung on strings, some still dripping blood, demonstrating the cruel method of punishment practised in these parts. Standing motionless on either side of the entrance, were a couple of hard-faced guards.

'Rose, stay close', Gallium said, trotting alongside some locals entering the city, as the area grew crowded.

The main high street of the city ran between rows of wall-to-wall housing, and was very much an entrepreneurial display of people buying, selling or bartering. At the end of a side alley was a snake charmer, playing a hypnotic tune on a narrow wind instrument called a pungi. The skeletal man was enticing a cobra slowly out of its woven basket, for all to be entranced. Stalls were packed tightly together,

227

laden with vibrant textiles and colourful spices, from sweet cinnamon and nutmeg to the fragrant herb coriander. Adjacent to this, a local woman was preparing flat bread to accompany a traditional clay-dish recipe, which had been bubbling away in a wood fire oven; and next to her, yet another was painting a pretty henna pattern on a lady's arm, similar to a tattoo. Up ahead, a group of mischievous children were mimicking an old blind man, who was desperately feeling his way through the crowd with his long wooden stick.

'Steady, Noble', whispered Rose in his ear, as she stroked the side of his neck.

'We'll have to walk from here', Gallium said, jumping off Ironbark and leading both horses to a nearby trough at the side of the dusty street. 'Try not to draw attention, Rose, and keep by my side', he said, looping the horses' reins loosely around a wooden post.

'I'll be vigilant', Rose said, using her hands to scoop up water from the tin trough to cleanse her face. Her stomach churned from nerves, as well as hunger.

'My friends, you must wait here', Gallium said, calmly instructing the horses. 'I will call if we need you.'

Using the trough water, he began washing the dried dirt off his arms and head; before long the water had evaporated under the relentless sun.

'Rose, I spy a tavern over there; we need food, and maybe we'll find Malachi.'

Gallium took Rose firmly by the hand and confidently weaved a way among the chaotic crowd. The noise level from the city folk was ear-shattering, combined with plenty of unavoidable pushing and the vendors' thrusting produce into their faces.

Suddenly, a hand grabbed Rose's shoulder from behind.

'Oh, mercy me', a voice croaked.

Gallium and Rose both turned, only to see the blind man.

Looking directly past their shoulders, the blind man held a finger to his lips, and leaning close, whispered, 'My lady it is I.'

'Malachi', Rose whispered back.

It was indeed the wizard, disguised in rags, with a bandana to cover his markings and head.

Malachi nodded and, standing between them, linked one arm in Rose's and the other in Gallium's.

'Spare a thought for a blind man who's lost his way.'

Malachi played his part well, croaking out a request for Rose and Gallium to lead him to the tavern where all would be explained. With no one suspecting a thing, they dodged the bustling crowd, stepping along a sandy path to enter the tavern.

Immediately on entering this smoky establishment, it seemed a thousand eyes were upon the strangers. The tavern's frequent visitors were merchants in fine, rich robes, seated on embroidered cushions and smoking clay water-pipes. Draped lavishly across the ceiling were spice-coloured silk scarves, while from the ceiling hung mosaic lanterns emitting a low light. Rose, still arm-in-arm with the 'blind man' Malachi, kept her eyes fixed on the floor, as they walked nervously to a corner booth. Gallium went to order refreshments at the bar. He was greeted—or rather, grunted at—by a tall, hairy-looking man with only one eye in the middle of his forehead.

'We don't want beggars in here unless you are going to pay', the one-eyed barman scowled, bent heavily with his arm on the bar, and staring at Gallium with his bulging eye.

'I'm no beggar and I can pay for all of us', Gallium said in a controlled manner, tossing a small red Jurien gemstone onto the bar.

The cyclops, growling to himself, snatched the stone and examined it, holding it up to the light of a lantern. 'What do you want?' he snapped.

'Wine and food for now', Gallium said smugly, as he flashed some of the other gems in his hand.

'I'll get someone to bring it over to your table', said the cyclops, keeping an inquisitive eye on the warrior.

Walking casually back to rejoin the others, Gallium surveyed their new surroundings.

'My lady, I'm so glad you made it through the desert', Malachi said across the table.

'Well, we encountered some difficulties on the way; incidentally how was your ride here?' she asked, rubbing her dry, tired eyes and suppressing a yawn.

'Let's say, travelling at night with only magic as your weapon, has its advantages', the wizard said, tapping his fingers on the tabletop. 'It's great to see you both again, my fine friends.'

'I trust you won't be disappearing again soon?' Gallium said sarcastically, seating himself down next to Rose. 'What's the plan now?'

'I have somewhere for us to stay tonight', the wizard said quietly. 'We can discuss our next course of action there.'

A moment later, a servant girl wearing a pair of burnt-orange, baggy trousers and a cropped tasselled top, broke up their conversation, as she humbly served their meal. All three started tucking into the food like starving orphans.

'Do you think that anyone suspects who we are?' Rose asked Malachi, guzzling wine as though it were water.

'Not if I can help it', he replied softly, keeping up the facade, as he felt his way around the table, in between drinking and eating. 'I'm sure "you know who" has ordered the local authorities to look out for us, so we must be on our guard—hence my disguise.'

'I agree', Gallium responded, moving the jug of wine away from one thirsty Rose.

Just then, a busy little man with an obvious limp hobbled over to their table.

'You like smoke?' he said waving a water-pipe, and revealing a gaping grin.

'Er, no thanks', Gallium said, politely pushing the pipe away from his face. 'We're not staying long.'

'Very good sir, very good.' The small servant bowed his head, mainly at Rose, and hobbled away.

A short while after, Gallium happened to notice that the barman was deep in conversation with the limping waiter, who was pointing his stumpy finger at Rose.

'It's that annoying waiter again', Gallium mumbled discreetly to the others. 'And he's pointing right at you, Rose.'

'My lady, he must have seen your crystals, tuck them away', Malachi advised from the side of his mouth. Right away, Rose shrewdly brought her hand up, tucking the gems behind the rag around her neck.

'We should go', Gallium quietly suggested, casually wiping his mouth with the back of his hand, his eyes still fixed on the curious cretin.

'I feel a bit woozy', Rose said, rising unsteadily to her feet.

'Guide me to the alley around the corner and I will lead you the rest of the way', Malachi said to them both. 'There we can change into something less conspicuous.'

'All right, follow my lead in case it turns nasty.' Gallium got up and ushered his companions out, none of them making eye contact with anybody.

All three made it past the impersonal stares and back outside into the dirty streets. Mumbala's trades were drawing to a close and soon nothing except scurrying desert rats roamed the gutters. Nightfall was upon them. A torch bearer, whistling his way through the city, was lighting the street lanterns that hung from the eaves of the clustered terracotta houses. In the background, a chorus of prowling cats could be heard. Rose and company passed through the city's streets, its never-ending walls occasionally displaying huge wooden doors, each at least two-men tall.

'I wonder who lives beyond these walls', Rose said with a hiccup, swaying slightly. She tried to catch a glimpse of what was concealed through the cracks in the door.

'Only the fortunate ones live in the gardens of paradise, so I've been told.' Then, Malachi came to a sudden halt. 'Ah, there it is.'

A short walk ahead was a gypsy caravan, stationed at the end of an alley. It was a decorative little wagon, with outer wooden panels painted with a colourful floral design, but it had no form of transport.

'I sense we are not alone', Malachi said to the others, standing between them.

Gallium detected two hostile shadows on the ground opposite and spun around, narrowly avoiding the swing of a blade. Two soldiers of Mumbala had

232

followed them, one of them grabbing Rose from behind, tugging the rags from around her neck to reveal the crystals.

'It's the girl!' the solider said, before sending a blow to Rose's head with the heavy pommel of his sword, and dropping her unconscious to one side.

'Rose!' Gallium shouted, but his way was blocked by the other threatening soldier.

Instantly, Gallium whistled loudly for Ironbark and Noble, while Malachi, using the power of air, blew a breeze strong enough to temporarily halt the other soldier. The hefty soldier who was fighting the warrior, kept swinging his blade and missing, as Gallium dodged and weaved out of harm's way. The sound of the two rapidly approaching horses then momentarily distracted the soldiers. Ironbark advanced, kicking up his front hooves and causing one of the soldiers to fall to the ground. Taking advantage of the situation, Gallium punched the same soldier in the kidneys, and then swiftly drew his sword from Ironbark's keep, before plunging it into his adversary. Malachi's foe was showing no signs of retreating, so, creating balls of flames with his hands, he flung them at the soldier. His clothes aflame like a human torch, the soldier fled for his life. The two victors looked on, tired but triumphant.

'Others will return. We must leave at once', Gallium stressed, rushing over to where Rose lay.

Standing guard over Rose was Noble, gently pressing his nose to her face. Although not moving, Rose was still alive. Gallium lifted his wounded princess and laid her on a small bed inside the caravan.

'She's going to be fine', Malachi assured the warrior. 'Quickly, fasten the horses to the wagon.'

Gallium proceeded to remove the horses' saddles and deposit them in the caravan, then fastened the stallions securely to its front. The warrior took the reins, ordering the horses to ride as fast as they could. The little caravan's wooden wheels spun wildly over the gritty lime-stone streets, as they made their way through the city. As they approached the city's entrance, little did they know that the warrior was about to face an even greater challenge. The passage was heavily guarded by a dozen or more soldiers, all armed and equipped with an enormous net that they had spread across the ground to capture their master's prize.

'Malachi, do something!' Gallium yelled, trying to keep the horse's momentum, and charging straight towards the only way out.

Positioning himself next to the warrior, the wizard cast a powerful spell, extending an arm in front, his palm vertical.

'Veni tempura sabia veni! Hold on everyone!' Malachi grabbed the iron rail at the front of the caravan.

The path leading out of the city dissolved like the sands of time, sweeping the horses and the little wagon with its precious load, over the moving sand and out the other side of the city's entrance. Most of the soldiers were left buried under the wave of sand that now blocked the great archway. The gypsy caravan bounced onto the ground then stopped, undamaged. Gallium and Malachi were thrown from either side of the wagon, landing a little bruised on the ground.

'Where am I?' Rose said, after being thrown from the bed onto the wooden floor and looking about the caravan's interior. She clambered up and sat on the edge of the bed, holding her head, while the powerful pink crystal soon healed her small injuries.

'Let's get back behind the reins and keep moving', Malachi said to Gallium, dusting himself off and climbing up to the front of the caravan. 'I was told of a plantation nearby; Noble can lead us there.'

Noble responded, his mark shimmering, and took charge alongside Ironbark.

Gallium climbed inside the wagon and sat next to Rose.

'Are you all right?' he asked, putting an arm around her.

'Yes I'm fine', Rose answered with a sigh. 'What happened and where are we?'

'This is Malachi's travelling wagon; we were seized by the guards of Mumbala, but Malachi used his best magic trick by far and we made it past them.'

'Thank God for Malachi...and you', Rose said, putting her head on his shoulder. 'Gallium, our quest is almost over, and come what may, I'm glad I chose you.'

'The quest may be drawing to a close, but our journey has only just begun', he said.

Together they admired the jewelled night sky through the top half of the caravan's rear stall door, the smell of incense lessening the further away they rode.

That same night, the Shadow Master was informed by the General of Mumbala of their escape, via a magic spyglass.

'Be that as it may, General, I am the master of my game, so let her come, this time I will be ready', Borago said undiscouraged. Straddled across his lap, Azria fed him another grape.

Chapter Twenty-Five—The Devil's Lair

Somewhere between Mumbala and the Shadow Master's lair, the little wagon and its important passengers arrived safely at an area filled with exotic rubber trees, their shiny thick leaves clumped together, and oil palms with leaves fanning out in giant splendour, providing ideal shelter from the damning sun. Having stationed the caravan under one tall tree, Gallium wandered over to inspect another one. Looking up at it, he felt how ribbed the bark was and with a satisfied grin, took off his boots and began to climb it. Using his belt as a harness around the narrow trunk, Gallium held on tight to each end and proceeded to walk up the tree, his body acting as an anchor. It was a humid night, however, and Gallium struggled to keep a firm hold of the belt, as his hands perspired in the heat. Once at the top, the panting warrior perched on a wide branch and searched the distance with his spyglass, to see if the enemy had followed. Fortunately, there were no signs of movement or flaming torches to suggest otherwise. Making his way steadily back down, Gallium happily reported to the others.

'The coast appears to be clear', the warrior said, re-entering the caravan.

'Right, well, while I was waiting for you both in Mumbala, I came by a traveller who traded this caravan for my horse, his having sadly passed away', Malachi explained to the others, kneeling on the floor.

Rose was sitting on the bed with legs bent, absorbing the wizard's every word.

'I also did a little probing and learnt that the Shadow Master lives high in the Mercury Mountains.' By now, Malachi had removed a table knife from his leather satchel. 'Every evening he is entertained by Mumbala's finest talent, which brings me to my next plan.'

'Are you suggesting we go in dancing?' Gallium said, leaning up against the stable door, arms folded.

'Well, not quite', Malachi answered, tucking the tip of the blade into a gap to prise open the caravan's floorboard. 'Tomorrow at dusk, the entertainers will be passing here on their way to the Shadow Master, and I propose we join them', he said, pulling traditional costumes, all spangled and bright, from under the floorboards. 'Gallium and I will disguise ourselves in these as gift bearers.'

'Whoa! That's not exactly fighting material', Gallium said, with a show of hands.

'And you Rose', Malachi said, ignoring Gallium's remark, 'will be our gift, rolled up safely in this rug.'

Placing the garments to one side, he then dragged a large dusty old rug from under the bed.

'Once inside, we will unravel Rose, who will be concealed with the swords, and with a bit of magic, the deed is done', the wizard concluded confidently, sitting cross-legged on the floor. Gallium gave Malachi a sideways glance, still unsure.

'It's all right, Gallium, I think this plan could actually work', Rose said, holding up her costume to assess it.

After setting up camp, Rose remained inside the caravan for the night, while her comrades respectfully retired to a tent. The Illuminata lay restless, her mind racing with thoughts of the past

237

and of tomorrow, making it hard to fall asleep. Unexpectedly, there was a knock at the wagon's rear entrance.

'Who's there?' Rose said, sitting up in bed a little startled.

'Rose, it's only me.'

'Gallium, what is it?' Quickly wrapping a blanket around her shoulders, Rose unbolted the rear stall door, and let him in.

Gallium crept into the caravan with only the moonlight to guide him.

'I wanted to say goodnight', he said, quietly. 'Remember I am only a stone's throw away if you need me.'

'I know; truth is, I doubt I will get much sleep tonight', Rose said, unnerved. 'I can't stop replaying in my mind all that we've been through and imagining what is yet to come.' She slowly turned away with her arms folded and fingers twitching nervously. 'What if I fail?'

'Then we fail together', Gallium said, stroking her hair with his fingers, as the silky strands cascaded down her back. 'But that is not what I think will happen, for you are powerful; I have seen what you are capable of.' Gallium slowly turned Rose to face him, moved in closer and placed a tender kiss on her forehead, before returning to the tent.

The quest had been such a turbulent one, so far, that the experience was taking its toll on the precious princess. The noise from the tropical insects and birds outside was almost deafening, and Rose tossed and turned in her bed until she eventually fell asleep, exhausted. During the sultry night, her fears had manifested into images of war on the innocent—Rose saw herself trudging over a battle field, when all at once, a cruel image of the Shadow Master's hand

238

reaching out for her throat, forced her to wake in a sweat of panic. Jolting upright, short of breath, with the blanket clinging to her clammy legs, Rose was relieved to know it was a bad dream. Wiping the sweat from her face with the blanket and slowing down her breath, she held on to the crystals, which began to glow. Reclining once again on the bed, Rose turned her thoughts to more pleasant ones, such as memories of time well spent with her Vervain family, or of fairy encounters in the Whispering Wood, or dancing with her warrior at the reunion, and thus gently drifted back to the land of dreams.

The warm mid-morning air was drifting in through the trees, as Rose got out of bed, feeling somewhat jaded. She strolled over to where the others lay in their tent, as dust blew along the ground past the caravan.

'Good morning', Rose called from outside, with a stretch.

'Good morning my lady, did you sleep well?' a refreshed wizard said.

'Yes, eventually', she said, not wishing to relive her nightmares. 'I take it Gallium is still asleep?'

'Either that or still sulking over his less-than-threatening costume', Malachi chortled. 'Well, I'm just going to sit under that tree and gather my thoughts for the day; care to join me?'

'Actually, yes', Rose said, wide awake.

Taking a few steps to a shaded spot, Malachi demonstrated how to sit with legs crossed, one hand on each knee, palms facing up. 'Now, let me guide you; start by taking in a few deep breaths.'

'Before we begin, I have questions', Rose said sharply.

'What is it?' he said.

239

'I was wondering firstly, what is to become of me, Malachi?' she said anxiously rubbing her hands. 'That is to say, can you predict the future?'

'You still have doubts and that's perfectly normal', the wizard said soothingly, turning to Rose. 'The truth is, I can't predict.'

'Can't or won't?' Rose asked.

The wizard sensed her emotions were running high.

'My dear lady, the only person who knows the future is Omnio himself. We simply have to keep the faith.' Malachi repositioned himself and closed his eyes. 'Now, meditate with me, it will prepare you for your journey ahead.'

'I suppose. I'm still trying to make sense of it all.' Believing Malachi wouldn't respond to any more questions, Rose surrendered with a sigh and sat down next to the wise wizard.

'Just breathe', Malachi instructed, taking in a few slow deep breaths himself. 'Clear your mind of any thoughts by focusing on your breathing, in...and...out, two, three, four', he said, masterfully. 'And tell yourself: I am amazing, I am brave, I am strong and I can do this.'

In her meditative state, Rose could visualise herself in lucid form as a warrior princess standing on a mountaintop, wearing crystal armour, her eyes sparkling with light. A bald headed eagle perched proudly beside her; she caressed its head with her finger, as the whistling wind blew through her long flowing hair. She knew a feeling of complete empowerment.

Amid this calm, Gallium found his beloved and the wizard in deep concentration. He decided to leave them be, and went to explore the area for signs of danger—and food.

Far away, in the unsettled market town of Vervain, where heavy rain had drenched the ground, King Yarrow was overseeing a tournament, with Sir Dill's help. The reason for the test of agility was to potentially recruit more men for King Yarrow's army. Men of all ages had come from within the kingdom and beyond, each taking his turn to complete a set of tasks. First, they had to compete in a sword fight, but not to the death; second, they must joust with a straw-filled dummy swinging from a tall wooden frame; and third was a test of archery, the target being another fake human. All hopeful recruits lined up, stating their cause and swearing an oath to the king. Down the line was a young boy, with a dirt-smudged face, holding a sharpened wooden stick.

'Why are you here boy?' the king asked the lad, who wasn't even old enough to grow whiskers.

'Begging your pardon, King Yarrow, but my father was killed by the bad men of the Shadow thingy, and I want to fight him', the boy said, demonstrating such courage as he held the long stick, his pigeon-chest thrust out.

'What is your name, boy?' King Yarrow asked, moved by the lad's bravery.

'My name is John, sir', he said, wiping his nose on his already soiled sleeve.

'Well then, John, do you have a mother?'

'Yes sir, and two little sisters', the boy said, eagerly answering the king's questions.

'You are indeed a brave young man', King Yarrow said, lowering himself to the boy's height and placing a hand on his petite shoulder, 'and I'm sure one day you will make a fine soldier, but I think you are needed more elsewhere.' The king, as father-to-son, spoke to him again. 'You must go home and protect your family, as I am sure your father would have expected.'

The boy did as the king advised, stepping down from the wooden podium, still grasping his stick, and marched all the way home.

During the tournament, a large yellow butterfly fluttered towards the king and spoke to him in a familiar voice, loud enough for all to hear.

'Your Grace, I have news', Morgana announced as she flew through a shower of fairy dust, to transform publicly in to her true shape.

'People of Vervain, the Illuminata has arrived safely in the Shadow Master's realm', the fairy queen said, turning slowly on the spot.

Immediately, the tournament was stopped at the command of Sir Dill; everyone paused for their guest.

'And soon she will come face to face with the Shadow Master himself.' Morgana stopped turning and looked at King Yarrow.

'I pray she makes it home, but instinct tells me I should ride to be by her side', King Yarrow said truthfully.

'Your current deed is enough, for Pangaea will come to depend on you and your men', she predicted. 'I hope you will all find the courage you need, to lift this terrible curse from our beautiful Pangaea.' Quicker than a humming bird's wing, the fairy queen changed into a little blue bird and disappeared into a nearby tree.

The whole crowd waited in anticipation for a word from their king. Their ruler rose from his seat, and simply said:

'My people, you heard the fairy queen, there is no time to doubt or delay; therefore, let the tournament continue', he said, signalling with a raised hand.

As the afternoon moved forward, back in the Anaconda realm the heroic trio were preparing for the evening's event. Rose and Gallium were practising their sword fighting skills in the warm evening air, to the sounds of nocturnal creatures.

'I look like a genie in this', Gallium frowned as he examined his garb, which consisted of a royal-blue truncated, cone-shaped hat, a similar blue waistcoat with gold trim, and low-waisted baggy trousers, also royal blue.

'Yes, minus the three wishes, of course', Malachi said, comfortably wearing the same outfit and magically creating a mirror by throwing water from his palm onto a tree trunk. Standing in front of the enchanted glass, he wrapped a bandana around his head again, added an eye-patch, and finally, a full beard.

'Come on 'genie', on your guard', Rose said teasing and taking up a fighting stance.

'Very funny', Gallium said, twirling his sword freely. 'I'll be fighting to victory on the day, with or without armour.'

'That's the spirit', the wizard said, magically transfiguring a rope ladder from the highest branch of a rubber tree and proceeding to climb it.

'Oh I see, he gets a ladder, I get blisters', Gallium said.

'What are you doing, Malachi?' Rose enquired, staring up at the wizard in the umber foliage.

'I'm certain they will be passing soon', Malachi said, shouting down, referring of course to the dark lord's entertainers.

The circus of entertainers was travelling towards the Mystic Mountains. With some on horseback and others in caravans similar to Malachi's, the spiralling wagon wheels and pounding hooves created a dense cloud of reddish dust on the distant horizon,.

'I was right! I see them', Malachi said, and began a speedy descent down the rope ladder.

'How can you be certain?' Gallium said, swatting another mosquito on his neck.

'I borrowed your spyglass of course', Malachi said, casually handing the brass object back to Gallium. 'Now, let's ride, before we lose them.'

With adrenalin coursing through their bodies, Rose and Gallium took up their places aboard the pretty wagon. Once the companions were in place, the warrior shook the reins and they were off, leaving the plantation far behind. The horses galloped in tandem across the dry plain and reached the convoy as rapidly as the setting sun.

'Halt, who goes there?' called one of the performers, trotting over to them on horseback.

Gallium slowed the horses down.

'Samir, it is I, Malachi. We come as gift-bearers for the master, as agreed', Malachi said, lifting his eyepatch.

'Malachi, my friend, you made it', Samir said, giving a huge grin, which raised a thick black moustache. 'Forgive me, I did not recognise you', he said, sitting astride Dewdrop. 'Stay closely behind the others and follow.'

Samir was the wizard's informer and the brother of servant-girl Azria. He was a man with great muscles, which showed through his impressive acrobatic costume. Gallium led the wagon to the back of the procession, and they carried on with their journey at a steady pace.

'What agreement might that be, exactly?' Gallium questioned.

'Samir and I agreed to help each other, as his sister has fallen prey to Borago; together we will fight for her rescue, and our cause', Malachi said, nobly.

Gallium didn't say another word, thinking instead of how many souls had fallen victim to this menacing being.

Before long, the road became a treacherous one, steep and rocky, the hardened crust of lava masking the true danger beneath. The group of players went on up the Mercury Mountains, as the monstrous glassy black castle came into full view. The front of the castle was framed by two tall obsidian towers, with many lit torches scaling the sides, and wide steps leading up to huge, impressive wooden doors. Reducing speed, the entertainers arrived at the base of the entrance.

'Are you ready, Rose?' Gallium said, as she leaned out from the front, in between the two men.

'Yes, onwards we must', she whispered, her eyes reflecting the flaming torches on the monstrous structure ahead; her linked crystals began to glow.

Malachi set about taking over the reins and stopped the caravan near the entrance, a few feet away from where the rest of the party were stationed. Jumping down, he ran to the rear of the caravan, from where Gallium dragged the rug, unrolling it on the ground. Rose lay down at one end of the rug, with the swords in sheaths placed flat on her front. Once she was in position, the wizard and the warrior began to roll the rug and the Illuminata up together. After which, the two imposters carrying, the fake prop, joined the cast at the back of the procession. The centaur guards patrolling the gate recognised the crew from their costumes and granted them passage into the Great Hall. The warrior and the wizard, the rolled rug high upon their shoulders, focused on keeping their balance with every step. With every inch closer to his nemesis, Gallium felt the tension rising from his gut and the sweat trickling down his back (although the sweat was more from the hot climate). Once the performers finished showing off their talents, the gift bearers shuffled towards the throne, stopping mid-point to lower their precious gift to the floor. There was an uncomfortable silence as all eyes, including Borago's, were upon them. The unsuspecting Shadow Master was intrigued, leaning forward from his throne with an elbow on one knee and rubbing his bristly jaw.

'My lord, we bring you a gift from our city', Malachi announced, in a slightly deeper tone, his chin to chest.

Malachi, with a nod to Gallium, started the unravelling. The only thing Rose could hear was her palpitating heart. Quickly, the rug unfolded and out popped Rose, springing to her feet with both swords in hand. Pumped with adrenalin, she deftly tossed Gallium his sword, as everyone in the hall fanned out, ready to defend themselves.

'Azria, we have come to save you!' Samir gallantly called from one side. His dear sister, kneeling beside the Shadow Master, looked pleased to see her brother and immediately tried to get up. But Borago restrained her with a heavy hand on her shoulder.

Samir was armed with a cutlass and ready to fight.

'Kill the men, but the girl is mine!' the Shadow Master said, standing by his throne and gripping his powerful staff.

Galloping their way into the Great Hall and charging straight at the civilians, came the centaurs armed with long spears. Gallium and Malachi fought furiously, one using a sword, the other magic. Driven by duty, Rose confronted the Shadow Master.

'I have come to claim the Orbicular Rock', the Illuminata said firmly, pulling her sword from its sheath; but, before she could move, Samir had another agenda.

The desperate man rushed at the evil master, eager to kill him. Undaunted by the attack, the Shadow Master didn't retaliate. Instead, he grabbed Azria off the floor by the arms, and held her in front of himself like a human shield. Tragically, Samir drove his sword into the beautiful dancer, his lovely sister Azria. Releasing her final breath, the defenceless girl fell to the floor, blood pouring from her wound. Horrified by his action, Samir dropped the sword and froze.

'Azria, what have I done?' Samir cried, collapsing over his sister.

The Shadow Master seized his moment, blasting the sword from Rose's hand with his staff. 'You fools, did you really think you could defeat me with your circus trick?', the Shadow Master sneered, creeping closer to Rose with an icy stare. 'I knew all along you would come.'

Suddenly, the grief stricken Samir tried once more to kill Borago, running at him with a pointed blade, but was silenced forever by General Taurus's spear, the cracking of his spine indicating a direct hit.

With that, Borago immobilised the Illuminata using the powerful rock, dragging her across the floor towards him. She lay at his feet, numbed and bruised. The Shadow Master then pulled Rose up off the floor by her arm, forcing her towards the Mercury Well chamber.

'Gallium!' Rose cried, struggling to free herself.

The warrior, momentarily distracted by a centaur's attack on Malachi from behind, had to act fast. Bounding off the back of a terrified juggler who was crouched on the floor, Gallium landed straddled across the four legged freak, and stabbed him in the neck. Clambering quickly off the dead centaur the warrior threw a look at Malachi.

'Go! I can hold them for a while', Malachi yelled, throwing yet another fireball into the face of a centaur.

Gallium rushed in the direction of the Mercury Well Chamber, where Borago was buckling the final strap around Rose's wrist, as she lay helpless on the stone table of a huge crushing wheel. Borago had purpose-built the wheel from the obsidian rock-face of the Mystic Mountains, using the power of the Orbicular Rock; it was the only thing capable of destroying the Illuminata and the precious crystals. Borago gave the command to commence the execution. Once dead, Rose's spirit would enter the Orbicular Rock, thereby increasing its power.

The circus performers now joined forces with Malachi, seizing whatever arms they could, such as wall-mounted spears, cutlasses, and heavy candelabras. The stilt walkers kicked a way out, while another acrobat back-flipped his way to the fireplace, reaching for a sharp poker which he launched straight through the chest of an oncoming centaur. The belly-dancers screamed in sheer terror, trying to escape the onslaught, as the Great Hall turned into a bloodbath.

'You're too late', the Shadow Master said, as Gallium entered the chamber. 'After she and the stones are crushed, I will have ultimate power over Pangaea.'

The wheel of black stone started to turn at an alarming rate, corkscrewing its way down a pole from the ceiling.

Without a moment's hesitation, the warrior went for the Shadow Master, wielding his sword. Suddenly, a huge spiked club stopped Gallium in his tracks. It was Otto, Borago's faithful troll.

'Otto, I release you to attack this fiend', the Shadow Master said, turning a key to unlock his shackles.

The giant troll lumbered towards the young warrior, holding the spiked club up high. Gallium swung his sword, but Otto easily dislodged it. The troll hammered on at Gallium, who jump-rolled across the floor, dodging every thwack. Eventually, Otto closed in on the warrior and, with his enormous hand, held him up against the wall just as if he were a boy. Gallium tried in vain to squeeze out of his grip.

Incapable of assisting as she lay beneath the descending wheel, Rose wriggled helplessly, her wrists chafing at the leather straps. Realising it was pointless, the Illuminata tried to think of another way to save herself. Closing her eyes, she imagined the wheel stopping, but the curse was too strong and the wheel continued to spiral down, although rather more slowly.

Meantime, the troll was about to strike the warrior, when, bending closer to Gallium, he looked closely at his face.

'What are you waiting for, you imbecile?! Kill him!' the Shadow Master yelled, watching from the well.

Ignoring his master's taunts, the troll slowly lowered his arm. Somehow, the troll mumbled the word 'son', and then, like the sky after a storm, it all became clear.

'*Father?* Is that you?' Gallium gasped.

Otto let out a groan, eyes welling up, as he hugged his son.

'Yes, how touching, your father is in fact a troll. I used a clever curse', the Shadow Master boasted, stepping closer. 'And now I command you to sleep.' With a bolt from his staff, Borago struck the giant right between the eyes. The troll fell hard.

'Father!' Gallium cried, examining his father who lay motionless.

'Now, to curse you', the Shadow Master said, advancing towards the warrior.

In a fit of rage, Gallium grabbed his sword from where it lay, launching it like a spear at Borago, but the Shadow Master stopped it mid-flight with the Orbicular Rock, forcing the weapon to drop to the floor. Disarmed but determined, the warrior lunged at Borago's legs, grappling him to the ground. The staff fell free from the Shadow Master's grip, and Borago had no choice but to fight by hand. Having the advantage, Gallium gripped the Shadow Master by the throat as he lay on the floor.

'I swore an oath I would kill you!' Gallium said through gritted teeth.

The Shadow Master was choking under the warrior's tight hold, when Malachi ran down the steps of the chamber, carrying the Renaissance Sword.

'Gallium!' the wizard shouted, as he slid the majestic weapon across the floor to him. 'Use it to destroy the wheel!' Malachi then turned his attention to the top of the steps, launching a fireball at an intruding centaur, which retreated to lick its wounds.

Picking up the sword, Gallium kicked Borago hard in the stomach, disabling the dark lord for a moment, then rushed over to the turning wheel of stone, now just inches away from Rose's body. The warrior swiftly drove the enchanted steel through the wooden corkscrew as though it were putty. Immediately, a bright light radiated from the magical blade, filling the gloomy chamber as the sword stopped the wheel from spiralling down any further.

'Damn you—all of you', growled the Shadow Master, crawling back to his feet.

The warrior unstrapped Rose and they hugged tightly, forgetting their place for a brief moment. Behind the Shadow Master, Otto was regaining consciousness, and saw Borago about to conjure another curse—this time aimed at his son. Vehemently, Otto kicked the staff out of Borago's hand. The powerful tool went somersaulting through the air and hit the hard floor; the rock broke free from its clasp, rolling over to Rose's feet. Borago watched in horror, massaging his injured hand, when a friendly voice within the chamber spoke.

'Rose, take the rock', it said softly.

Without hesitation, the Illuminata bent down to pick up the Orbicular Rock. Now holding it in her hands, the rock instantly connected with the Illuminata, emanating a vibrant glow.

'How is this possible?' Borago gaped.

In that instant, from a shadow behind the well, stepped a familiar figure—Morgana, adorned in a poppy flower gown.

'You!' Borago snarled, eyebrows raised and veins pulsating at his temples.

'Hello Borago; it has been a long time', Morgana said calmly.

'Why...why did you leave that night, without a word?' he said, avoiding her beauty and leaning on the edge of the well for support.

Morgana was once the love of Borago's life for a short time, but one night she vanished, leaving the then pirate king alone and broken-hearted.

'I had no choice. As the Fairy Queen, I am duty-bound to Pangaea', she said, moving like a cloud-driven breeze up to Rose. 'And—to our daughter.'

'What?' he said, his eyes protruding. 'Liar!' Borago skulked over to Morgana, remembering the night she had seduced him. 'You used me!' He went on, pointing a trembling finger only inches from the queen's face.

'It cannot be true', Rose said, equally stunned and almost letting go of the rock.

'It was the only way to guarantee the capture of the Orbicular Rock and the eventual demise of the Shadow Master', Morgana said, showing no signs of remorse. The fairy queen stood behind Rose, placing her hands gently on the Illuminata's shoulders to calm her.

'Only she who has the same blood can touch it and claim it', the queen pronounced.

In the background, Otto suddenly started to change form.

'Father, you are returning!' Gallium cried, leaving Rose's side to go to his father.

Otto was no longer a hideously disfigured troll, but the former Captain Aiden McLarty. The Shadow Master's powers were fading fast; cracks started to appear in the walls and the ground began to quake, as the tyranny shrank to its end.

Realising this, Borago attempted to snatch the rock from Rose's clasp, but like a ball of flames, it singed his fingers and he retracted. Furious that Rose could not be harmed, Borago pulled a dagger from his belt and in a frenzy threw it at Captain McLarty. The dagger pierced the good captain's heart like a bolt of lightning, and instantly he was dead. Gallium could not believe his eyes; words failed to part his lips and he fell to his knees beside his father's body. Amidst the sorrow, the Shadow Master took a smoke bomb from his pocket, and throwing it to the floor, escaped up the stony steps. The spiralling smoke filled the chamber, causing the others to cough and feel their way to safety. Up in the Great Hall, the massacred Mumbalians were all that was left, obstructing the way out. Running past the victims, Borago continued to make his way up a battlement tower, with Malachi in close pursuit.

'You will have to do better than that, wizard!' Borago jeered down the staircase, after Malachi had missed him with a fireball, losing his balance due to the earthquake.

Once at the top, Borago was greeted by his loyal golden gryphon, Castro, which was waiting to fly his master to safety. With the tower cracking under the earth's pressure, the wizard was convinced he should retreat back to the wagon, in the hopes of finding the others there. The centaurs, led by Taurus, had regrouped and were galloping at great speed away from the destruction, in the direction of their master.

In the chamber, the diminishing smoke revealed Gallium hugging his father, as he lay on the obsidian floor. Carefully, Gallium pulled the deadly dagger from McLarty's chest, throwing it into the well with a loud cry.

'Goodbye father', he said, his breath catching.

'I'm so sorry Gallium. I wish I could bring him back', Rose said, standing next to him.

The Mercury Well Chamber was crumbling and more loose rocks were falling.

'There's no time. You must leave at once', Morgana's voice echoed, but the queen was nowhere to be seen.

'Come on Rose', Gallium said, holding back tears and pulling the Renaissance Sword out of the crushing wheel. 'We've got a murderer to catch.'

The wheel of stone started to crack, and piece by piece it fell into a deep rupture in the ground. Now in a frantic hurry, Gallium grabbed Rose by the hand and rushed out of the collapsing castle, trying hard to avoid falling debris. Through the remaining doorway they ran, and were soon reunited with Malachi at the wagon.

'Where is he, that blackguard?!' Gallium barked, peering inside the wagon, hoping to at least find him tied up.

'I'm afraid Borago has escaped', the wizard said.

'Aaaargh!' Gallium punched the lower half of the wagon's rear door.

'Please, Gallium, I promise we will find him', Rose said, healing the warrior's sprained knuckles with a gentle touch.

'My lady, you ride with Gallium on Ironbark and I will ride on Noble; we must leave at once', Malachi urged as he mounted, having already loaded the horses with supplies from the caravan. 'The wagon remains here; it will only slow us down.'

'No more the fool; next time we get him', Gallium asserted, jumping up on Ironbark behind Rose.

'Indeed, let's head for the border', Malachi instructed.

The three friends rode faster than the north winds, leaving behind a trail of broken volcanic rock and lava spewing from the centre of the Mercury Mountains, creating a glowing path of immeasurably hot, molten ooze.

Chapter Twenty-Six—The Briny

Boat

After their rapid get-away, the devoted trio once again found the hollow of the globular tree at the edge of Anaconda, where Gallium told Malachi of the travesties he and Rose had discovered inside the Mercury Chamber.

'Gallium, my deepest sympathy; your father truly was a good man', Malachi said.

'Mark my words, Borago is going to wish he'd never met me', the warrior said, before wandering over to Ironbark for some space.

Rose had already retreated inside the hollow of the tree, to gather her thoughts and examine the Orbicular Rock closely.

'My lady, are you all right?' Malachi enquired, entering the spacious trunk and removing his eyepatch.

'Malachi I can't believe it, he's, my father.' Rose was slumped on a blanket staring hypnotically at the glassy rock, mesmerised by the mysterious swirls of smoke within.

'I realise this is a shock for you, but try to see him for who he really is, a merciless man and one who will stop at nothing to get what he wants', the wizard said, sitting beside Rose.

'You are right; he could never be my father', Rose said, with a catch in her throat. 'I am nothing like him and I never will be', she declared, placing the Orbicular Rock back inside a suede satchel, while Malachi produced the Book of Legends.

'Now, let me see', the wizard said, changing the subject. 'According to the book, we need to return to the Fatum Realm.'

'Perfect, I must speak with Morgana', Rose said, standing tall.

'Of course, but I'm afraid it will have to wait', the wise wizard said, putting away the great book. 'The road to Dorsal Bay is our next stop and we will need our strength.'

Sitting comfortably upright, Malachi closed his eyes and added, 'Come, meditate with me.'

Rose huffed out a breath, and after brief consideration did the wise wizard's bidding.

From the Mystic Mountains, the sea of lava had covered a large area north of Anaconda, extended as far as Mumbala. Once famous for its hustle and bustle, Mumbala was now an abandoned, lost world. Most of its citizens had fled, although an unfortunate few remained immersed in its structure, under the thick burning magma.

The enemy was still at large, making his way to another part of the land. A time of change was coming.

After a short nap, Malachi, with an enormous sense of responsibility for the emotional pair, thought it best they rode on again.

The three travellers soon proceeded with their journey to the Fatum realm. As they moved from the one realm to the other, the hard ground became softened by the early morning dew; fresh moist winds cleansed their tired dry bodies. Gallium held on tight to the reins and to Rose, now asleep on the back of Ironbark. The two stallions wearily trotted into a clearing in the trees, arriving under a warm, spectacular sunset. Here, Gallium laid Rose on a thick patch of clover and grass, in perfect slumber.

The warrior covered them both with a blanket and rested along-side her, while the wizard sat deep in thought.

'Queen Morgana, the Illuminata needs you more than ever for the final stage of her mission', Malachi communicated through thought. 'We are at the mercy of your realm; please guide us safely.'

'I am always here, Malachi', Morgana whispered, appearing in his mind like a vision of loveliness. 'Trust Noble, he will not fail you.'

'What about Borago?' Malachi said. 'I failed to stop him escaping.'

'He has many loyal followers and will try to form an even greater army; it is vital you succeed in this mission.' Morgana paused for a moment. 'When you reach Dorsal Bay, call upon Triton, King of the Sea. He will help you sail to the Island of Onesta. And— take care of my daughter.' In a veil of light, she vanished.

'Of course, consider it done, my queen', said the wizard, before drifting to sleep.

Queen Morgana's prediction came to pass. The Shadow Master found safe haven at Port Oreon, where he reunited with his centaurs. Despite not having the powerful rock, Borago held leadership over his kind: he owned a considerable amount of wealth, hidden in coves around the port—in fact, he owned all of Port Oreon—and not forgetting, he was still in possession of the emerald crystal ball.

The morning after a restful sleep, Noble instinctively led the way to Dorsal Bay, passing through low shrubs as they continued along the muddy banks of the Dorsal River. The sun shone intermittently from behind the clouds, making it a perfect day to travel. The mouth of the river gradually grew wider as it touched the distant ocean and around the corner was a pebbly Dorsal Bay, its waves tranquil. Malachi, Rose and Gallium stood admiring the view from the edge of the shore.

'Triton, I have here the Illuminata and we humbly request the Briny Boat to take us to Onesta', the wizard called loudly and waited.

At first nothing happened. Then, sweeping from the west, came a warm breeze.

'The Illuminata you say', King Triton boomed in a big deep voice, causing ripples across the waters.

'I am the Illuminata'. Rose stepped forward, the sand crunching under her boots, and removed her necklace, holding the chain of gems aloft. 'I bear the crystals of Pangaea.' Immediately the precious stones shone like a lit beacon.

Just then, a melodic sound from across the sea gradually grew louder. It was the sweet notes from a pan-pipe.

'I see something over there', Rose said, looking at a place across the ocean, as she lowered the crystals and fastened them again around her neck.

A swell in the body of water started to churn and a sailing boat floated in from the blue. It was no ordinary wooden boat, but one made entirely from strips of driftwood woven together. Seaweed fringed parts of the boat and barnacles studded the hull. Perched on a wooden seat in the stern, was no ordinary sailor, but a merman. He was plump and strong, navigating the boat through the water solely by means of his fishtail; at the same time he blew into an enchanted pan-pipe. The Briny Boat gently moored near the shore as the merman ceased playing.

'Greetings from King Triton, I am Fillius—at your service', he said in soothing tones, his fishtail still hanging in the water.

'Pleased to make your acquaintance', an intrigued Lady Rose said. 'I am Rose and these are my friends, Gallium and Malachi.'

'I am here, by order of the sea king, to navigate you to the Island of Onesta.' Fillius offered his hand to welcome them on board.

Malachi instructed the horses to wait by the shore until their return, then climbed into the boat after the others. With a blow over the pan-pipes, Fillius set course for Onesta.

Chapter Twenty-Seven—Land

Ahoy!

Cruising along at a steady pace in the rustic boat, Dorsal Bay was soon a mere speck behind them. A cool, gentle sea breeze blew across the calm ocean and clouds floated lazily in the sky, while the spray from the salty waves misted their faces. Rose stared aimlessly into the sea with a dreamy expression, although her thoughts were far from calm or serene. Gallium held Rose's hand, as he too tried hard to ignore the feeling of hurt and anger at finding his father only to lose him again. Occasionally, a pod of dolphins swam playfully alongside, enjoying Fillius's merry tune. After a while, the light from the sun reduced to a haze and the mood changed to a more sinister silence. Further they drifted through a wall of dense low fog. At this point, jagged rocks began to surface, like huge stalagmites, causing the little boat to sway. A ghostly mist now masked their vision

'What is happening?' Gallium said, as all of them held onto the edge of the boat, swivelling their heads in all directions to scan the area.

'Do not fret, the rocks are only for foes who may try to reach the Island of Onesta without King Triton's permission', Fillius said reassuringly and carried on playing his pipes.

A short time passed and the fog parted like curtains to reveal the beautiful Island of Onesta. Its tropical surroundings of crystal blue sky and turquoise waters lapping gently against the white sandy beach contoured by numerous palm trees, created a perfect picture.

'This view looks familiar', Rose said, her eyes taking in every detail.

'Yes, it's like the one from the sacred painting that holds the Book of Legends', Malachi said in astonishment.

Soon they arrived at the white sandy shores of this hallowed Island.

'Welcome to the Island of Onesta', Fillius said, directing his passengers ashore.

Promptly, the merman and the bespoke boat submerged gradually below the waves, leaving the three passengers standing on the beach to explore their new surroundings.

'By my recollection, the book suggests we head for the centre of the island, where we will find the Cave of Creation', Malachi said.

'Fine, let us follow you, Malachi', Gallium said, drawing his sword just in case.

Venturing bravely from the sandy tranquil beach they soon encountered the overgrown undergrowth of a hot and humid rainforest, causing Malachi and Gallium to use their swords to hack a way through the strangling vines that grew heavy around the old trees. The trees, which were infinitely tall, had buttressed roots growing from the bases of their trunks. Lagging a little behind, Rose became aware of a sort of supernatural presence. Tingling but unafraid, she looked with interest at every living thing along the way. There must have been a thousand different-coloured orchids growing; a humming bird was hovering over a huge iridescent flower, its wings whirring wildly. Increasingly, a concoction of animal sounds could be heard—whistling bugs, squawking macaws, rasping toucans. The jungle truly was a vibrant and colourful place, but it had hidden dangers, too. The ground was dry one minute and a squelching, swampy mess the next, due to the frequent heavy rains. By now, the men had sweat running down their faces and torsos. The humidity intensified along the way. Gallium stopped for a moment to take a breath, and looking round, realised that Rose was nowhere to be seen.

'Malachi, where is Rose?' he said, frantically separating low foliage and ferns in case she had fallen. 'Rose, where are you?'

The unruffled wizard, instinctively looking up, spotted Rose wrapped in the coils of a lengthy boa constrictor.

'There she is', Malachi said, pointing the way.

Gallium, aghast, was about to start climbing the tree to reach for her, when a few arrows suddenly struck the boa constrictor. It fell to the ground with a bounce, still curled around Rose, fortunately cushioning her fall. The two men hurried over to where she lay.

'Rose, are you all right?' Gallium asked, lifting the gigantic dead serpent off, and helping the princess to her feet.

Rose was gasping for air, after almost suffocating.

'Do not make any sudden movements; we are surrounded', Malachi said, in a low voice.

Rose, Gallium and Malachi stood back to back in a prism shape, under ambush from the native tribe of Onesta—the Nwee people.

Chapter Twenty-Eight—The Nwee Tribe

The Nwee men, also known as the 'tree people', were standing with their spears at the ready and not wearing much. The stick-like men prowled ever closer, mimicking wild cats on a hunt.

'Lumi, Lumi!' One of them said excitedly, pointing at Rose's gems.

Gallium moved to stand protectively by Rose.

'Se Lipan', a Nwee man said, gawking at Gallium; Lipan meaning warrior.

Another one stepped forward, recognising the markings on Malachi's forehead.

'Sim se Malachi?' he whispered, brushing aside the wizard's fringe with the tip of his spear, for a closer look.

Malachi felt he ought to comply and stood motionless, and then the Nwee man turned to his people. 'Se Malachi!' he said joyfully, as everyone dropped to their knees.

'Should we be concerned?' Gallium said from the side of his mouth to Malachi.

'I think they recognise who we are. I will attempt to speak to them', Malachi said, stepping forward with his hands up. 'People of Onesta, we come in peace. We are here to find the Cave of Creation.'

There was a pause as the tribe softly chanted their names. At that moment, an elder rustled forward from behind a shrub. Compared to the other tribesmen, he was decoratively dressed, wearing a necklace made from multi-coloured feathers and animal teeth. He stood proudly before Malachi,

263

demonstrating the palm of his hand, which bore an intricate spiral tattoo of a mandala.

'Welcome! We are the Nwee people, and we have been expecting you', he said with a warm smile. 'My name is Chief Rumi. Come, follow me to our village.' With a broad grin, Rumi moved in the direction of home, and everyone casually followed.

The jungle gradually became less overgrown. The sounds of children's laughter could be heard, and a smell of burning woodfires tickled their noses. Walking between oversized shrubs and into a clearing, Rose and company saw row upon row of trees with towers around their trunks, cleverly constructed from twine and branches, allowing an easy climb up to platform tree houses. The roofs of the dwellings were robustly fashioned from sago palm leaves, while the floors were made of thick tree bark. The houses were at least twenty men high. At the centre of the village at ground level, was a round hut, where the community would congregate. This was also Chief Rumi's home.

'Come, sit, you must be hungry', Rumi said, as he instructed one of the village wives to prepare food.

The round hut was a little crowded, but comfortable. They all sat on palm leaves in the middle of the floor around a chopped tree trunk that served for a table.

'How is it you know my name?' Malachi said, focusing on Rumi's face.

'Your name means 'wise wizard' and the story about you all was written on the walls of the Cave of Creation by the God Omnio himself', Rumi said in a throaty voice, holding his finger in the air.

'So you know where the Cave of Creation is?' Rose said, absorbed with interest, as one of the Chief's children sat sweetly next to Her Ladyship, stroking her arm.

'As guardians of Onesta, it is our duty to protect, but also to welcome the Illuminata', Rumi told them, smiling at Rose. 'The Keeper of the Cave is the Green Man; only he can allow safe passage to the sacred location. I will take you to him when the first rays of light wake my children', Rumi chortled, patting one of them on the head as he weaved passed, playfully chasing a sibling. 'And they sleep little, ha-ha!'

One of the women entered the round house with a banana leaf platter of food. Gallium's jaw dropped in horror when he saw what was put in front of him. An assortment of roasted bugs on wooden skewers, edible flowers and raw honeycomb. Looking wanly at Rose, who was tucking into the palatable grubs, Gallium almost vomited.

'Eat, warrior, you must keep up your strength', Rumi teased, giving him a playful slap on the back.

Gallium didn't wish to appear rude, and so he bravely tucked in, trying not to betray his disgust with each crunchy bite, although Rose noticed his face turning slightly green! Nonetheless, Gallium finished his course with a satisfied belch and everyone laughed, especially the locals.

That evening, some of the tribesmen and women put on a celebration dance in honour of their guests. It was a tribal festival, the dancers clad in colourful plumed costumes; their feet bounced rhythmically off the ground to the beat of a drum, while the women sang joyfully. At the centre was a large fire which sent swirls of embers floating up into the night sky. It was a perfect end to an extraordinary day.

Chapter Twenty-Nine—The Green Man

The birds of the jungle were singing a sweet salutation to the sun, as it rose on this paradise island. Gallium jerked awake to a hauntingly familiar smell, as more grubs on a skewer were thrust in his face by a giggling local boy.

'Up now, we will eat, then I will take you to see the Green Man', Rumi said bright-eyed, as he stood over the three friends, surrounded by more curious children.

The Nwee women brought woven palm-leaf baskets filled with a selection of fresh fruit—they recognised pineapple, pawpaw and others they had never seen before. A young girl presented Rose with the gift of a flower, positioning it in her hair. Just then, a naughty spider monkey scampered in and, to Gallium's surprise, jumped onto his shoulder.

Once the meal was over, the three guests were escorted to the sacred cave by Rumi and two other men from the village. A short walk brought them to another tree construction, only this time, there was no house at the top. Instead, suspended from treetop to treetop, was a walkway. Rumi guided them up a wooden ladder and along the bamboo boardwalk; Rose gingerly stepped forward without looking down, telling herself to trust all was well. The atmosphere was peaceful and the view truly breathtaking; for miles and miles, they could see a sea of green against the clear blue sky. Rainbow lorikeet birds flew up, perching among the foliage while spider monkeys swung skilfully from branch to branch.

There were a few more bridges, which they crossed with ease, until Rumi grabbed hold of a huge vine and slid back down to the ground. The rest of the group followed him. The plant life in these parts appeared denser and the trees in the distance were staggeringly taller. They then noticed a tinkling sound, and looking up, saw millions of emerald wand-shaped crystals hanging from the canopy of branches, the sun's rays highlighting the green gems. Rumi stood pensively with his eyes shut, while everyone observed attentively from behind him. The chief placed his tattooed palm on a huge moss-covered mound.

'Oh green and wise one, I bring you great news', he spoke loud and clear.

Gallium eye-balled the area, failing to see anyone green or human, whereas Rose, breathing lightly by Rumi's side, controlled her excitement as they waited for the magical encounter. Deep within the earthy mound there came a rumbling sound, accompanied by a slight tremor, and from beneath the green, there gradually emerged a giant being in the form of an old fallen tree. Rising creakily with a stretch, the giant woke from his slumber. Strips of old bark fell away to the ground, leaving the Green Man towering over the Nwee and their visitors. He was covered in thick damp moss, and had a friendly, human-like face and pixie-like ears; also, curly roots for a beard, green moss for a moustache, variegated leaves for hair, and two long branches for arms. There was one more thing, something quite magical: the Green Man's body was alive with tiny, sparkling emerald fairies living among the foliage and crevices. Now and then, one would show its shy pretty face, peering out from behind a leaf, its large crystal green eyes shining.

'What...is the...purpose of...your intrusion?' the Green Man asked in a slow, ancient voice, blinking the soil out of his eyes.

'It is I, Rumi. I bring you the Illuminata, oh ancient one', he said humbly, nudging Rose's arm, signalling her to step forward and greet the giant being.

Some of the fairies flew past Rose's face, as the Green Man lowered himself in slow motion down to Rose's height. Without hesitation, Rose held up her hand to the Green Man's cheek. It felt warm, and like a magnet their energies connected. After a few seconds, Rose prised her hand away, catching her breath.

'You are indeed...the Illuminata and everything...pure leads back...to you', the Green Man said standing up again. 'Know this: good shall always...prevail.'

'That is most reassuring', Rose said, tilting her head up, in complete awe of the being. 'Will you guide us to the Cave of Creation?'

'You have...not far...to travel', the wise being said, turning round majestically to face the group of trees behind him. Unexpectedly, he then blew on his hollow wooden thumb, producing from his elbow a horn-like sound that vibrated to everyone's core. 'Reveal...the sacred...steps of Onesta', he boomed.

To everyone's amazement, the surrounding undergrowth and trees began to move in a shuffling manner, uprooting and hopping to one side, to show a weathered stony path. In the foreground, a group of gigantic trees grew at the foot of a mountain. As one, these lanky trees pulled their rooted stumps out of the earth, creating a great divide at the base of the mountain.

'Go now. A path has been made', the Green Man said, lifting his mossy brow to the peaceful blue sky and adding sombrely, 'But hurry...a storm, is coming.'

'Do you mean the Shadow Master?' Malachi said.

'The shadow still lurks', the Green Man sighed, his breath rustling the leaves; the fairies shuddered at the very mention of the evil one's name.

The storm the Green Man alluded to, was the new and powerful army that Borago had created with the help of his most trusted allies— Captain Nine-tails Johnson, the centaurs, and the witches of the Well, who were freed from their entrapment when the well was destroyed by the earthquake.

'I see no steps', Gallium said, shading his eyes from the sun with his hand, and walking briskly ahead to investigate. Suddenly, the warrior could walk no further. Something hard and low to the ground was preventing another step.

'I think I've found it', Gallium called to the others. Up the side of the mountain, he saw a hundred or more steps, cleverly carved into the side of the prominent mound. Face-on, the steps were camouflaged, creating an optical illusion. The grey-brown slabs of stone led straight up to the cave entrance. Within moments, Rose, Gallium and Malachi, loaded with the Orbicular Rock, Book of Legends and Renaissance Sword, commenced their ascent. Rumi waved them goodbye and wished them well, before returning with his men to the village.

Chapter Thirty—The Awakening

Having taken twenty or more steps towards 'heaven', Rose's legs began to feel heavy with effort, and her head buzzed with thoughts of what was to come. The day was light and warm, the sky blue as the ocean. Staying focused, the intrepid trio continued their climb; deep-down knowing the final hurdle was literally just ahead.

Across distant lands, Borago's army of centaurs, pirates and ghostly witches had split up and were entering the borders of each realm via Bloodwood Gorge. From aboard the ship Exodus, they surged onto the shores of Fatum like a swarm of feisty bees; the Shadow Master's wrath spread at an alarming rate, the centaurs' spears leaving a trail of death, while the pirates slashed their way through towns and villages with no remorse. The ghostly witches, Hemmatia and Marelda, flew around terrorising any living creature, before turning them into stone with a single foul breath. With a lust for revenge, the Shadow Master ordered the legion of villains to hunt down Rose, and this time—kill her.

The Kingdom of Vervain was soon alerted by Morgana, the dreaded news causing an atmosphere of unrest, as the citizens prepared to defend their humble homes. Women and children were ordered by Queen Aveena to seek refuge in the castle basements, while the men remained to stand and fight—families painfully torn apart, all because of one man's greed. King Yarrow recruited an army for this war-of-all-wars, positioning men strategically around the castle grounds, heavily armed and ready to die for the cause. Vervain was on its guard, all the while praying Rose had made it safely to the Crystal Masters.

In the meantime, the chosen ones reached the top of the sacred steps, exhausted from their long climb. Resting on a nearby rock, Rose felt glad of the wondrous view beyond— she could see the entire island, framed by golden beaches and the shimmering sea.

'I think it's this way, my lady', Malachi said, moving in the direction of a gravel trail.

The trail stretched ahead to a huge dark opening in the mountain, shrouded by a creeping plant. Malachi picked up some brushwood and magically set fire to it, producing a torch for each of them. Continuing down a passageway, they were suddenly confronted by a cloud of bats flying out of the cave's mouth, screeching at a high pitch. Rose, Gallium and Malachi covered their ears for protection from the horrible sound, until the nocturnal creatures had gone.

The cave gradually widened, the further the trio went, the walls showing signs of decoration. On one wall was a mural depicting a familiar story. Studying the henna-painted images and symbols, Rose traced her fingers carefully along the remarkable workmanship. The first symbol showed a shooting star plummeting to earth, below it a gemstone shaped like the rose quartz crystal, and a female figure with lines like beams of light coming from her body—it was a representation of the Illuminata. Beside that image was the warrior holding a sword and across from him was Malachi, with the four symbols above, exactly the same as his birthmarks.

'Look, it's us', Rose said with a smile.

'Rumi was right', Malachi said, observing curiously as they moved slowly along.

Moments into the cave's depths, wall mounted torches miraculously lit themselves, while a beckoning light guided the three companions safely in the right direction to the next cavern. It was a little warmer here, and breathtakingly beautiful with its clear quartz surroundings and glistening mirror-like rock pools. It was a sight to behold.

'I feel lighter than air', said Rose softly, pirouetting on the spot, as any aches or pains rapidly disappeared.

Malachi reached the opening of another hollow, this time even more beautiful.

'I believe this is the way, my lady', he said, peering in at the glowing lavender chamber. Stepping into the next cavern they saw that it was made entirely of pure, purple amethyst crystal. This was the centre of the Cave of Creation; the key to the past, present—and future.

At the centre of this glowing space was an altar of purple granite while, right at the back all in a row, were the four amethyst crystal tombs in which the masters lay dormant. Malachi approached the altar steadily, the others in tow, then took out the Book of Legends from the painting and laid it on the altar.

'My lady, you must position the Orbicular Rock carefully in the cleft of the altar', the wizard instructed, flicking to the relevant page of the hallowed book. 'According to the book, you must read aloud what is written.' Malachi took a step back, and stood poised beside Gallium.

'It says I must break the Orbicular Rock open by using the Renaissance Sword', Rose said. 'Only then will the masters' spirits be released—whew', Rose said, becoming fully aware of the magnitude of her assignment.

'Continue, my lady', the wizard encouraged, tapping her arm.

'I am peace, I am love, and I am the Illuminata.' Rose's voice echoed throughout the cave, sending ripples across the rock pools and tremors up the walls.

The crystals around her neck shone brighter than ever. She drew the sacred sword from its sheath before announcing, 'And I release you!'

With one full swing of the shining blade, Rose cracked the Orbicular Rock wide open. The power of the mighty sword flung her backwards onto the floor, rendering her unconscious. Gallium hastened to her aid, but distressingly could not revive her. The explosive sound of the fracturing rock shook the altar and released the four spirits. Like wisps of white smoke travelling through the air, they went down a small hole at the head of each tomb. Amazingly, Rose now began to glow and levitate towards the altar; a force had taken over her body, lowering it onto the granite top, her eyes still shut tight.

Gallium was speechless, watching on in wonder and concern.

Malachi was hastily fumbling the pages of the old book, to find the next part.

As he uttered the ancient words, Rose's necklace magically unfastened and hovered above the Illuminata's body, as one by one, the precious gem stones slipped off the chain, whizzing through the air to each tomb and down the same channels as the spirits. Next, the tombs radiated a violet light and faint angelic voices could be heard chorusing from within. The stalactites began to crumble from the cave's ceiling, forming a fine purple dust that sprinkled the ground, as the stone roof of the cave slid open to reveal a burnt-orange sky. For a brief moment, there was a dead calm. Not a murmur, not a sound, nor a flicker of light, nothing moved— until...

With a grinding noise, the lids of the tombs gradually slid off and dramatically crashed to the ground.

Malachi fell to his knees, hailing this glorious moment.

'Oh great masters of our time, return once more and ever be divine', he chanted.

Meanwhile, Gallium hopelessly tended to his pale Rose with sinking heart, softly stroking her cheek with a trembling hand and praying for some movement, she being cold to the touch. Abruptly, the Book of Legends slammed itself shut, and from the tombs, the masters rose one at a time. All four sat tall, drawing in deep breaths, then stepped out of their stone-encased beds, reawakened.

Lapis was the first to present himself; a tall and slender male with a lucid complexion, his role was to create harmony and protection. Up next was Zincite, a fuller male figure with a jolly grin, he too emitted a lucid presence. Zincite's role was to anchor pure source energy to the earth. Following Zincite was Amazonite, a young male with a white turban wrapped about his head. It was his role to heal the hearts of the good. Finally, there was Perlana, a female of pure heart, whose role it was to plant purity and grace into the earth.

All four Crystal Masters now stood silently in a row, their gems glowing with energy atop clear crystal sceptres. The sceptres showed veins of liquid energy from their bases up to the encrusted gem stones.

For Gallium, panic was setting in.

'She's not breathing', he said, putting his ear to her face. 'Malachi, do something!'

The task of cracking open the Orbicular Rock meant that Rose's life had been sacrificed for the Crystal Masters' return.

'Gallium, forgive me, there is nothing...', Malachi said quietly, rising slowly to his feet.

The warrior jerked his head round at the wizard, his eyes narrowed.

'You knew, didn't you? You knew this would happen!' Gallium rasped. Flinging himself on Malachi, he began to pummel him with his fists, but was soon stopped mid-action, as Lapis created a force field around the wizard, using the crystal sceptre.

'Please, you must help her', Gallium begged, surrendering on his knees. 'I swear to love her even after my soul has left this body.' The warrior's desperate plea to the Crystal Masters was evidence enough for them to know that he meant it.

Amazonite went to where Rose lay and looked upon her drained complexion.

'This is the Illuminata, who gave her life to restore ours', the young and wise master said to all present. 'In the name of love, I will heal her pure and godly heart.'

Picking up the rose quartz crystal from the altar, Amazonite placed it over Rose's heart space. Then, with one hand above Rose and the other holding the sacred sceptre, he summoned the power of healing, through thought. Malachi placed a hand on Gallium's shoulder, as the two men witnessed the miracle. The colour soon began to reappear in Rose's skin and her fingers began to twitch, as the Illuminata breathed in life. Amazonite, withdrawing, rejoined the other masters.

'Thank the masters, you're alive', Gallium said, with his forehead touching hers.

'Masters, we thank you', Malachi said. 'And, if I may, we are in vital need of your help. Our world is being destroyed by the Shadow Master.'

'Your world is not yet broken, but we will help heal it', Lapis said, in a smooth and calm voice.

'Let us call upon the White Crusaders of Veritae', Zincite announced, looking up through the centre of the cave, where the sky was now a shade of deep purple, as night fell.

Chapter Thirty-One—The Tempest

While this miraculous event was taking place, the venom of Borago continued to leach into every realm. The once blooming Airlastua, with flowers galore, was now crushed underfoot, tainted with the blood of the slaughtered. In the north, the villagers of Tregonia had been turned to stone by the Sisters of Darkness, Hemmatia and Marelda. Much of the Fatum realm also clearly showed signs of a mindless, bloody attack. Now the horde were progressing to the once-peaceful Kingdom of Vervain, casting a black veil over the surrounding beauty and draining the lives of many.

Later that night, the Shadow Master arrived at the door of King Yarrow's bedchamber and burst into the monarch's room. The two old adversaries were now face to face.

'To die a slow death would be a pity, for a man like...you', Borago whispered darkly.

'I don't know how you got past my guards, but this will be your final destination', King Yarrow said, leaping from the bed and grabbing his sword from beside it.

Running towards the dark lord, the king drove the sword into Borago's black heart; then the good king woke in a pounding sweat, realising it was all a bad dream.

'Yarrow, it pains me to see you so troubled', Queen Aveena said, stroking his back.

'How can I sleep, Aveena, when my people need me', the king said, getting out of bed to put on his robe. 'I must be ready to lead the men into battle...' the king said, pacing the floor. 'You must retreat to the basement with the other women and children.'

'As you wish', the queen obeyed, as she dressed suitably for her task.

'Aveena, if the kingdom should fall...'

'No, I will not.'

'Hear me, please; take your leave through the underground passage, the tunnel leads to safety.' Wrapping his arms around his woeful queen, the king concluded, 'And may God be with you.'

Outside the castle walls, the thunderous noise of destruction could be heard, swelling from the south. The smell of death was increasing; it was indeed time to fight for their lives.

Back at the Cave of Creation, Rose, Gallium and Malachi observed as the masters stood at each of the four corners of the altar, laying down their crystal-mounted sceptres in a cross formation, so that the stones touched the broken Orbicular Rock at the centre of the slab. Still holding on to the sceptres' shafts, the masters went into a deep trance, and began to illuminate. The sceptres' glowing ducts of energy then connected to the Orbicular Rock, repairing the broken pieces. The renewed sacred stone loosed a vertical jet of light, which streamed into the exposed night sky. Like a radiant key, the beam of energy unlocked the heavenly realm of Veritae, and the God Omnio sent forth the White Crusaders. These saintly soldiers did not speak or show their faces; instead, armed with spiritual swords, they imbued their steel helmets and silver armour with a ghostly presence, gliding down from the sky on winged white horses. The swords looked like blades of glass, but were most powerful. The Crusaders waited outside the cave in their hundreds for instructions. The masters and company made their way up yet more steps hidden deep within the cave, and in no time at all, they met with the White Crusaders.

'Warrior Gallium, it is your duty to lead the White Crusaders in battle', Lapis said.

'I consider it an honour', Gallium said, bowing his head. 'Don't worry I will return', he told Rose, standing beside him.

'No need, I'm coming with you', Rose said.

'As it should be', Lapis said, softly holding Rose's hands. 'You will each take a winged horse and fly to Vervain.'

Accompanying the White Crusaders by valiant decree, were Gallium, Rose and Malachi, flying in the direction of war-torn Pangaea. At the same time, the Crystal Masters flew on horseback to the ends of each designated realm, to initiate the healing process.

Chapter Thirty-Two—For Truth and Justice

Arriving on the outskirts of Vervain, Gallium and his winged army surprised the enemy with an aerial attack. The White Crusaders, circling the frightful scene, shot lightning bolts from their swords at the pestilential pirates and criminal centaurs. Gallium swiftly made his winged descent, heading straight for the battlements of Vervain. He quickly dismounted and rushed to report to the king.

'Gallium, am I glad to see you! What news of Rose?' King Yarrow cried, as the two locked forearms.

'I am here, Your Grace', Rose said, running to the king and hugging him.

'It is good to see you, Rose', said Prince Burdock, by his father's side.

'My lady', bowed Sir Dill.

'Sir Dill, take the Lady Rose to the queen for safety', King Yarrow ordered.

'No, please, I did not come this far to give up now', Rose said passionately, showing the sacred sword.

The king could see the determination in her eyes and the strength in her stance, realising once more she was born for this mission.

'Well then, Sir Dill, see to it that they are properly attired', King Yarrow said. composing himself. 'Let us unite and undo what has so wrongly been done.'

After Rose and Gallium were appropriately suited-up for battle, they shadowed the king on the front line behind the castle gate, waiting for the marauders to break in. Malachi, on top of the battlements, had his own score to settle with the Sisters of Darkness, who were full of fury.

Still the Shadow Master was nowhere to be seen, choosing instead to witness the deaths of many via his crystal ball, from the safety of the ship Exodus. He watched as, like thousands of ants, his villains plagued the once peaceful realm.

'Steady men, lock...draw...loose!' King Yarrow ordered his archers to loose arrows through the gaps in the portcullis; Sir Dill took charge from the battlements, as the siege spilled into the castle grounds.

A group of Vervain's soldiers, using a towering trebuchet, swung a ball of flames at the Shadow Master's villainous mass. Still they came, the bandits scaling wooden ladders in an attempt to get over the castle wall, all the while being fired on with more arrows. Gallium felt compelled to meet up with the White Crusaders and, sneaking away, took to the sky on his winged horse.

Meanwhile, the Sisters of Darkness accepted the challenge from the wise wizard, and the aerial combat commenced. Malachi flung fireball after fireball, but the sisters' powers had grown stronger since leaving their prison in the mercury well. A thousand bees swarmed from the hags' mouths, only to be diverted at the hands of Malachi using a fierce wind spell to force them into the face of an attacking pirate down below. The witches retaliated by flying at lightning speed around the wizard, creating a burning wall, but this too did not last long. Malachi used sweeping hand movements to quench the flames with a strong, ice-cold wind, turning the flames into icicles that dropped uselessly to the ground. All the while knowing the hags' weakness, Malachi waited for an opportune moment.

'You're no match for us, I could turn you into a slug, sliding on your belly', Hemmatia said, with a loud cackle.

The wicked pair ascended into the night sky once more. Merging together to form a gigantic crow, they swooped down towards the wizard. Malachi seized the moment and pulled the sacred painting from his satchel. The witches were closing in fast, as he unfolded the magic piece and held the depiction up to the witches, who were cackling their way down, ignorant of what lay ahead.

'Aqua secrato veni!' the wizard shouted.

Spectacularly, the holy water splashed out of the painting like a tidal-wave, completely soaking the hags. Their loud shrieks echoed eerily, as the sacred water melted them away.

'You're a wicked wizard!' Hemmatia said, shrinking fast, with Marelda contorting beside her.

The wizard didn't say a word, instead he looked on in relief, knowing his job was done. Eventually, all that was left of the two hags was a gluey, yellow mess, fizzing and bubbling on the surface. Malachi slumped to the floor, exhausted, then rolled up the painting before joining the battle below.

Meanwhile, on re-joining the flying army, Gallium made his announcement.

'My lords, I say we fight on the ground and drive these scumbags back from where they came.'

At once, the White Crusaders unified, raising their swords in agreement.

'Follow my lead!' Gallium called, and swiftly they flew down after the warrior, blasting adversaries out of the way.

With Gallium at the centre, the Crusaders quickly formed a line of defence, positioned between Vervain castle and the enemy. Then, as they were fending off the enemy, something miraculous happened: a mystical voice spoke to the warrior.

'Gallium it is time, become the true warrior you were born to be.' The voice was that of the God Omnio.

No sooner said than done, Gallium, motionless on his powerful winged horse, observed in amazement as his body was encompassed in magical liquid gold, which instantly solidified into armour. His hands, too, were enveloped in precious gold gauntlets and his steel helmet was overlaid with a crown of gold, befitting one of greatness. The fiery winged army was now galloping at great speed side by side, trampling those who got in the way. All at once, their divine swords were mystically changed into titanium rods, locking end to end horizontally, forming an indestructible pole, a mile in length. The golden warrior took hold of the mystical pole and was instructed again through thought, by the God Omnio.

'Warrior, use the pole's power to drive the enemy out.'

The force-field of the pole began blasting everything within close range, while driving the remaining scum, in a panic, all the way back to Anaconda.

Within the castle walls, meanwhile, the action was intensifying and urgent help was needed. Even the lovely Rose, equipped with the Renaissance Sword, was fighting skilfully alongside her compatriots in one corner of the courtyard, while pirates and centaurs sliced and hacked their way in, showing no mercy. The king and Sir Dill were steadfast, fighting alongside one another at the castle gates. Rose was embroiled in the fighting, when a centaur flung a spear at her, grazing her shoulder. In answer, she plunged the sword of greatness into the charging beast's chest. The centaur stretched out his long arms, reaching for her throat—in vain, instead collapsing in death. Suddenly, a wild pirate loomed behind Rose, about to hack into her back.

'Look out, Rose!' shouted Prince Burdock, as he bravely thrust himself between the two, jabbing at the pirate.

At the warning, Rose turned sharply.

'Ahh! Burdock, you are hurt', she said, eyes wide with shock; tragically, the pirate's cutlass had left a deep gash in the prince's chest, during his heroic act.

'It was worth it, my lady.' The noble prince gently felt her cheek, then fell to the ground, clutching his bleeding wound.

Sir Dill saw it all and quickly responded, carrying the prince's body to a sheltered spot against a wall, where he could examine the injury. Sir Dill shook his head regretfully, and gently closed the deceased lad's eyes.

'Burdock, no, no, no!', Rose wept, kneeling beside him. 'I could have saved you.' Rose desperately tried to cover the gaping gash; her hands were saturated with the prince's blood as the tears streamed down her face.

'Forgive me, my lady', Sir Dill said, helping Rose to her feet, and propping her up with his arms. 'But now is not the time to grieve.'

Then, noticing her injured shoulder, Sir Dill began to lead the fair princess to safety.

'No', Rose said firmly, lightly pushing Sir Dill away. 'I owe it to Burdock to stay and fight.' With more attackers coming their way, they both returned to the combat.

A hefty bandit brandished his double-edged sword at Rose in a mad figure of eight, thinking her an easy target. He was soon proven wrong.

'Ahhhhhhh!' With an anger driven by great sorrow, the Illuminata flung her opponent flat on his back, and showing no mercy, drove her mystical sword into his chest, finishing the job with a twist.

Fearless, Lady Rose soldiered on, battling twice as fiercely. All the while, caught up in the fighting, the king was unaware of the tragedy that had occurred.

The Crystal Masters, meanwhile, finally reached their places of origin. In the Neve realm, Lapis stood at the edge of Lake Lunga; Zincite positioned himself at the Cliff of Promise; Amazonite was poised at the top of the Aurora Mountains in the Airlastua realm, and Perlana, arriving in the Sirenuse realm, halted on the shores of Coral Bay. Together in conscious intent, they gripped their crystal sceptres, plunging them with great force into the ground, all the while keeping a firm hold. The energy plummeted down, sending universal power throughout the land, the divine source healing from beneath the earth's crust, as it turned everything back to how it once was. During this surge of the Crystal Masters' joint power, the whole of Pangaea became lit up like a beacon, as nature was gradually restored and foliage and flowers bloomed once more. The civilians that had been turned to stone dissolved back to their original form.

At the border of Anaconda, the White Crusaders, led by the golden warrior, drove Borago's remaining mob into the ravine of Bloodwood Gorge. Those that escaped, fled across the realm. The yellow dawn now rose over all the troubled land. Witnessing their victory from the top of a hill, Gallium despondently rode his horse back to Vervain, in the sad knowledge that his father would never return. The sacred soldiers with their swords restored, lined up on the edge of Bloodwood Gorge. As one, they drove their swords into the hard ground with shattering force, dislodging the Anaconda realm and causing the huge part to detach and sink slowly through the thrashing waves, down into the depths of the ocean. The beast-afflicted realm was no longer part of Pangaea.

Once some sense of normality was restored, the majestic White Crusaders flew back to Veritae in the sky, the gateway disappearing, as it clouded over. Having dutifully restored Pangaea, the Crystal Masters returned on winged horses to the castle of Vervain, where joyful scenes greeted them: civilians threw down their weapons, rejoicing, while others reunited with their families. But for most, the aftermath meant the slow rebuilding of their homes and burying of their dead.

Sadly, King Yarrow was informed of his son's death and brought to the prince's body, now lying in his bed.

The grieving queen was draped over her son, while Rose caringly held her hand. The princess' mind was heavy with guilt, wishing she could have saved him.

At that moment, the Crystal Masters quietly entered the bedchamber.

'Please, bring back my son', the queen begged, addressing the masters from Burdock's bedside.

'We cannot bring back a mortal from the dead', Amazonite responded gently.

'Could you not give him my life in exchange?' the king pleaded, standing over his son's pale body.

'We are restorers of Pangaea and we can undo most evils, but alas not this', Lapis conveyed sorrowfully. 'We will return now to Onesta, and leave you in your peace.'

The Crystal Masters respectfully left the room in single file, but before departing from the castle grounds, they had another act of kindness to perform. Miraculously, by the power of their sceptres, the godly four repaired the broken mess, each stone replaced, and Vervain castle was restored.

What should have been a time of celebration in this castle, had ended in sorrow, as Gallium and Malachi stood watch in silence at the back of the prince's chamber. And all the while, the evil Borago was still at large with the disgruntled Captain Nine-tails floating aboard the ship Exodus, left to contemplate their fate.

And so, for every end there *is* a new beginning...

33381735R00169